𝕳ermitage, 𝖂at and 𝕾ome 𝕯ruids

Or

We're Going on a Murder

The Investigator's Apprentice.
The Investigator's Wedding
The Investigator's Kingdom
The Boundless Chronicles of Brother Hermitage
Return to the Dingle
Murder Can Be Murder
Murder 'Midst Merriment

Brother Hermitage Diversions
Brother Hermitage in Shorts (Free!)
Brother Hermitage's Christmas Gift

Audio
Brother Hermitage's Christmas Gift
Hermitage and the Hostelry

Howard of Warwick's Middle Ages crisis: History-ish.
The Domesday Book (No, Not That One.)
The Domesday Book (Still Not That One.)
The Magna Carta (Or Is It?)

Explore the whole sorry business and join the mailing list at
Howardofwarwick.com

Another funny book from The Funny Book Company
Greedy by Ainsworth Pennington

Hermitage, Wat and Some Druids

Or

We're Going on a Murder

Being further

Chronicles of Brother Hermitage

by

Howard of Warwick

From the Scriptorium of
The Funny Book Company

The Funny Book Company
www.funnybookcompany.com

© 2015 Howard Matthews

ISBN 978-1-913383-01-5

Cover design by Double Dagger

Hermitage, Wat and Some Druids

Contents

Introit

The lone Norman was scrambling back down the scree-sided hill much faster than he had gone up it. With each half stumble and blow from some bouncing piece of specially sharpened rock, he cursed himself for ever having gone up there in the first place.

Perhaps he'd be able to see his way out of this God-forsaken country if he climbed one of its interminable hills? Stupid idea.

He should have just followed one of the rivers to the sea. But that would have meant passing through the habitations of the completely mad people who lived here. And he'd seen how that ended up. From a distance, thankfully.

He glanced back over his shoulder to see if the pursuit was still with him. Of course it was. That was the way his luck ran. Of all the endless, deserted stretches of rain-battered, bog-filled land to choose from, he selected the very bit with some lunatic living in a cave. A very jealous and very lunatic lunatic, judging from the reaction.

All he tried to do was get out of the wretched rain for five minutes. The stuff fell out of the sky pretty much constantly so surely he could be spared a bit of cover.

How was he to know the cave was occupied? It was a miserable hole in the side of a hill which no one in their right mind should be living in. And there was no one in their right mind living in it. No one in their right mind who had got a sword from somewhere. A sword? In a cave? With a lunatic?

He kept running.

The stones under his feet were bouncing up to hit his calves and ankles, and the stones from his pursuer were raining down on his shoulders and back. And the rain was falling on both.

He knew a mission from King William was not something to be ignored, or managed badly. The things the king would do to him would make falling down a rock strewn hill in the rain chased by a mad man with a sword feel like a stroke from a jester's bladder. But the king was miles away. More miles away than the Norman thought possible. The man with sword was right behind him.

He knew where his priorities lay. He would explain the situation to the king later. Later meant he could spend all the intervening time still being alive.

Just then, the wretched hillside fell away under his feet. The hill had been steep enough as it was. Now it tipped even further and he went down. Down onto the sharp stones.

He felt the cuts and grazes on his hands as he slid down the slope which might as well have been paved with broken glass.

Looking in the direction of travel he saw the scree drop straight into the waters of a small but deep and dark lake. He could see it was dark, he just knew it would be deep. Perhaps, once in the water, he would be able to swim away. Or sink with the rest of the stones. Probably the latter.

While still moving he managed to dig his right hand into the ground and slowly spin his body round that he was going down backwards. There was no point trying to protect his hands, which were doubtless already cut to shreds.

As his feet dug into the scree he began to slow. Relief spread through him as he realised he would be able to stop before the water. The relief was only momentary as he now had a good view of his pursuer who was handling the steep slope very well indeed and holding his sword high at the same time. Most impressive.

At least his last sight would be of the mad man who was going to do for him. Better the sword than the lake, he thought.

He looked up into the eyes of the cave-dwelling swordsman. 'You!' he exclaimed, with more surprise than he had felt for a very long time.

Caput I: Here Be Dragons?

With more outrage than he had felt for a very long time Brother Hermitage put his hands on his hips. 'Wales?' he asked. He had felt a lot of outrage for quite a while now, and it was stirring quite unfamiliar feelings in his sedate character. He was never easily provoked, as his brother monks, who spent a lot of their time trying to provoke him could testify. His emotional range normally stretched from mildly annoyed to moderately satisfied, and he rarely reached those dizzy extremes. Now, he was feeling positively testy.

He could only gaze at Le Pedvin, King William's second in command and chief frightener of Saxons who had mentioned the dread place.

Hermitage had been given his own personal prophecy about Wales and it didn't end well. Of course he really only believed in prophesies from the Old Testament prophets, and they never mentioned Wales. This had to be a coincidence. If it wasn't a coincidence he was in real trouble. The sort of trouble that only gets mentioned in prophesies.

'Yes, Wales.' The Norman waved an inaccurate map of Britain in his right hand as he lounged in a comfortable chair in his camp tent; the tent with his attendant soldiers, the ones with all the knives and swords.

Hermitage's mouth was open but wouldn't work properly it was so outraged. He appraised the figure of Le Pedvin, hoping this was some sort of joke. He would have to admit the Norman was not known for his jokes, or humour of any sort really. Apart from ill-humour of course, the man had a lot of that.

Even appraising the figure was a problem as Le Pedvin didn't really have one. His face was as ragged as a week old corpse and the patch over one eye only enhanced the impression that the man had started dying some time ago, but hadn't quite finished yet. His reputation for wielding a sword was hard to believe. Wielding it for hours on end straight through people who stood in his way, apparently.

Le Pedvin's lone eye examined Hermitage in return and it was clear that the sight of the young, even-faced and bright-eyed monk gave it no pleasure.

That eye moved on and fell upon Wat the Weaver. A few years older than Hermitage, much better dressed and with considerably more experience behind the eyes and under the mop of curly dark hair. The weaver was trying to look bored at being asked about Wales – and was failing.

The eye paid no attention to Cwen, the third person facing the Norman's chair and the youngest of the group. He'd met her before and even cuffed her out of his way once, but as she appeared to be a servant, she didn't register. If he'd been told this young woman was a talented weaver, and spent most of her time ordering the others about, he'd have laughed heartily; a hearty laugh from Le Pedvin being akin to the terminal wheeze of a ferret choking on the bones of a baby rabbit.

'We've only just stepped back in England,' Hermitage protested, seeing where Le Pedvin's finality was about to send them. And they had only just stepped back off the boat from Normandy, where they'd been looking into another one of the murders that seemed to follow Le

Pedvin around.[1] Hermitage found himself wondering if, one day, he'd be asked to look into the murder of Le Pedvin himself. That would be nice. No, it wouldn't, he reprimanded himself. All murder was evil.

'You're just in time then and heading in the right direction,' was all the Norman had to say.

'Not more murder?' Hermitage asked, familiar despair preparing itself for a bit of a romp around his head. Being dispatched by Le Pedvin to investigate a murder in Normandy had been appalling and their encounter with the man at the castle Grosmal had been awful.[2] Hermitage had little confidence Wales would be any better.

'No,' Le Pedvin replied sharply.

'Really?'

'Well,' the Norman hesitated. 'Yes. Probably.'

He nodded a silent order to one of the men of arms who stepped smartly out of the tent. It was clear Le Pedvin had sent the man for something, hopefully a better map. Hermitage folded his arms and waited. It was an unusual feeling, being in demand, having something Le Pedvin wanted, which Hermitage felt put him in a position of strength. Of course he knew that anything Le Pedvin wanted the man would take, probably by force. Still, it was nice to bask in the moment.

After a very short time the guard returned, dragging something along as he backed his way into the tent. Definitely not a map then. Perhaps a trunk full of maps. That would be interesting. The backward travelling man

---

[1] The reason for their stepping back is nicely explained in *Hermitage, Wat and Some Murder or Other*. Perhaps you'd like to buy that as well.

[2] An awful experience neatly explained in *The Garderobe of Death*, available from shops with books in them. You could start a collection.

elbowed them out of the way and deposited his burden at their feet.

'Ah,' they all shouted, as they saw what it was.

Wat's "ah" was a knowing and simple confirmation that this was exactly the sort of thing he'd expected.

Cwen's was a stifled "ah" from someone who didn't want to appear surprised by anything.

Hermitage's was a much more normal "ah". The sort of high-pitched noise that the person hopes will propel them rapidly away from the dead body that's just been dumped in front of them.

'What's that?' Hermitage followed his "ah". His voice still up with the bats.

'It's a body.' Le Pedvin seemed puzzled by the question, 'Surely you've seen enough of them to know what one looks like.'

Hermitage had seen enough bodies. More than enough. He'd have been happy to stop before the first one. 'I have seen far too many.' He tried to make the criticism stick on Le Pedvin, but the man was far too slippery. 'Where did it come from?' he demanded, still thinking it was the most outrageous thing to throw before him.

Le Pedvin frowned. 'Outside,' he said. 'You just saw the guard bring it in? I do wonder how you manage to investigate anything sometimes.'

'I know it came in from outside.' Hermitage laid his contempt on thick, which was still pretty thin. 'Where did it come from before that?'

Le Pedvin looked at Hermitage as if the monk was speaking a foreign language. 'Wales?' he asked, clearly unhappy that Hermitage had not been paying attention. 'One of our number went to Wales and now appears to be dead. You're going to find out what happened to him and who made it happen.' He explained this as if to a child.

'Appears to be dead?' Hermitage was squeaking again. 'He doesn't appear to be dead. He's actually doing it. Right here.' He held out his arms to draw attention to the corpse on the floor. 'As far as I'm concerned this poor fellow doesn't come under the category of maybe a murder, he's a firm yes.'

'I don't mean him.' Le Pedvin was full of scorn for the monk's stupidity.

'There's another one?' This shocked Hermitage, although he tried to tell himself he shouldn't really be surprised.

'That's what you're going to find out.' Le Pedvin rolled his eyes across the roof. 'This is just a messenger' He nodded to the body on the floor. 'Staggered in from Wales, delivered his message and died.' Le Pedvin scoffed at the inadequacy of the modern messenger.

Hermitage offered a silent blessing to the one who had now departed to deliver his very final message.

'Had he run all the way?' Hermitage asked sympathetically. If that was the case it was no wonder the poor man had died.

'Could be,' Le Pedvin acknowledged without interest. 'Although it was probably the curse that killed him.'

'The what?' Hermitage asked, very slowly and very carefully.

'The curse,' Le Pedvin confirmed, as if everyone knew this. 'The druid curse.'

Hermitage could tell he had turned pale, even from the inside. The little blood that usually kept his face on the light side of pallid, had left for somewhere safer. Somewhere the discussion didn't involve druid curses.

'The druid curse?' he asked, unhappy to let the words pass his lips.

'That's what he said,' Le Pedvin nodded towards the deceased again.

Hermitage gaped.

'Well,' Le Pedvin explained, 'more sort of screamed repeatedly, to be honest.'

'Why us?' Hermitage bleated.

'King's Investigator?' Le Pedvin pointed out. 'King William made you his Investigator. Therefore you investigate things for him. He wants this investigated, therefore you do it.'

Hermitage had to admit this was a very sound and well-constructed argument. He didn't want to do it, therefore he shouldn't, seemed to get him nowhere.

'And you think this other man of yours is as dead as this one. You want him avenged?' Wat asked.

'Not really,' Le Pedvin sniffed. 'It's only Martel, who'd care? What we can't have is people going round killing Normans. They'll all think they can do it.'

Now that was heartless, even for Normans.

'And when you've found out what happened, you can bring his killer to your workshop in Derby.'

'Why there?' Wat sounded rather worried that Le Pedvin was using his home as a landmark.

'Because we're heading north for a spot of harrying and it'll be on the way.' Le Pedvin paused and consulted his map. 'I think,' he said, turning the parchment in his hand.

Wat frowned deeply.

'Oh, and of course if you're not there, in what shall we say?' The man pondered as if adding up barrels of cider on his fingers. 'A week to get to Wales, week to find Martel's killer, week to Derby? Three weeks? Yes, in three weeks we'll burn the workshop to the ground and kill everyone in it.' Le Pedvin completed the plan.

'Is that really all you can do?' Hermitage's outrage flared once more. 'Every time you want something, you threaten to burn places to the ground and kill everyone.'

Le Pedvin smiled his thin, horrible smile, 'Think of it as our secret weapon.'

'It's not very secret.'

'That's why it works so well.'

'Well it's not going to work for long. What happens when you've burned everything to the ground and killed everyone?'

Le Pedvin held the monk with his one eyed gaze, 'We've won.'

There was nothing in the cold, lifeless face Hermitage wanted to engage with, so he moved on. 'Have you any idea whereabouts he might have been?'

'Whereabouts? Of course not,' Le Pedvin scoffed. 'Have you got a map of Wales?'

Well naturally Hermitage didn't have a map of Wales. Who did? What a ridiculous suggestion.

'So we just go to Wales, start at the bottom and work our way to the top looking for a single dead Norman.' Hermitage tried to make it clear the whole idea was ridiculous.

'Got it. Shouldn't be hard to find. You can take this,' Le Pedvin held out the parchment map which was still grasped in his hand. 'It's been drawn up by Ranulph de Sauveloy. Ghastly man, but knowledgeable. It's the best we have.'

'Is this it?' Hermitage asked with obvious disappointment.

'Unless you've got something better?' Le Pedvin

enquired mockingly.

Hermitage shrugged. No one knew of any events in Wales so how could they make a map? Hermitage had heard of some ludicrous new approach to map making where you looked at the ground around you and drew a picture of that. What use this would be to anyone he couldn't imagine.

He peered at some tiny scribble in one corner of an otherwise randomly drawn shape of Britain.

'Here be dragons?' he read in disappointment at the speculation and unimaginative superstition.

'Yes. de Sauveloy wants you to spot one while you're there and do a picture.'

There seemed nothing more to say, Hermitage just looked blankly at the empty space on the parchment in front of him, thinking it was a fine summary of this situation, a void about to be filled by something horrible.

There was a shuffling at the back of the tent which diverted their attention just as the silence was about to get embarrassing. A flap was thrown aside and two more soldiers entered the space. They examined the contents of the tent with some disdain and then grunted a signal back the way they had come. They held the tent flap open and stood back to make way for King William.

Caput II: Because the King Says So.

'Aha.' The voice of the king climbed right inside Hermitage's habit and scared all the hairs on his body to attention.

'My Investigator and his weaving friend,' William observed as he strode into the tent like he owned it. Which he did, along with the country it was pitched on. He clasped a sheaf of documents in his left hand while his right held a leg of some animal or other, bits of which sprayed from the royal mouth as he spoke.

On their previous encounter Hermitage had thought the man physically quite unassuming but nonetheless terrifying. Nothing much had changed. The king hadn't grown in stature, he was wearing the simple garb of a solider, or at least someone who spent most of his time fighting people, and his head carried the bizarre Norman haircut. But there was still that look in his eyes. The look that asked you why you weren't dead, and said if you wanted to be, he could help.

Cwen stood at the back, not bowing. She was staring at the king, looking singularly unimpressed. She had frequently said what she would do to King William should she ever meet him. And here she was meeting him. Hermitage hoped to goodness she wasn't going to try any of the things, even one of the more harmless ones, of which there weren't many. If the king saw what appeared to be the eyes of a servant staring at him impudently, he would probably dismiss the servant, but keep their eyes.

'So.' William settled himself in Le Pedvin's vacated chair and thumped the arm with the handful of parchment. 'You're off to Wales to find Martel then.'

Hermitage tried to say yes, but his voice wouldn't come out in the presence of the king. He nodded and bowed at the same time, which he hoped conveyed the right message.

'Excellent. Doesn't really matter if you can't find him, or you find bits of him.' The king took a bite of his animal. 'Just make sure you bring back the gold,' he added nonchalantly.

The silence in the room this time was very heavy and Hermitage didn't know what to do with it. He had the urge to attack it with a lot of words, many of them pointless but all of them comforting, at least to Hermitage.

Le Pedvin sighed, 'I hadn't actually mentioned that,' he said pointedly.

'Well that's what we want,' William replied, as if it was obvious. 'No one cares about Martel, it's the gold he sent word of. The gold this idiot was supposed to collect.' He gestured at the body on the floor, which he had clearly noticed, but which he had ignored completely. They were probably laying around everywhere he went – or were after he'd left.

'As far as this lot know,' Le Pedvin went on, as if the others weren't there, 'they're looking for Martel's killers. Now that we've revealed the gold they might take it for themselves and never come back.'

William stared at Hermitage, who tried to appear the sort of monk who wouldn't dream of taking a king's gold. He wouldn't anyway, but he thought it important to look the part.

'They wouldn't,' William said confidently. 'No one in their right minds would take the king's gold. Just imagine the awful things that would happen to them if they did.'

Hermitage simply put all the sombre commitment one monk could get into a shake of the head.

'There you are,' William confirmed Hermitage's acquiescence. 'And the weaver and this impudent servant who keeps staring at me will do the same, won't you.' He barked these last words right in Cwen's face as he dropped his meat and bounded from his chair in one wolf-like leap, burying the space between them.

Cwen shrieked. William stared into her eyes with his look of impending death and eventually she swallowed and nodded her head.

'Excellent.' William was instantly back in good cheer, and returned to his chair.

Hermitage thought it best to get back to the matter in hand, in case William took a shine to killing someone, just for the practice. His voice came out as if carried into the room by a troop of particularly timid mice, 'Martel sent word of gold then your majesty?'

'He did. Mountains of it, apparently. People wandering around draped in the stuff. So, Martel, being seven different sorts of an idiot, we sent a messenger to get it.'

'This poor fellow here.' Hermitage noted the dead body and wished William would at least acknowledge it.

'Him?' The King gave the corpse a sideways glance. 'No, don't think so.' He turned to Le Pedvin, 'This isn't the first one is it?'

Le Pedvin gave his sigh another outing. 'No, it isn't. But they didn't know that either.'

Hermitage was horrified, 'How many have there been?'

'Two,' King William said.

'Three,' Le Pedvin corrected. William frowned at him.

'If you count Hector de Boise.'

'Oh yes,' William was happy with the correction. 'But he wasn't a messenger. He was a knight.'

'A knight?' Hermitage was getting beside himself again. He looked to Wat and Cwen, either for support or for an escape route. He was gratified to see that they both looked very worried.

'Absolutely,' the king said, as if Hermitage was daring to question Hector de Boise's knighthood. 'Bloody good knight as well. Excellent back hand.'

'And he's dead?' If messengers and knights were meeting their ends on this task, what chance did a monk and two weavers have?

'I think he must be,' King William mused. 'This messenger brought some of de Boise's bits back with him. Pretty vital bits by the look of them.' He cast a disinterested nod at the corpse of the messenger.

Hermitage's brain and body were not capable of functioning under this sort of onslaught so they stopped. His mouth dropped open and he stood frozen in fear and anticipation – and anticipation of fear.

'Just bring as much gold as you can carry and then we'll go and get the rest. After I've harried the north.'

The only burning question in Hermitage's mind was the one about not doing this at all please? Surely the failure of two messengers and a knight was reason to send an army. Or not to go at all? If he pointed out that they were being sent to a certain death, William would probably think that was a very good reason to get on with it.

'Did Martel give any indication of where the gold was majesty?' Wat asked.

Hermitage saw this was a very good question, it might

avoid the dangerous tramping about all over Wales asking about gold.

'Of course.' William had gone back to his parchments and looked up in apparent surprise that they were still there. 'The druids have got it.'

'The druids.' Hermitage said the words slowly, so they wouldn't frighten him all at once. 'Hence the curse that killed the messenger.' He nodded to himself, keeping remarkably calm, he thought. They were being sent into Wales to steal druid gold. Cursed druid gold. The first thing Hermitage was going to look for when they got out of this tent, was the nearest privy.

'That's them.' William seemed unconcerned 'Apparently they've got piles of the stuff. Every one of them wears a big lump round their neck, and the old ones have swathes of the stuff dangling from them.' William's eyes narrowed slightly as some thought skulked around his head. 'Easy enough to chop the head off an old druid, I'd have thought.'

'Unless you're a messenger of course,' Wat said with real feeling. 'Or Martel, or a knight,' he added. 'A fully armed, bloody good knight with an excellent back hand.'

William found this comment unhelpful and threw his attention back on Hermitage and Wat, 'Just get some gold and bring it back,' he barked. 'I expect Martel was killed by a druid after he'd revealed their gold, so you can find out which one and bring him back as well.'

'Just get some gold off the druids and bring it back,' Hermitage repeated in a daze. 'Along with a killer druid.'

'What is the matter with you people?' William's patience was expiring. 'It's a simple enough instruction, now get on with it.' He waved a hand to dismiss them from his presence, and beckoned Le Pedvin to join him in examining one of his documents.

Hermitage's mouth opened, ready to release a wide ranging exploration of the issues facing them, but his eyes saw the look on the king's face and he closed it again.

With silent agreement, and a new found understanding of just how closely death was treading their footsteps, they turned to leave the tent.

'Where are you going?' Le Pedvin asked, without looking up.

'Er, Wales?' Hermitage suggested. Honestly, you couldn't do right for doing wrong.

'That's right,' Le Pedvin confirmed. 'But we're about to leave for London so we'll take you with us. Make sure you get off on the right foot.'

'Aha,' Hermitage simpered, 'That is good. Save us a lot of time. Thank you very much.' His enthusiasm sounded like the last squeak of a blackbird in a pie shop.

Caput III: What's The Time?

'Oh go on, go on.' The children were tugging at Wulf's white robe, which was not really showing the right respect for his position. He was still only an acolyte, but really. They wouldn't have gone anywhere near the Arch-Druid's robe, let alone tugged it. Once he'd learned how to curse their souls to be devoured by the Gods, they'd leave him alone.

It was a warm summer's evening and the last light of the departing sun threw its final beams over the Welsh hills to illuminate an immemorial scene. As the illumination died away, the Gods once more started to place the stars in the sky, which was always a bit of a relief, and the shapes in the valley shrank in the insubstantial presence of darkness.

That night's ceremony at the great stone circle had come to an end, The Arch-Druid, with Wulf in attendance, had invoked the Gods to deliver the crops and so that was one job to tick off the list. Now the villagers could relax and the children wanted Wulf to do his magic. Some of them called it a trick but the Arch-Druid pressed the idea into their heads that it was magic; mainly by nearly pulling their ears off to make it clear.

Wulf raised his eyes in question to the Arch-Druid who responded with that look of disappointed acquiescence he always had to hand. The old man's robe was the whitest, his hair wildest, and the gold dripping around his neck glinted in last light of the sun and the first of the moon. He was the personification of authority.

With a curt nod, he indicated Wulf could go ahead.

The children clapped their pleasure and even the adults gathered to watch. Gathered outside the circle of course.

Wulf drew breath and strode his standard paces across the grass until he was at the centre of the circle. Marked by a simple slab of granite buried in the ground, this point was equidistant from all the stones of the circle. Exactly equidistant.

It was more than just the middle, it was the centre, the centre of everything the circle represented. And it was just what Wulf needed. He turned north, south, west and east in turn, gazed to the sky and held his arms out, indicating that he was ready.

The crowd breathed out, breathed in and spoke the great question. The question he would have to answer with nothing but the stones and the stars.

The question shuffled from mouths and ran around the enclosing woods, burning itself into the stones and into his ears.

'What's the time mister Wulf?'

Wulf knew he could do this better than all the other druids but didn't know why and couldn't explain it. He suspected even the Arch-Druid couldn't match him.

Where other acolytes had to examine each star in the sky in relation to its neighbours, and then compare them to the position of the stones, the whole thing leapt into Wulf's head ready-made. He didn't have to work anything out, he simply read the circle. He couldn't understand why everyone couldn't do it, and used to say so quite often. Which did nothing for his popularity.

He took breath and made a point of looking towards the correct star.

'By the reckoning of the Christians,' be began, 'it is the year ten thousand and sixty eight.' Some of the older druids still fought against the pagan nonsense of the Christian calendar, but it was hard to ignore when the rest of the country used it.

No reaction from the crowd; children could do this.

'The month,' he went on, turning slightly, 'is Augustinus.'

This brought some unimpressed murmurs.

'The twenty third.' Wulf stated with confidence.

The murmuring became acknowledgements of a job being done satisfactorily.

'The hour is ten and one quarter,' he slowed, 'precisely.' He emphasised the moment with a snap of his fingers.

Relief spread around the circle at the completion of the task and the senior men nodded their told-you-so's at one another. The children clapped until clapped into silence by elders and betters. Wulf had done it again.

But there was something new in his vision. He held up a hand to stop the noise. Something in the mithral stone spoke directly to him. 'Tomorrow will be fine,' he said. Well anyone could see that from the clear sky. 'But rain will spread from the west by early afternoon.'

Again, not much that an educated guess in this part of the country wouldn't have hit on the head. Rain usually spread from somewhere most days.

'Next week will start rainy but will clear by Wodensday and the rest of the month will be fine.'

There was muttering now.

'The wheat in the lower field will be ready for harvest in three days. The sheep must be brought down from the high pasture on the third of October. Old mother Carlac's winter fever will return on November the ninth.'

There was so much to tell; his head was filling up faster than his mouth could empty it. He was ready to go on at some length when strong arms took him from his place and pulled him back.

As he moved from the centre of the circle the details disappeared. He glanced up at the sky and could still see the time to an unbelievable accuracy, but the knowledge that had seemed so obvious, was gone.

He struggled against the hands that held him and eventually turned to see the Arch-Druid. The man clearly wasn't going to let go. In fact his attention was as much on the crowd as it was on Wulf. The muttering of those around the circle had become quite pronounced.

'Wulf Barelock has done well,' the Arch-Druid announced in loud clear tones to the assembly. 'The ways of the seer may even be open to him but only I, your Arch-Druid and Invoker can judge. I must take him from here and examine him.'

The muttering of the crowd died down a bit. There was no longer that underlying grumble which told Wulf he had been showing off again.

The Arch-Druid gazed into the sky. 'The God's tell me that mead must be drunk,' he announced.

Well, that took everyone's mind off anything but the mead. Now the adults were clapping and the children were scowling, knowing perfectly well how this evening was going to end up.

'We'll talk in the temple,' the Arch-Druid hissed in Wulf's ear.

If Wulf had been puzzled about what was going on, he was now ready to leak into his robe. The Arch-Druid wanted to talk to him in the temple. Everyone knew what that meant. Why not simply say "let's get the sacrificing knife and see what the inside of your stomach looks like."

...

Another pair of eyes frowned down on the scene from a hiding place among the trees on the side of the hill. These eyes had witnessed many things since they had started watching the village and its druids from a safe distance. A lot of the things seemed strange and pointless but a few were intriguing, and one or two were positively alarming.

This was an entirely new and unexpected development and the chin below the eyes was stroked in a thoughtful manner. This would need further observation. All information was useful, and anything that indicated a weakness of some sort, doubly so. The Arch-Druid down there seemed particularly put out. And that was just what the observer hoped for.

The eyes turned to the top of the hill and the figure scrambled up away above the tree line to the cave among the jumble of rocks, which was home now. No one came up here, not any more.

...

The square face of the outer temple wall emerged through the dark wood as if it was coming to meet them. Sacred oaks stood sentinel on either side of the entrance, their limbs raised in supplication to the stars. The close timbers of the outer wall glowered down at Wulf.

'Right,' the Arch-Druid said, turning his back to the temple. 'Tell me what you saw.'

Wulf faced his master. 'I, er, I saw the stars and the moon and could tell the time through the patterns in the sky and where they were above the stones.'

'As you've been taught,' the old man acknowledged. 'But you haven't been taught to read when the crops will come in.'

'No,' Wulf dropped his head. 'I didn't really see it, it was just sort of there.' He shrugged.

'It was just sort of there,' the Arch-Druid imitated Wulf's voice in a very mocking manner and was clearly not satisfied with this explanation. True to form, he reached forward and clipped Wulf sharp round the ear.

'Ow,' the acolyte responded. He thought he'd been acolyte long enough for the master to stop hitting him.

'What were you looking at?' the master barked. 'Quick now.'

'The mithral stone,' Wulf blurted out, without really understanding why he had forgotten.

'Ah.' The Arch-Druid seemed satisfied with that answer, which gave Wulf time to rub his ear. 'And?'

'It just looked as if the weather was going to change later on.'

'The mithral stone looked as if the weather was going to change?' The tone was now mocking and challenging, speaking to Wulf as if he was stupid as a tree. As it had since he was eleven.

The old man ran a hand over his face. 'I suppose I should be grateful to see this in my lifetime,' he said in dark tones. 'But I suspect it's a whole load of trouble in a robe.'

'What is?' Wulf asked.

'It's the Sight.'

'The Sight?'

'The Sight of the seer. You always were a troublesome child,' the druid went on, this Sight business plainly being Wulf's fault. 'Always questioning everything and coming up with answers before the others.'

Wulf could only agree with that and he had the bruises

to show.

'I knew from the earliest days you'd make the priesthood.' The druid nodded.

Well that was a bit much. Wulf wished that had been mentioned seven years ago, before all the agonies of the acolyte. A bit of encouragement now and then wouldn't have gone amiss.

'And I had a suspicion there'd be more. Perhaps a bard but maybe, just maybe a seer.'

The seers were great men, usually old and wizened, who, through years of selfless dedication and denial, were able to read the future from the state of the world. Becoming a seer was always a bit of a dream of the acolytes, but they rather hoped the gift would come naturally, selfless dedication and denial not being high on their list of things to do. And the one seer they had met gave most of them the shivers.

'And I'm a seer?' Wulf asked slowly. He hadn't even started to consider dedication and denial, and here he was, a seer.

'Don't know how else you'd explain it,' the Arch-Druid grumbled.

'But then why's it trouble?'

The Arch-Druid sighed his sigh at ignorance revealed. 'You know yourself, all seers are old men of great authority and wisdom.'

'That's what you told us.'

'Then that's what's true. You on the other hand are neither old, nor of great wisdom. If a wise and ancient seer turns up and wants to reveal what's going to happen, he generally cackles and laughs a lot. Might even dance about a bit to make people think he's mad.'

'Why?' Wulf didn't understand this at all.

'What would you do if someone came and told you in a calm and sensible manner that your cat was going to die tomorrow, and then it did?'

Wulf had to admit that sort of thing didn't go down very well. The cry of evil fluence was a popular one which seldom ended happily.

'But if an old loon comes dancing around the village singing an obscure song about cats and the afterlife, and then your cat dies? Well, you think that old man has been blessed with special powers and you probably give him a free meal.'

Wulf shook his head in amazement.

'It's all part of the training,' the Arch-Druid explained. 'The training you haven't had. And stone sight is the worst kind of all.'

'Stone sight?'

'The sight that tells you useful things and in detail. Just the sort of things people want to know. When will it rain, when will the frost come, when to harvest, when to plant?'

'Well that's good surely.' Wulf thought that sort of thing would make him quite popular.

'And the sort of things people don't want to know in detail. When the plague will come, how many will die, when there will be a famine, fire, flood. People don't like bad news. They don't like bringers of bad news in general, but they really don't like bringers of bad news who are always right.'

'What do we do then?' Wulf asked, suddenly feeling rather helpless and hopeless.

'We have to keep you alive.'

'I'm all for that.' He hadn't even imagined the question would be up for debate.

'Stone-seers are as rare as singing sheep. Only a stone-seer can build a circle in the first place, and do you know how long it is since the last new circle was built?'

Wulf considered the question carefully, it was probably one the Arch-Druid had asked before, and tried to pull Wulf's hair out for not knowing.

'Er,' he hesitated and screwed up his face in the manner of all children who are trying to drag from their memories some fact that they know isn't there. 'No,' he eventually admitted.

'Me neither,' the Arch-Druid responded with disarming honesty. 'So it must be a long time ago.'

'So,' Wulf said with a realisation that scared the spit from his mouth, 'I'm supposed to make a circle?'

The Arch-Druid shrugged, 'Who knows? No one's ever met a stone seer so the Gods know what you're supposed to do. The best we can do is keep you alive long enough to find out.' He lapsed into silent thought. Wulf tried not to look into the temple, the nine wooden statues of the Gods were in there somewhere and he wasn't ready for them yet.

'There's only one thing we can do,' the Arch-Druid announced, brightly. 'We need to see Lypolix. He'll know.'

Wulf's stomach sank. Many of the events of the acolyte's life had been challenging, some had been alarming and a few had been disturbing. Then there was Lypolix.

...

In the darkest recesses of the sacred wood, they found Lypolix the seer. All the acolytes were brought before the old man of the trees as part of their initiation. It was the part guaranteed to make those without a strong constitution go running for their mothers.

The body was small and bent, whether by old age or all the things that hung from it was hard to tell. If the small pots, pans, bits of plant, bones, twigs and dried rodent corpses that dangled from the arms and neck on lengths of twine were taken away, the man might be able to stand up straight. The tears in the figure's robes exposed bits of the wrinkled old man which people really didn't want revealed, and which took the word "wrinkled" to horrible extremes.

On top of this panoply of the peculiar was the head. And this made the rest of the body look positively wholesome. Random lengths of matted grey hair sprung in all directions. That there was face at all was only given away by the eyes, which peered from the depths like a drowning owl. They peered at Wulf though, and Lypolix cackled again.

'That's how you do it,' the Arch-Druid said with great respect. 'You could learn a lot from Lypolix.'

Wulf was pretty confident there was absolutely nothing he wanted to learn from Lypolix. He thought there might be some things he could catch, but not if he kept his distance.

The cackling went on a bit longer until the face looked straight at Wulf, which was rather disconcerting, 'The stones,' the mouth said, before the words were buried in yet more cackling.

'That's all it takes.' The Arch-Druid was nodding in appreciation. 'A good long cackle, a couple of words and leave it at that. No need to go telling people what date things are going to happen. Just cackle "crops" and shut up.'

Wulf was wondering if this was all there was to the

encounter, a lesson in cackling.

'And in his younger days Lypolix did an excellent dance of the madman.'

Wulf was sure a dance was unnecessary.

'Yes.' Wulf nodded to Lypolix as he did to mad mother Gwynn, whose only word these days was "thicket."

'In here,' Lypolix tapped the side of his head.

'A vision.' The Arch-Druid nodded authoritatively.

With the revelations about the methods of the seer, Wulf looked with new eyes at Lypolix. He realised the old man really was a cuckoo.

'We are gathered,' the great seer announced, with barely a cackle at all and his hands raised.

The Arch-Druid looked on in awe, hand raising was clearly a significant development.

'The acolyte of the stones.' The wizened finger came down again and hovered in the direction of Wulf, who smiled politely.

'The Arch-Druid.' The finger moved along. The Arch-Druid bowed his head in humble acknowledgement.

'And Lypolix.' The man even went to the trouble of pointing at himself.

A silence descended on the grove, the oak trees standing patiently, waiting their turn to be dragged into all this.

'It is the Prophecy,' Lypolix hissed into the night air, as if he'd been saving a special breath for just those words.

'The Prophecy,' the Arch-Druid repeated in a voice with so much awe he could be mined for the stuff.

'There will be more.' Lypolix breathed. 'More will come. More for the stones. We are not enough, but more will come. Even now they come. The monk. We must have the monk of the Christian God. Called, they are. Called I say. They cannot resist. There will be one for every stone and every stone will have one.'

Well that added up, even to Wulf. For years he had thought of the old seer as a figure of fear and respect. Tonight he had started to look on him as a rather harmless old loon, the type you would throw twigs at, or dunk in the pond. Now he found himself in the middle of some prophecy or other, he saw the sort of loon to be avoided. The sort who arrived in a village just before all the dogs disappeared.

'And when they are all here,' Lypolix paused, dramatically and Wulf looked on, expectantly. 'Then we can get on with the sacrifices.' The old druid cackled, as if looking forward to second helping of oats.

Caput IV: All Druids.

Travelling through the countryside on a Norman cart was not a comfortable experience for the small team of Saxons. They got things thrown at them by both sides.

The journey itself was pretty awful but the destination didn't bear thinking about. Wales. Hermitage reasoned that it couldn't really be all druids and dragons could it? If everyone was a druid who did all the work? If the sky was awash with dragons, how did anything get done at all?

But it was all fitting together in a rather horrible way. Years ago he had been told to go away from his monastery and study the ways of the druids, and other outlandish groups, so that the church could damn them more effectively. Well, he'd been told to just go away from his monastery first, the bit about the druids had come later. And of course he had done his work well. He only ever did his work well.

Many of the groups he encountered made a field full of March hares look like one of old Abbot Hender's silent contemplations on death. These were people who not only talked to the trees, they listened to the replies and then went off and did what the foliage told them.

Compared to most, the druids had been quite sensible. Plainly heretic and deserving of their fate, but at least you could talk to them without them whooping at you and skipping round a yew tree waving a dead fox in the air.

And old Theletrix had told him. Quite matter-of-fact, as if discussing the weather, the druid had said that Hermitage would go to Wales, he would attempt to take from the druids and would come to his end. But Hermitage did not believe in prophesy, well, not the ones come up with by druids. They were just normal people. Wrong, but normal.

The only reasonable view to take was that Wales was just like everywhere else. The people were just people and they only did the things people did. Obviously they did them in Welsh, but that was hardly life threatening. A trip to Wales would be absolutely no problem and in fact would be educational and informative.

He reached over and grabbed Wat's sleeve, 'We can't go to Wales,' he howled. 'We'll be eaten alive.'

'Oh, pull yourself together for goodness sake.' Wat, stirred from his reverie and brushed Hermitage off. 'It's no different from anywhere else.' The weaver gave the monk a very disappointed look, and even Cwen coughed her contempt.

'Look,' Wat went on in whispered tones as the cart trundled along, 'I didn't tell Le Pedvin or William of course, I wouldn't tell those men their heads were coming loose, but I've been to Wales before. It's not a problem.'

Hermitage regarded his friend with the old familiar admiration. He had known Wat would have the solution to the problem, and he did. 'You've been to Wales?' he asked in tones of awe.

'Of course. I'm a tradesman, I go where the trade is. There are so many superstitions about Wales that most people stay away. Leaves the market open for those of us who are prepared to make the journey. And of course the prices go up as a result.'

'Ah,' Hermitage said with real interest. But then a worry popped up in his head. He had a large space in there where he kept his worries so there was always one ready for action. 'So your trade was tapestry?'

'Of course.'

'The old tapestries.' Hermitage was cautious.

'Yes.' Wat's tone was of someone who knows they are about to get an earful of trouble.

'Oh Wat.' Hermitage let his disappointment gush out.

'They were very profitable.' Wat defended himself with money. 'Wales didn't get much in the way of sophistication.'

'I would hardly call tapestries full of naked people cavorting with one another sophisticated,' Hermitage admonished.

'I did one of a monk once,' Wat offered.

'And was that decent?'

'Oh no.' Wat was quite firm. 'Definitely not.'

'And the Welsh bought these disreputable works?'

'As quick as I could churn them out. They liked the outdoors. Very popular, the outdoors.'

'Scenes of the country and the natural world?'

'Mainly naked people cavorting outdoors, to be honest.'

Hermitage had run out of sighs.

'We're still living on Welsh gold.' Wat patted the pack on his back.

This gave breath to one of Hermitage's oldest and most familiar worries. In accepting the weaver's hospitality he was accepting his past, and the methods by which the hospitality became possible.

As usual he reasoned that he could continue to take the hospitality as long as he continued to complain about it.

'And you heard it from Le Pedvin.' Wat smiled. 'England's got thousands of Normans, all very much alive and looking for trouble, Wales has only had four, and they're all dead.'

...

Towards the end of the day, as the late summer evening descended cautiously over the landscape, the party approached a field full of tents. If Le Pedvin's camp had been bustling and busy this one was a beehive of Norman soldiery.

The tents stretched endlessly along the south bank of what must be the Thames. The river was broad and wide, or rather the space it occupied was. The tide was out now and the expanse of river looked like nothing more than a dribble down the chest of man who's fallen asleep in a field of mud.

On the opposite side of the river there was building work. Wooden scaffolding could be seen wandering up into the air, and even from this distance men were visible, swarming over it. A lot of them. Doing a lot of building.

'All right, you can leave them here.' Le Pedvin's voice barked out a command as he rode up on his horse.

Hermitage felt genuine relief that they wouldn't be going into the camp, they were being released to start their journey to Wales. Actually that was worse, wasn't it? His sense of good and bad was being eroded by the continual absence of any good by which to measure things.

Le Pedvin noticed Hermitage gazing at the structure over the river.

'The Tower of London,' he announced.

'The what?' Hermitage didn't know if this was supposed to mean anything.

'The Tower of London. That's what we're building. On top of the old Roman fort, we're building the Tower of London.'

Only one thought occurred to Hermitage, and as usual it had to be let out. 'Why does it want a tower?'

Le Pedvin looked at the monk as if he was very stupid indeed. 'Got to have a tower.'

'Have you?'

'Of course. First thing you have to do, build a tower. Defend against attack.'

Hermitage pondered the idea that if the Normans weren't so violent all the time, they wouldn't get attacked. And then they wouldn't need the tower. He knew ideas like this never went down well. 'I see,' was all he said.

'Well.' Le Pedvin dropped disdain from the back of his horse, which itself looked at the small Saxon band as if they were something nasty stuck to its hooves. 'You can head off to the druids and their gold, and we'll see you in Derby in three weeks. Won't we.'

'Oh absolutely, of course, no question,' Hermitage blurted out.

'Laden with gold I expect,' Le Pedvin added.

'Oh laden,' Hermitage confirmed. 'Very laden. Really very laden indeed. Hardly able to walk, probably.'

'Pleased to hear it. And just to make sure things go well I'm prepared to help you out some more.'

'More help,' Hermitage managed to say. 'How lovely.'

Le Pedvin stood in his saddle and scanned the surrounding men. Finding what he wanted, he beckoned someone to join them.

Without any apparent movement of the throng of men around them a new figure appeared at their side.

'This is, erm,' Le Pedvin paused, as if trying to remember the new man's name – or make one up. 'John.'

A quick glance was sufficient to get the measure of this

fellow. His age was probably the prime of life, but he was built to make starving cats feel better about themselves. And he had a look in his eye that said he would do things a starving cat would be ashamed of. He was only slightly larger than Cwen but his wiry frame could be built of solid metal. The face was long and drawn, cheekbones prominent and dark eyes brimming with secrets you really didn't want to know.

He gave Hermitage the shivers and the monk quickly knew why. The man reminded him of Le Pedvin.

'John will make sure things go well. Look after you, that sort of thing.'

Hermitage suspected that Le Pedvin's idea of looking after someone would not be a happy experience.

Le Pedvin now beckoned Hermitage and Wat close, and whispered so John could not hear. 'The king may trust you not to run off with his gold but I don't trust you to walk upright. John here thinks you're looking for Martel and doesn't know anything else. I suggest you don't tell him.'

Hermitage nodded his head and shook it at the same time.

'He really is the sort of man who would run off with a king's gold if he knew about it. Probably making sure anyone else who knew wouldn't speak of it. Most likely because he'd cut out their tongues.'

'And he's here to help?' Wat queried with a desperate laugh.

'He's here to help me.'

'Oh good.' Wat strode off in disgust. 'Thanks very much,' he called back.

'That's settled then,' Le Pedvin said to them all. 'You know what you've got to do, now get on with it.' He

35

wheeled his horse around and headed off to the middle of the camp without a backwards glance.

Hermitage and Cwen exchanged shrugs and set off after Wat. At least John had the decency to follow them at a distance.

When the weaver's grumbling died to a silent sulk, Hermitage risked a question.

'So, er, where do we go now? It'll be dark before long, I expect we'll need somewhere to camp?'

'I do know of an inn near London Bridge.' Wat was hesitant, as if it might not be good enough.

'Ah yes? What's it called?' Hermitage asked, equally cautiously, suspecting the place might be full of Wat's tapestries.

'Don't know.'

'Don't know?'

'Tends to change its name each time the king's tax man comes round. You know. Come to tax the Inn of the Horse. Oh, no such Inn of that name round here sir, this is the Inn of the Walking Man, has been for as long as I can remember.'

'Friends of yours then,' Cwen concluded.

'I am known to the Inn keeper.'

'I think perhaps we had better make haste?' Hermitage suggested.

'Eh?'

He directed their attention back down the track where a cloud of dust indicated that some Normans were on the move again. Saxons found out after dark were generally frowned upon, usually because they made a mess on the conquerors' horses when they were trampled to death.

...

The inn had no name at all when the small band

arrived, having run the last stretch to make it. Even John seemed anxious not be out in the open after dark.

The Inn Keeper explained he was waiting to see what sorts of names the Normans liked for their inns before re-naming his. Wat suggested The Abject Surrender would go down nicely, Cwen came up with The Norman Bastard, while Hermitage's best advice was to close the place completely and go on pilgrimage.

Thanking them for their comprehensively useless ideas, the inn keeper directed them to a corner table, where he brought them food and drink.

A large jug of beer and leathern mugs, a loaf of bread and a pot of steaming stew occupied most of the table and the four of them tucked in. John ate as if it was a distasteful necessity.

Hermitage had the opportunity to consider the man at close hand as he leaned over his food, and he had an overwhelming urge to send him on his way. He had been told about people who generated instant dislike; those who carried with them some indefinable aura of "otherness", and scattered it liberally. They didn't have to say much, or anything at all. They didn't have to do anything. They just stood there and within a few moments people wished they would go away.

Many of the people Hermitage encountered; brothers, priors, abbots, bishops, nobles, peasants, beggars and the like had suggested that he had a fair portion of this aura himself. He could never get them to put their finger on exactly what it was that he did, or said, which annoyed them so. He had been told he didn't need to say or do anything, he just had to be.

He pointed out that being was hardly something he had any control over, and they said that was a perfect example of what they were talking about, which did nothing to help Hermitage.

The second jug of beer disposed of and the sun well doused in the cold bath of night, there was unspoken agreement that it was time for sleep.

The inn keeper led them to a simple chamber at the back of the building, a ground floor room of rough earth with a single cot low in one corner. Cwen made it silently clear that the cot was for her.

'Be just us tonight.' Wat slid a coin to the inn keeper and winked to make the message clear. John would have to sleep outside. Le Pedvin's man didn't baulk at this, in fact he gave Hermitage the distinct impression he would be sitting up all night staring at the door. The fact that the man had said not a word to any of them so far, was starting to get to Hermitage in a way he didn't know he could be got to.

...

Settling down for a night's sleep. Hermitage's head was well provisioned with another night's load of disappointment and worry.

Sniffs and snuffles, sighs and wriggles settled into a collection of gentle breaths as the three of them drifted off to sleep.

At some indeterminate point Hermitage surfaced from the world of sleep, the reality of the real one making him thankful once more that it had all been a dream.

It was still dark and so he tried to settle his mind back towards sleep. Then he heard what had woken him.

There was a shuffle outside the room. Not by the door, across which Wat's sleeping form moaned and complained in its sleep, but behind the wall beyond Cwen. The single window in the place was a small opening high in the wall opposite the door, and it was no way big enough for anyone to get through.

'Ahh,' Hermitage cried out, leaping to his feet and backing away from the window, straight onto Wat, who had started to wake at the cry.

'Ahh,' Wat said as Hermitage trod on him.

'Ahh,' Cwen said, waking quickly and clearly convinced she was under attack.

'What is it?' Wat, half asleep, half angry at being woken. He got to his feet.

'The window,' was all Hermitage could say.

'What about it?' Cwen asked, sounding entirely angry that she'd been dragged from some very satisfactory dream.

'Something came through it.'

'Something came through the window?' Wat seemed unconcerned about things coming through the window.

The room was as black as the back room of an Inn in the middle of the night, and so all they could do was keep still and see if anything moved.

Nothing did. If anything had come through the window it had stayed where it was. There was no sound of shuffling from the other side of the wall and no snuffling animal wandered the floor.

'What is it?' Hermitage hissed, hoping not to be heard by whatever it was.

'How should I know?' Wat hissed back.

'Perhaps it's a snake?' Hermitage suggested.

'A snake?' Cwen almost laughed. 'Why on earth would a snake be climbing through our window?'

'Someone pushed it through.'

'Someone pushed a snake through the window?' Cwen snorted. 'How much beer did you drink, Hermitage?'

'I heard a noise outside,' Hermitage explained patiently. 'On the other side of the wall. Someone was out there. Then it moved to the window and something was dropped through.'

'But why a snake?'

'Someone wants to do us harm.'

'By dropping a snake through the window?' Wat was as impressed with the idea as Cwen. 'This isn't some story Hermitage. Nobody drops snakes through windows in real life. If it was a snake it could hardly jump around the room and bite us all. If it was a viper, who's to say it would bite anyone anyway, they're timid things, run away at the first sign of trouble.'

'Well,' Wat corrected himself. 'Sort of slither away I suppose. And who in their right minds goes round picking up vipers and dropping them through windows? One thing guaranteed to annoy a viper I'd have thought, being picked up and dropped through a window. So unless you heard a pronounced "oh bloody hell I've just been bitten by a viper" coming from outside, I'd suggest it wasn't a snake.'

'All right, all right.' Hermitage felt rather annoyed that his concern for their safety was being dismissed so comprehensively. 'What was it then?'

Wat moved and edged forward in the darkness, the sound of his feet scuffing across the floor. He covered the ground, clearly sweeping his foot left and right to see if there was anything there at all.

'Oh,' he cried out.

'What?' Hermitage asked, thinking Wat would feel a bit silly if he'd just been bitten by a snake, it being a mark of Hermitage's innocence that it never even occurred to him to say "I told you so".

'Nothing. Just a bit of a surprise. There is something here.' He could be heard bending down and scrabbling to pick something up. 'It's some sort of plant.'

'A plant?' Hermitage was puzzled but pleased that something had been found. And that it wasn't a snake. 'Who'd drop a plant through a window?'

'A farmer?' Wat suggested.

'What's a farmer doing running round in the night popping plants through people's windows?' Cwen did not appear to be taking this seriously.

'Maybe he'd run out of snakes?'

'Perhaps it's poisonous,' Hermitage suggested, trying to get the two of them to address the situation.

'Have to be pretty bloody poisonous to kill people just by being in the same room.'

'Maybe it's poison Ivy,' Cwen suggested with a snort. 'That can climb.'

'Very helpful.' Wat moved towards the window, his shadow blocking out what meagre light there was, 'I can't see what it is. Hermitage, you know stuff, can you tell?'

Hermitage was grateful he was thought of as knowledgeable, but identifying plants in the dark was not something he was prepared for.

He nearly jumped out of his habit when there was a scuffle outside and the door was thrown open. John stood on the threshold, candle in his left hand and sword in his right.

'What's going on?' he demanded, as if accusing those in the room of disturbing his night.

'That's what we'd like to know.' Wat threw the accusation back.

'I heard you lot shouting about. Come to see what's going on,' John explained. 'Sounded like you were being attacked.'

'We're having plants thrown at us. Found this on the floor.' Wat held up the plant so it could be seen in the candle light.

They all looked and could identify it easily.

'Mistletoe,' Hermitage whimpered, fear at the plant of the druids descending on him like a cat falling out of a tree. Drawing upon all of his Christian learning and his studied rejection of pagan philosophies – a rejection born itself from a deeper understanding than most, he appraised the implications of a simple plant, and drew the only possible and reasonable conclusion. 'It's the curse,' he howled. 'Druids. We're doomed!'

'Druids?' John was alarmed and looked round the room as if expecting to see one under the bed. 'Le Pedvin didn't say anything about druids.'

Hermitage turned to pace up and down the room, pacing always helped his thoughts get moving and made the fears subside, a little. He glanced up at the window where the first splashes of dawn were bothering the sky. And then he screamed.

The others jerked their heads up, saw what had alarmed Hermitage and variously gaped or gasped.

The window frame now looked like nothing so much as a nicely framed picture of a druid. A big, scary druid, with beard and staring eyes. This was explained by the fact that a big, scary druid with staring eyes was sticking his head through the window.

Caput V: Prophecy, Prophecy.

'Erm, this Prophecy?' Wulf asked, trying to sound like he knew really. 'Which one is it, exactly?' Life was full of prophecies. You couldn't walk ten yards in a market without someone offering you a prophecy. He would have to admit that prophecies from mad druid seers in sacred groves at night would probably be more reliable than most. He certainly didn't like the idea of a prophecy full of sacrifices. They were always such messy affairs.

'You will build it,' the seer prophesied through a pointing finger, which always added to the effect.

'I'll build the prophecy?' Wulf didn't think much of that as a prophecy. Prophesying another prophecy wasn't going to get anyone very far.

'No,' Lypolix replied, cackling mysteriousness replaced by irritation that he wasn't being understood. 'You will build it.'

'Well that's excellent,' Wulf said, trying to sound cooperative. 'And what is it exactly?'

More cackles.

'I hope you're taking all this in.' The Arch-Druid spoke up. 'Ask a direct question and get a cackle in reply.'

'Very helpful, I'm sure.' Wulf was finding the constant noise from the seer irritating. 'I'm hardly likely to burn him as a witch am I?'

The Arch-Druid took a step forward and clipped Wulf round the ear.

'Ow,' Wulf cried, with a glare at his master.

'Just because you're a stone seer doesn't mean you don't behave.'

'You'll build it,' the seer went on, gazing into the air of the grove in what was apparently a mysterious manner. He waited until there was complete silence. Then he waited some more until an owl hooted. 'The Grand Complication,' he announced

'No.' The Arch-Druid's awe was having trouble keeping up.

'Aye, aye,' Lypolix cackled out. 'No less, no less.'

'This is incredible.' The Arch-Druid had a good stare at the same bit of mid-air which was occupying the seer's attention.

Wulf gave it a hard look as well but couldn't see anything. No materialisations, no spiritual wisps, no images created by a swarm of midges. Very disappointing. He looked to the Arch-Druid again and it was clear he was going to have to confess that he had not the slightest idea what a Grand Complication was. Mindful of his ears, Wulf half put his hand up to ask a question, 'This erm, Grand Complication?'

'Yes?' Lypolix turned his attention back to the here and now.

'What, erm, what is it?'

'What is it?' Lypolix screeched, either offended that Wulf didn't know, or appalled that anyone could ask such a stupid question. 'What are you teaching acolytes these days?' he directed the question at the Arch-Druid.

'Not about the Grand Complication,' the Arch-Druid replied defensively. 'It's hard enough getting the equinoxes to stick in their heads, never mind advanced ideas like The Grand Complication.'

The two old men lapsed into a session of mutually disappointed head shaking that did nothing to explain what a Complication was, Grand or not.

Wulf tried another tack. 'Where exactly will I build it?' he asked. Perhaps this would move things on from what The Grand Complication actually was. As a newly anointed stone seer he used his mystical powers to conclude that it probably had something to do with stones.

'I have started,' the mad old seer announced. 'You will finish.'

That was really less than no help at all.

'Aha.' Wulf gave his knowing nod again. At least he hoped it looked knowing from the outside.

'Come, come, see.' Lypolix beckoned them to follow him deeper into the woods.

Wulf thought that was probably a very bad idea, but could see he had no choice.

Lypolix led and the Arch-Druid followed, pushing Wulf ahead of him.

'We're all taught about The Grand Complication,' the Arch-Druid explained as they tramped on. 'Or at least the idea of it. You would have been if you'd entered the priesthood. It's been handed down through all the generations from the ancient ones.' The words "ancient ones" were accompanied by the traditional nod of the head. The nod which indicated the great debt the modern world owed to the ancient ones.

Of course it would be the ancient ones, wouldn't it. The wretched ancient ones who were the bane of every acolyte's life. "The ancient ones could do this in their sleep." "If you don't remember the dates of the equinox the ancient ones will come and steal your spirit." "Don't make me fetch the ancient ones." All the threats and worries of a young druid's life emerged fresh and full of life from the ancient ones. As far as Wulf and the other acolytes were concerned, if they'd ever met an ancient one, they'd have taken him to the temple to find out what ancient entrails looked like.

Perhaps now that he was a seer of stones he could dash some ancient ones to death against quite a big one.

'But no one knows the details,' the Arch-Druid went on. 'We know it would be a large circle and would have special powers but more than that has vanished in history. Taken with them to the spirit world by the,'

'The ancient ones,' Wulf snorted slightly. 'Yes, I can imagine.'

Lypolix cackled in a very straightforward manner. 'He will find the master, and Lypolix will give the others their power. But we must hurry,'

'Hurry?' The Arch-Druid clearly thought hurrying a task like this was as futile as shouting at an acorn.

'Oh yes.' The seer looked at them all significantly. 'They are coming.' He nodded at this as if interested to hear about it himself.

'They? Who are they?'

The Arch-Druid shook his head in disappointment. 'You don't ask the seer a specific question like that. Never get an answer.'

'Aha, they are coming, and we must hurry to be ready for them.' Lypolix was back to his obscure self and added a cackle for emphasis.

'You said a Christian monk?' Wulf pressed.

'The most important,' Lypolix confirmed. 'After the stone seer of course. And the Arch-Druid.'

Wulf was about to dismiss all this as so much seer

nonsense when they emerged into a clearing.

It wasn't a very good clearing, made by hand rather than nature, and there were still small trees and the remains of undergrowth dotted about. It was the standing stones that sent a shiver through Wulf. Three relatively small standing stones he had never seen before. Stones which did not seem friendly.

'I have started, I have started,' Lypolix cackled as he skipped into the clearing. He proceeded to hop and skip around what would be a circle when the rest of the stones were erected. He stopped at each stone in turn, patting it and stroking it in a very disturbing manner.

The Arch-Druid raised his druidic eyebrows, the ones which made the acolytes flinch. This place was clearly new to him as well.

'The stone seer will find the master stone,' Lypolix explained with something approaching clarity. 'The great stone to rule them all. It will call to him across the fields and he will fly to it.'

Wulf started to back away from the seer until he bumped into the Arch-Druid.

'Where are you going?' his master demanded.

'Oh, you know. Anywhere?' Wulf sounded hopeless. He tipped his head towards Lypolix, rolled his eyes and risked a bit of impertinence with the Arch-Druid. 'I think the seer is several stones short of a circle.'

'Of course he is.' The Arch-Druid missed Wulf's suggestion by a country mile. 'You heard him. You are to select the master stone.'

Wulf looked rather hopelessly at the mostly missing stone circle, the three upright rocks looking as if they could easily be handled by one man. If this was the start of a Grand Complication, it wasn't very grand.

'I don't know even where to start looking for some master stone.' He held his arms out, trying to take in the whole of the surrounding land.

Lypolix now gave up the very personal contact with his stones and advanced on Wulf. There was a look in the old man's eye which made Wulf pull his robe a little bit tighter.

When he drew close, a withered old hand reached out towards Wulf's face and without any sort of introduction tapped the acolyte in the middle of his forehead.

It was as if a fully formed and completed dream had been forced into Wulf's head, pushed in through the seer's finger. It had all the vivid life of a dream at the moment of waking, except of course, Wulf was already wide awake. It was a very uncomfortable feeling, and Wulf felt it offered some sort of explanation for Lypolix. If the old man had to put up with this all the time it was no wonder he was off with the swallows.

He saw the circle complete, he saw the master stone standing in its place, and he knew where it was now. He saw what this Grand Complication would do and he knew how to use it. Half of him hoped that, like a dream, this understanding would fade when he woke up. Or went to sleep.

'He sees, he sees,' Lypolix skipped off to let his stones know.

The Arch-Druid looked to Wulf for an explanation.

All the acolyte could do was nod. 'I can see the master stone,' he said with some surprise. 'I know where it's got to go and I know where to find it.' His voice was full of wonder at his own words.

The Arch-Druid nodded in a knowing, Arch-Druid sort of way, quiet satisfaction at a life of devotion coming to fruition.

'It's quite big though,' Wulf explained, as he started to appreciate the scale of the task.

The Arch-Druid nodded solemnly.

'In fact it's very big.'

'We will find a way.'

'It really is very big indeed,' Wulf tried to emphasise the scale of thing he had in his mind.

'It will be the work of the Gods,' the Arch-Druid droned. 'And the villagers will help.'

'Ah, yes.' Wulf was thinking that he wouldn't trust most of the villagers with a task as complex as moving a rock. Perhaps the ancient ones would need to lend a hand as well.

There was one element of his vision he hadn't mentioned, and didn't really like to. It would come out sooner or later. But then he recalled that the Arch-Druid was always difficult with things that came out later. And the old man had demonstrated his habit of hitting Wulf had not gone away. 'I, erm, I think the size might be the easy bit,' Wulf said cautiously.

Arch-Druidic eyes narrowed, 'And what would be the difficult bit?' he enquired, carefully.

Wulf took a breath and swallowed.

'Well,' he tried to sound nonchalant, 'I imagine that the erm, gold will be a bit tricky.'

'What gold?' the Arch-Druid asked slowly.

'The gold for the stone,' Wulf explained, with bright enthusiasm, hoping it would carry the audience with him.

'The stone has gold on it,' the Arch-Druid said, clearly accepting the fact, but not very happy about it.

'Oh yes,' Wulf nodded. It had to have the gold or the whole thing wouldn't work.

'And how much gold are we going to need?' the Arch-Druid asked in the tone of a man who has asked an army of rampaging beggars how much of your food they would like to steal. He even dropped a protective hand to the gold that hung around his neck.

'Oh, quite a lot,' Wulf said matter-of-factly and with a large smile, as if that made things easier. 'Probably more than we've got.' He turned his head and thought about the druid gold. The Arch-Druid himself carried the largest supply but there were torcs and a few other bits and pieces about. 'We might need to get some more from other druids,' he concluded.

He'd never seen that look on the Arch-Druid's face before. Disappointment, irritation, anger, fear, resignation and despair. All at once. And all expressed by a face which was mostly beard. This was clearly a problem.

The Arch-Druid offered no suggestions so Wulf moved away to the nearest stone of Lypolix's to show where the gold would go on the full-size version. As he drew close he frowned as he thought he saw a new feature on the upright rock. 'Is that blood?' he asked with a shiver, pointing at stains on the nearest upright.

'Very likely,' the Arch-Druid confirmed, emerging from his personal reverie about getting gold from other druids. 'Got to have a sacrifice to give the stones the power.'

'Ah yes,' Lypolix skipped over and stroked this stone in a very intimate manner.

Wulf hadn't realised anyone could be intimate with a stone until he saw this. But there really was no better word.

'And you did the sacrifice did you?' he asked, and

immediately wished he hadn't.

'Difficult,' Lypolix cackled. 'Difficult it was. Great sacrifice needed for the Grand Complication. Unique.'

Wulf really did not want to know what a unique sacrifice would be for Lypolix. Anything smaller than a chicken would probably get away, and he doubted the old seer could defeat anything bigger than a chicken. Probably a chicken then. Mind you, there was an awful lot of blood for one chicken. Perhaps the stones needed a chicken each.

'The sacrifice, the sacrifice,' Lypolix cackled as he danced round in a little circle.

'Aha,' Wulf nodded very cautiously.

'The Gods themselves,' Lypolix added mysteriously.

Wulf didn't understand what this meant. But then he thought not understanding anything Lypolix said was perfectly reasonable.

'The Gods?' The Arch-Druid asked. This seemed to mean something to him.

'Aye, aye,' Lypolix said, with as much significance as he could squeeze between two cackles.

The Arch-Druid stroked his beard and explained to Wulf. 'He means the Gods themselves helped with the sacrifice.'

'Helped?' Wulf couldn't see what divine help would be needed to kill a few chickens.

'Yes. They could have delivered the sacrifice to Lypolix, or struck them dead at the right moment, any one of a number of things. It's very rare for the Gods themselves to get involved in a sacrifice. I wonder what they did.'

Wulf noticed Lypolix's face dropping at these words to become, what was the word? Normal. He stroked his straggled beard and spoke in an almost human voice. 'The

Master Stone shall have him,' he whispered in a voice that would send shivers down a slab of solid granite.

'Erm,' Wulf couldn't help himself.

'Yes?' Lypolix snapped his attention to Wulf and the old seer was back. The old, familiar cackling, incoherent cuckoo-head.

Wulf wasn't sure he wanted to ask anymore. 'Who will the, erm, stone have? Exactly. If stones can have people that is?'

'The great sacrifice,' Lypolix explained, as if that should be obvious.

'Yes,' Wulf nodded. Another chicken then. Probably a very big one. He should have realised Lypolix would have personal relationships with the bird life.

'The master sacrifice for the master stone,' Lypolix went on. 'It shall have the monk.'

'Monk?' Wulf was lost, was there something called a monk-bird? Could be, he was never very attentive during the Arch-Druid's instruction on animals and plants. The stars were his thing.

'Aye. Even now he comes and the stone will be initiated in the blood of the Christian monk.' Lypolix rubbed his hands in happy anticipation.

Oh, ye Gods. He meant a real monk. An actual living person. He turned a shocked gaze to the Arch-Druid and was alarmed to see the old man didn't look at all put out by this. Perhaps all that chicken blood on the other stones wasn't actually so chicken-related after all.

'We're expected to sacrifice a monk?' Wulf couldn't stop his voice quavering ever so slightly.

'Oh, no,' Lypolix laughed at the stupidity. 'The Gods will kill the monk for us. All we have to do is watch.'

Caput VI: A Growing Quest.

'What do you want?' Wat demanded.

'I have come,' the man intoned. The voice was as deep as druid's should be, and the words came out in a slow chain, each one waiting until its significance had died down before making way for the next. This was a man who knew how to intone and probably did it regularly. Most likely he practised quite a lot and was recognised for the quality of his intoning. His words made it quite clear that druid ways were mysterious and were not about to be explained.

The face disappeared and the man could be heard walking round the outside of the inn. They waited patiently, no one having much to say until the full druid, head, robe, arms and legs, appeared at the doorway.

The beard was certainly in character, dark but with strands of grey gathering their strength for an assault on the main body. The dark brown eyes did look intelligent, but this druid was probably only middle aged and was not strewn with gold. Hermitage felt a momentary disappointment that even though they now had a druid, they were still going to have to go to Wales. He also felt ashamed that he had assumed the first druid he saw was guilty.

'Well, now you've arrived, you can go away again,' Wat growled. 'And take your mistletoe with you.' He searched around and found the plant lying by the door, picked it up and threw it at the druid.

The man caught the small branch and slipped it into a pocket in his robe with great reverence.

'I am here,' the druid said in an unnecessarily sing-song voice, as if that was supposed to explain anything.

'And soon you won't be.' Wat put his shoulder to the task of removing the druid and managed to get him to the door.

'No, look, really, you don't understand.' The druid's voice was suddenly a lot less mystical. 'I have come to join you.'

'Join us?' This did give Wat pause for thought. 'Join us in what?'

'Your journey. Your journey to Wales.'

There was a moment of silence, a moment of awe as this impressive figure dominated the room once more. Hermitage's wonder took an extra leap. The man had calmly announced that he was joining them on a secret mission that they had only just been given.

Wat broke the tension as he threw his hands in the air. 'Is there anyone who doesn't know we're going to bloody Wales? Who told you?'

'It is known,' the druid said mysteriously.

'Oh, very mysterious I'm sure. Of course it's known. I don't know why we don't get a bell and announce it in the middle of the inn. See if anyone else wants to come along.'

He looked to Hermitage, who had no ideas to offer.

'What's the point?' Wat went on, in high pitched exasperation. 'Well, we're up now, might as well all have a nice breakfast together while we discuss the health of Hermitage's mother.' He picked up his pack and strode from the room, brushing John and the druid aside.

Hermitage followed, rather alarmed to hear his mother being mentioned as he was reasonably confident she and Wat had never met.

...

After a desultory breakfast, with more glare passing across the table than the summer sunrise, the departure from the Inn with no name was a rapid and straggling affair. Wat was up front, striding along as if he wanted to leave everyone behind. Cwen followed, striding as best she could to show that she was not going to be left behind. Hermitage followed, wondering what the hurry was.

The druid was next, followed by John, who looked suspiciously about, as if ready to fend off an immediate attack. Neither of them appeared to be in any great rush to catch up with the weaver as he made a bee-line for the river.

....

The great River Thames could be many things. It could be an impenetrable barrier, it could be a magnificent highway. It could be a source of food for those on its banks, or a threat to their homes in winter. It could be an inspiration to poets as they translated its majesty into words, or to musicians as they told tall tales of its passage. It could be the subject of murals or tapestries and it could be a creature of legend and myth.

In years to come, its fish-weirs were going to cause real trouble - but thereby hangs another tale altogether.[3] To one particular pair of eyes, watching as the worried monk, Wat, Cwen, John and the Druid approached the bank, the River Thames could also be a nice little earner if you had a boat. Whether it was actually your boat or not was only splitting hairs.

...

Hermitage had drifted into the lead of the party and

---

[3] That tale is The Magna Carta (Or is it?), available for a very modest amount of gold.

almost leapt into Wat's arms as an apparition appeared before him. The approaching figure must surely have been washed up by some evil tide, or been thrown out of the slime by the foul creatures of the river who, after all, did have some standards.

There were legs and arms but they had all the substance of partly dissolved driftwood. The only reason the torso could be described as such, was because it was in the middle, holding the rest together. The head was positively alarming. There was a beard, or rather a bush of grey hair coming out of the bottom of the face, but it wasn't clear whether the beard was growing from the face, or vice versa. Above this fibrous mass was a grinning mouth and bright sparkling eyes which clearly said that someone was alive in there. A single tooth loitered in the mouth, probably waiting for just the right moment to leave, taking what final vestiges of sanity loitered in this accumulation of body parts.

The party had drawn together again now, and stood behind Hermitage, probably quite gratefully.

'Hello,' the bearded mouth spoke in a bright, squeaky, high-pitched voice which suited its source completely.

'Yes.' Hermitage acknowledged that the figure was actually alive and had spoken.

'I'm More the boatman,' the figure announced. 'Boat?' he asked in an enthusiastic flurry of beard, gesturing towards a large wooden rowing boat which nestled the bank.

Wat peered around Hermitage, 'Yes, we can tell.'

'Take you down the river?' More the boatman asked hopefully. 'Or up?'

'Or across?' Hermitage asked. He didn't know why he asked this. He just liked to have everything complete and its place.

'Ooh, no,' More sounded horrified at such a suggestion. 'I don't do across. That's ferrying. I used to do ferrying but I don't anymore.'

'Why not?' Hermitage was drawn into this bizarre discussion despite himself.

'I had a very bad experience once.' The old man nodded significantly. 'But it's a long and mysterious tale.'[4]

'Good,' Wat said. 'We don't need to hear it then.' He looked at the boat again, appraising its strength and safety. 'And you can take us up the river can you?'

'Oh, yis.' The old man nodded very happily. 'Boatman by appointment to King William, I am.'

Wat looked up and down the river bank, probably hoping to spot some other boatman who looked a bit more man, and a bit less left-over bits of a boat. There was no one. 'We're going to Wales,' he said, probably hoping to scare the boatman into leaving.

'Wales?' the old man squeaked, clearly impressed at such a great journey. 'Where's that then?'

'Where's what?' Hermitage asked, getting lost very quickly.

'Where's Wales?' the boatman asked.

Wat coughed lightly. 'I think we need a different boat,' he whispered quite loudly.

'West of here.' Hermitage couldn't help but explain.

'Oh, Staines way. I can take you there. And the tide's with us so make very good time.'

'We're not seriously going to get in this thing's boat are we?' Cwen had a look of revulsion on her face as she

---

[4]   Which is called The Domesday Book (No, Not That One), another essential purchase.

appraised the boatman.

'The boat looks alright,' Wat replied. 'The man? Definitely not.'

'If I don't get you there, you can have your money back.'

'Won't do us much good if we're walking to Wales along the bottom of the river will it?' Cwen observed.

'So,' Wat turned to More. 'How much?' He asked this as if expecting any reply to be ridiculous.

'To Staines?' More nodded and grinned. 'Well, it's usually fourpence, but there's five of you see.'

'Yes,' Wat said, slowly, cautiously, and with just a hint of threat that he could take his business elsewhere.

'So that's a, erm..,' More screwed up his face even more than time had already done, and gazed at the clouds while he worked this out. 'A pound.'

'A pound?' Wat's voice was high and shocked. 'No it isn't,' he said. 'Five people at fourpence is twenty pence. One shilling and eight pence.

'Oh yes,' More agreed. 'A shilling, that's the one.' He held out his hand.

Wat opened his mouth to object but realized it had been his offer. This More wasn't as stupid as he looked. Mind you, no one could be quite as stupid as More looked.

'Of course if you want to go to Wales, that's extra.'

'Let's get to Staines in one piece shall we?' Wat suggested.

More now scurried around taking people's packs, and stacking them in the depths of the boat, before he gestured them all to climb aboard. On the prow seat he placed the druid. This could be to set the balance of the boat, the druid being the largest of them all. Or it could be that rowing down the river with a large druid in the prow of your boat looked pretty impressive, and was probably good fortune.

Hermitage noted that More didn't seem at all disturbed by the druid, and generally appeared to be very happy with his lot. As his lot was plainly pretty awful, this could only mean that he was mad. On the river with a mad boatman. Marvellous.

With them all aboard, the boat was fended away from the bank and pulled out into the stream without sinking once.

...

The row along the river slipped quietly on for hour after hour. With the sun shining and the ripples no more than gentle sparkles on the surface of the water, Hermitage even found himself feeling quite relaxed, which was an unusual experience for him where boats were concerned. The Lord had miraculously walked on water, which Hermitage took as a sign that mortal man should keep away from it completely. His only experiences in boats had been bad ones. Still, there was plenty of time yet.

'At least old Bones of the River here seems to know his stuff,' Cwen noted as she trailed a hand in the passing water. She hastily withdrew her hand when something soft and lumpy bumped into it.

'Oh, yis.' More nodded as he pulled on the oars with a strength and efficiency that was very well hidden in his flimsy frame. 'I been rowing this river for as long as I can remember.'

'Probably about a week,' Wat commented with a laugh.

'You say you used to be a ferryman?' Hermitagewas

always uncomfortable when conversations drifted toward mockery, or insult.

'Oh, yis, that's right.' More sounded as if he'd only just remembered the fact. 'Down Gravesend way it was. Backwards and forwards I used to go. Regular as the tides. That was when I was rowing for the king.' It sounded like he was about to embark on his very lengthy tale. 'But me boat got burned after his man had used it. And not paid me for the trip. And there was three of them as well. Three at fourpence, I should have had a pound.'

'Shilling.'

'That's the one.'

More rowed on in silence.

'There was a snooty one,' he piped up for no good reason.

'Beg pardon?' Hermitage asked, wondering if one of the birds on the river was called a Snootyone.

'In me boat,' More explained. 'There was a snooty one and another, one who kept very quiet and wanted to go home all the time. Very sensible, if you ask me. Then there was some talkative Saxon who did nothing but complain, and the horrible one of course.'

'That's not three, it's four,' Cwen pointed out.

'That's right,' More agreed.

'A horrible Saxon?' Hermitage asked.

'No, no. The horrible Norman. All thin he was.'

That was a bit much coming from the man who made a sliver of parchment look like it had let itself go.

'And with an eye patch and all.'

The boat was already pretty silent, but now it became more so.

'Eye patch?' Cwen asked as nonchalantly as she could, her capacity for nonchalance being very limited indeed.

'Le Pedvin,' Wat spat.

'That's him,' More exclaimed, as he stopped rowing. 'You know him?'

'Oh, we know Le Pedvin alright.'

More looked at them all, his familiar inane grin was gone. 'Well as far as I'm concerned, any friends of Le Pedvin can get out and walk.' He nodded towards the river.

'We're no friends of his,' Wat explained, 'well, most of us.' He looked towards John, who gazed at the river to see if he could spot a Snootyone swimming by.

'It was him what put a burning stick in me boat,' More complained.

'He likes burning things to the ground,' Hermitage observed. 'It's what he does best.'

'So, how do you know him?' More asked. 'If you don't like him?'

'He keeps giving us jobs to do.' Hermitage explained. 'And then he threatens to kill us all and burn us to the ground if we don't do them. It's very unimaginative.'

'But effective,' Cwen observed with a disappointed scowl.

'Is this one of his jobs?' More asked.

Hermitage didn't like to say yes, in case More rowed them to the shore and made them get out.

'Yes, I'm afraid it is,' Wat acknowledged apologetically.

More rowed steadily on, with no more sign of wanting to get rid of his passengers. His paying passengers.

'What's the job then?' he asked after a few minutes, as if he'd only just managed to digest the facts.

'We're looking for someone,' Wat replied quickly, looking at Hermitage as if the monk might have blurted out something about gold.

'Oh yis?' More nodded. 'That'll be easy then. There's lots of people about.'

Hermitage frowned as he tried to make sense of this.

'Don't find me though,' More added. 'I don't want to be found by Le Pedvin. Not again. I can't afford the boats.'

'We're not looking for just anyone,' Cwen half shouted. 'If we were looking for just anyone we'd have found them straight away.' She shook her head at the idiot in charge of their boat.

'Well,' More responded equitably, 'I did wonder why you'd need a boat to find someone. There's plenty of people on land.'

Hermitage, Wat and Cwen exchanged glances that said they thought getting out of the boat soon would be quite a good idea.

Hermitage spoke clearly and slowly, 'We are looking for someone particular, an individual person. Just the one. With his own name.'

'Who you looking for then?' the master mariner enquired.

Cwen huffed her impatience, 'A Norman called Martel. 'Know him?'

'Yis,' More said, without surprise.

'Oh really.' Cwen's disbelief added to the weight in the boat.

'He was the one in me boat who wanted to go home. Nice chap.' More nodded happily, but then had a thought. 'Small world, isn't it?'

Hermitage, Wat and Cwen exchanged another look. This could not be right. There was no way they would wind up in the boat of a man who knew the person they were looking for. Coincidence wasn't even the word. It was as if someone had made up a ridiculous connection to put in a story, just to make the thing work.

'You know Martel?' Hermitage asked slowly.

'That's right,' More confirmed. 'He was the one who was quiet. There was rotten Le Pedvin with his eye patch. Another horrible know-it-all called, what was it?' More racked his brains, which didn't take long, 'Randolph?'

'Ranulph?' Hermitage asked, recalling the name of Le Pedvin's map maker.

'That's him.' More confirmed. 'Then there was the Saxon who complained all the time. I think he was called Mabbut, or something like that. He went north but didn't come back. And then there was Martel. He went north and did come back. Didn't look like he wanted to though. Seemed to be in trouble with old eye-patch-man, goodness knows what he'd done. Nothing was ever good enough for that man. Martel was being taken back for some sort of punishment.'

'Being sent to Wales,' Hermitage breathed.

Wat looked the boatman up and down before asking very carefully, 'So, you know what he looks like?'

'He's hard to miss with that eye patch,' More replied.

'Martel.' Wat kept his temper.

'Oh, yis,' More nodded.

'Can you describe him?'

'I've got a better idea.' The old boat man sounded very enthusiastic for his better idea.

'Which is?' Wat asked very cautiously.

'I'll come with you.'

'No,' Wat said. 'You won't. You'll tell us what he looks like and we can find him.'

'But if I was with you I'd be able to point to him. What if I suddenly lose the power of speech?'

'You'll lose the power of something in a minute.'

'And he would know me. I wouldn't be able to say, "that's Martel" at the first Norman looking type I saw. I expect he'd remember.'

'If he's been in a boat with you, he'll never forget. I doubt if he'll recognise you now though,' Wat explained with grim seriousness. 'What with him being murdered and all.'

Hermitage thought this was a good plan to make More see that going to Wales was a very bad idea. Hermitage was certainly convinced.

'Murdered?' More asked, in a saddened tone.

'To death,' Wat added with a grimace.

'Oh dear,' More squeaked. 'Still,' he brightened enormously. 'Perhaps he left me something.'

'Left you something?' Hermitage did not know what was going on.

'Yis. I liked Martel, we got on. Perhaps he left me some money when he died.'

'Got murdered,' Wat corrected, with some malice. 'Along with two other Normans, one of them a knight. You are not coming with us,' he said quite plainly. 'Absolutely no way whatsoever. There are too many of us already and we do not want you. Is that settled?'

...

'Well, that was inevitable,' Hermitage muttered to Wat as the six of them disembarked for the evening and set up camp, More included. 'It looks like everyone we bump into wants to come along. Almost like Wales is calling them.' He shrugged at this patently ridiculous idea.

Caput VII: The Scent of Gold.

In Wales, in the heart of it, in the great hall of the stronghold of Lord Bermo, who proclaimed himself ruler of quite a lot of it, the druids were the topic of conversation, once more. (Great Hall and stronghold being more by the way of convenient terms rather than actual descriptions.)

King William would have been very disappointed to hear that this conversation included several references to druid gold, his druid gold as he saw it. If Lord Bermo had any idea that this was William's view, he would have taken issue with him immediately.

Lord Bermo had a very physical approach to taking issue with things, most of which ended up so comprehensively damaged that they weren't an issue any more. People, livestock, furniture, nothing was safe.

Druid gold had long been a topic of interest, but the druids themselves were always there to get in the way. The druids controlled access to the Gods and that was that. Lord Bermo was a straightforward, practical and action-oriented chap. But he was also Gods fearing. Actually, he was Gods-terrified. He could lop the head off most things at a moment's notice but even he drew the line somewhere. It was much further out than where most people drew their lines, but at least it was there.

Now though, other options were appearing in his head, or rather were being dripped in through his ears. Apparently the Christian God was much more powerful than all the Gods of the druids put together.

Christian priests and pilgrims passed through this land and had been telling him this for years. The problem for Bermo was that the druid Gods were in the woods outside his window. The Christian God was miles away. This usually meant that the Christian priests and pilgrims became issues, which were dealt with in the usual manner. Their actually completing a passage through his land was so unsuccessful they had taken to going round instead.

This latest visitor had a very interesting view though. He was pointing out that if the druid Gods could be defeated by the Christian God then all the druid gold would become Christian. He then went on to explain that the Christian God didn't care for gold and the like and so Bermo could look after it.

The visitor had been with Bermo for several days now. That he was a stranger and was still alive at the end of those several days meant that change really was in the air.

On this evening, the fire glowed dull but hot in the middle of the floor. The stranger thought this was also a fairly accurate description of his host. He sighed as he went over the argument. How many more times? He knew English was Bermo's second language, but he was starting to have doubts the man even had a fully functioning first one.

'We have swords,' the visitor explained, nodding towards Bermo's sword on the table so the lord got the idea. 'We use them to chop the heads off the druids, which will make it easier to get the gold off.'

Bermo screwed his face up in thought. The visitor couldn't tell whether this was because the concept of such an overt challenge to established religious authority was raising fundamental doubts about the stability of society, or because he was trying to work out whether it was the shiny bit of the sword that did the chopping.

'Druids,' Lord Bermo mumbled in worry.

No, the visitor realised, the thoughts that were actually in Lord Bermo's head were about the giant squirrel-God which lived in the woods. Apparently, it also hid under the beds in the castle, ready to bite Bermo's bits off if he got too close so it could bury them back in the woods, where they would grow into something unspeakable.

It had taken two long evenings of barely coherent conversation to get to the bottom of that particular pit.

The visitor put his face in his hands. Again. 'The Christian God will defeat the squirrel,' he assured the master of the place.

'But even so,' Bermo drawled. 'Killing druids?'

'Killing pagans,' the visitor corrected.

Bermo frowned. 'I thought the Christians were the pagans.'

'Not any more. And you don't have to kill the druids,' the visitor explained, with a hint of annoyance. 'Not personally.'

'Don't think my men would like to do it either.'

'I'll kill the first one,' the visitor sighed heavily. 'Then, when the squirrel doesn't come and eat my bits, you'll see that it's alright. If the squirrel does eat my bits, you can blame me. How's that?'

Bermo didn't respond.

'Look,' the visitor used his hands on the table to explain the situation he had explained every mealtime since he'd arrived. 'King William will be coming this way looking for gold. He has a very big army and is very keen on using it to kill everyone in sight.' He put his right hand on the right hand end of the table.

'He will bring his army to kill you and the druids and take the gold.' The left hand represented Bermo. The right hand came across the table and flattened the left.

Bermo started at the sudden capitulation of his forces. 'William,' he scoffed. He clearly believed less in this King William than he did in the squirrel-God.

'That's right. The King William who has already defeated the Saxons. The same Saxons who defeated the Vikings.'

This did seem to register on Bermo's largely vacant face.

'But if you have the gold first you'll be able to pay for a bigger army to defend yourself and drive William away. Get some big Irishmen, they're always good in a fight.'

'So you want to kill a druid?' Bermo checked.

Perhaps, at last, the idea was sinking in. The visitor nodded and spoke as he would to deaf man at a distance. 'Yes please.'

...

'He wants to kill a monk,' Wulf hissed his alarm at the Arch-Druid. 'A real live monk. Not a chicken or a goat like we usually do, but a person.' They were outside the temple, where the Arch-Druid had stopped to pick up his staff. The long piece of carved oak leant the old man even more authority than he had already. And helped him hit people who were out of reach.

'One thing at a time. Let's just start with the stone, we'll worry about the sacrifices later.' The Arch-Druid's concern was clear in his voice. 'We haven't even got a monk,' he added.

Lypolix was there, weeing against a sacred oak.

Wulf gaped at the old seer. If he had so much as had the thought of discussing such an act, in secret with the other acolytes, all of them sworn to secrecy by the most hideous vows, the Arch-Druid would have removed his weeing apparatus with a blunt sickle.

'We go to the village,' the Arch-Druid called, trying to distract Lypolix from the task in his hand.

The seer cackled and nodded, re-arranged his robes and gave the oak a friendly pat.

The route to the village was clear and relatively short, although there were several twists and turns in the woodland trail.

At the first hour of the day the people of this modest place in the depths of the welsh hills found themselves wishing the sun would go back down again and leave them alone until their heads stopped throbbing.

The deerskin over the entrance to the village head's hut was thrown aside and a figure stepped out into the daylight. It immediately clamped its hands over its eyes and groaned loudly.

'Good morning Hywel,' the Arch-Druid boomed.

'No it isn't,' Hywel replied, dropping to his knees and resting his forehead against the ground, perhaps in the hope that the monsters in his head would migrate to the earth, and from thence to the hell from which they came. 'This is your fault,' the man added in a pathetic moan. 'If you hadn't shouted for the feast to begin as soon as Wulf did his reading, we wouldn't have drunk all the mead.'

'All of it?' the Arch-Druid was either surprised, impressed or disappointed. It was always hard to tell.

'Must have done. We can't find any more.'

'I'm surprised you're not dead.'

Hywel raised his head from the ground and dragged his eyes towards the Arch-Druid, eyes that looked like they had been pickled in honey, just before the bees found out where it had all gone and came to take it back. 'I think I am,' he groaned.

The Arch-Druid simply tutted in that way he had. The way which could make the Gods feel inadequate. 'We have a task for you,' he went on, ignoring Hywel's condition.

'A task, a task,' Lypolix cackled loudly and scittered about.

Hywel held up a hand, 'Whatever it is, I'll do it. Just get him to stop making that noise.'

'Right.' The Arch-Druid clapped his hands smartly together, which caused Hywel to wince and start to crawl on hands and knees back towards his hut. 'There's work to be done. Wulf, fetch the small cauldron from the temple compound and look for sorrel on the way back. I'll start a fire and get the hawthorn.'

'Aha,' cackled Lypolix. He raised a hand in acknowledgement of the Arch-Druid's plan and bounced off into the wood.

...

After a couple of hours of herb and plant selection and preparation, (ignoring most of the ingredients Lypolix had found, many of which were still moving), several minutes of mumbled and incoherent incantation, which Wulf tried to pick up but which he suspected were deliberately mumbled and incoherent, and another hour of careful steaming, boiling, stirring and straining, it was ready.

The villagers, having figured out quite quickly what was going on, queued up at the small cauldron to get their portion of the Arch-Druid's famous cure; morning-after-the-mead-before.

It was a famously bitter concoction. Not bitter in the

way ale or some herbs are bitter, but bitter in the way that it obviously hated you. From the inside out. How anyone who ever tasted this stuff could even thinking of drinking again was a mystery.

The villagers took their portion and then they gagged. After that they vomited, they screamed and swore oaths to every God they could remember that never again would they do whatever it was they'd done to deserve this. They would double their temple contributions, and do anything as long as no one made them ever put this foul distillation of purified venom to their lips again.

When they had finished thumping the ground with their fists, seemingly convinced their eyeballs were about to drop from their heads, they sat back and took deep breaths.

Heads were clear. Stomachs were settled. Appetites rekindled and a thirst for pure, clean water was overwhelming. In the space of a few short moments they started to think that actually, if the Druid's concoction could make them feel so much better, perhaps they might celebrate midday with a small mug of mead. Except of course, as some recalled, it had all gone. They'd better start another batch.

...

'A circle?' Hywel asked when they were all seated round the village table, 'a stone circle? Another one?'

This table was a magnificent piece of furniture which merited its own hut. For as long as anyone could remember it had been the place where the issues of the day were discussed and dealt with.

The myths and rumours that surrounded this magnificent example of the carpenter's art were as dark and complex as anything the druids told. According to your preference it had either been carried down from the top of Mount Snowden by a magic goat, been sailed up the coast as a boat by a Dragon that had lost its fire, or been found at the bottom of the deepest gold mine by the God of darkness who had used it to hold the lamp of eternal night.

There was even some fanciful nonsense about it simply being some old king's table which he used to gather his knights around before they went off and did brave deeds. But that was far too dull to be true.

Wulf thought it quite appropriate that the table was round when the subject under discussion was his new stone circle.

'Wulf is a stone seer, which Lypolix has confirmed, and we are to make The Grand Complication, the stone circle of all stone circles which will allow us to see all there is to see. This village has the honour of putting the master stone in place.'

'Just us?' Hywel seemed doubtful about this being quite such an honour. 'How big is this master stone?'

'It is magnificent,' the Arch-Druid explained.

'I'm sure it is. Just how big is magnificent? Bigger than the stones we've got.'

'Oh yes.' Wulf suddenly felt some enthusiasm for his master stone.

Hywel's doubt had made camp on his face. 'And how exactly are we to put this magnificent, big stone in place? You told us the Gods and the Ancient Ones built our circle.'

That was a good point, thought Wulf. The Arch-Druid was always reminding the villagers of the power of the Gods and the Ancient Ones. It would be a bit hard to explain if the villagers were now asked to dig a hole and haul the stone about without any mystical help.

The Arch-Druid explained carefully, 'That was that one, this is this one.'

To Wulf's surprise, this seemed to be perfectly acceptable to Hywel.

'Still,' the villager frowned, 'must take a lot of time, shifting some master stone. How are we going to get the rest of our work done if we're all playing with stones? Crops don't harvest themselves you know. And where are we going to get this stone from anyway?'

'Wulf will identify the master stone, some of you will have to attend to your normal tasks while the rest work on the stone.'

'Hm,' Hywel did not sound convinced.

'And of course the Gods will want to see the work progressing,' the Arch-Druid threatened.

Wulf could see that Hywel was torn. The man clearly didn't want to lose the time that would be needed in the coming months simply to see the village through the next winter. But on the other hand, angering the Gods was completely out of the question. From a simple boil to a hideous death, everyone knew what the Gods could do if they felt like it. And the Arch-Druid was the only protection.

Wulf thought perhaps a bit of encouragement might help.

'The stone will be big but I'm sure we can manage,' he said with a smile. 'And once we cover it with the gold everyone will see what a good job we've done, including the Gods.'

For some reason the Arch-Druid had his head in his hands.

Hywel looked at them one at a time, very slowly. A

complete change had come over his countenance and he seemed to have a new found enthusiasm for the task. 'What gold?' he asked very carefully.

Caput VIII: The Stone of Stones.

After a surprisingly enthusiastic and rapid climb up into the hills above the village, Hywel and the Arch-Druid sheltered under the overhang of a cliff.

Lypolix had wandered off to do some cackling and Wulf was scouring the hillside for his stone.

This side of the mountain had crumbled and fallen over the ages, and left a jumble of rocks strewn down its side like a runny nose on a winter morning.

Away in front of them the valley floor fell to the village, and beyond that to the woods of the Druids. They must be some one hundred and fifty feet above the floor of the valley and the climb had been steep.

Above them, drilled into the top of the mountain was a cave. The place was so far above the grass line it wasn't even worth the sheep going that far. The stone-hunting party would certainly not bother going up there. But that was not known to the pair of eyes that looked down the hill from the cave, trying figure out what on earth was going on. The eyes had never seen so many people come this far up the hill and so it hid behind a rock from which it could observe in safety.

The weather was normal for this height; universally damp. That was also normal for all the other heights, but at least from up here you could see more of it.

Eventually, Wulf stopped his fidgety questing and sat down on a flat area of bare rock.

The Arch-Druid and Hywel risked stepping out into the drizzle.

'Well?' the Arch-Druid asked.

'Oh yes.' Wulf beamed a smile that didn't belong in this weather.

Hywel looked about and couldn't immediately see anything especially impressive.

Wulf simple patted the monstrous slab he was sitting on.

'What?' Hywel went over to join the young Druid. 'Can we see this stone from there?' He sat next to Wulf and surveyed the landscape.

It was all very well druids saying that something needed doing, but they tended not to get involved in any of the actual doing. They did the looking on and barking out instructions.

'You're sitting on it,' Wulf explained.

'Sitting on what?' Hywel got up and tried to look at the seat of his leggings. For a bright village leader, he was being particularly thick.

'The stone,' the Arch-Druid said, in as calm a voice as he could manage. 'I think you are sitting on the stone Wulf wants.'

Hywel turned and examined the stone stretched out before him. He didn't need to do so in detail.

'This?' he half screeched.

'This is it,' Wulf confirmed with great satisfaction. 'Of course we'll have to give it a top dressing and remove some of the irregularities on the side, but this is the one.'

'You are joking.' Hywel certainly was.

'When did you last hear a druid joke?' The Arch-Druid asked.

Hywel knew several druid jokes, none of which was repeatable in front of a druid. 'This,' he gestured at the slab of rock, 'is not a stone.' He held his arms out to indicate the size of the thing.

'What is it then?' Wulf asked.

'It's, it's..,' Hywel struggled for a suitable description. 'It's the ground,' he concluded.

'The ground?'

'Yes,' Hywel was insistent, and sounding slightly hysterical. 'The rocks and stones rest on the ground. This is what they rest on. I could build a decent sized house on this thing. It's not meant to move. If it needed moving the Gods themselves would have to come and do it.' He was becoming positively excitable.

'It'll probably slide down the hill alright, once we get it moving,' Wulf encouraged.

'You're not meant to move the ground. It'd be easier to leave this where it is and move the rest of the world.' Hywel now walked the length of the stone and squatted down to estimate its breadth as it lay on the slope of the mountain.

'There's always a way,' Wulf smiled.

'No there isn't,' Hywel was very clear. 'That's a ridiculous thing to say. There isn't always a way to do a whole list of things. There isn't always a way to drink the sea, or fly like a bird, or, or.' Hywel had run out of things there wasn't a way to do. 'It simply can't be done.'

'Nevertheless, we have to do it.' Wulf was still smiling.

'There you go again.' Hywel had regained some of his control and sat next to Wulf on the stone once more. 'Wulf,' he said, sounding as if he was going to explain to a five year old that the fact his puppy had been taken away by wolves did not mean the puppy was now a wolf. Although it still meant they wouldn't be seeing the puppy again. 'When it's said that something can't be done, it means doing it is not a question of "nevertheless". It means finding something else to do instead. Moving this rock,' he patted the rock, 'is a thing that can't be done, which means we find something else to do. In this case we find a much, much smaller rock.'

'But I need this one.' Wulf tried a smile. 'I can see it's difficult.'

'It's not difficult Wulf,' Hywel went on. 'It's bloody huge. This rock is enormous, gigantic. It will be unbelievably heavy and, and,' he searched for the right word, 'unmovable.' He had found it. 'This rock is unmovable. You cannot move an unmovable rock. You can't move an unmovable anything. It's what the name means.

'And it's no good you sitting there and going all druidic on me. And it's no good the Arch-Druid coming in with the will of the Gods.' He glanced at the Arch-Druid to fend him off. 'If this rock was meant to be moved, it wouldn't be unmovable see?'

'But it isn't unmovable,' Wulf stated simply. 'If it was unmovable we wouldn't be able to move it. That would be madness. This rock is movable. Just not very easily.'

'Not very easily?' Hywel was starting to squeak again. He calmed himself and took another tack. 'Wulf, this stone here, the one you want, is bigger than big, isn't it?'

'Oh yes.' Wulf was happy to accept that. 'It is very big indeed. In fact,' he went on with clear satisfaction, 'it's quite probably the biggest stone that's ever been moved for a circle.'

'There we are then. He paced up and down the length of the stone. 'I mean,' he said, stroking his chin and sucking in his breath. 'You'd need at least a day of digging out just to get the levers in for one end. And they'd have to be whole tree trunks. Even if you got rollers under one end and levered up the other, the whole thing would probably shift and take out whoever was at the bottom.

'You'd need a harness pinned to the mountain and we don't have enough rope. And of course we're half way up the bloody mountain and we'd need every man, woman and child to get the thing done. And then we'd have to think about the casualties. No.' He came to his conclusion. 'Sorry Wulf, it can't be done.'

The Arch-Druid stepped up and laid a druidic hand on Hywel's shoulder. 'I think you've just described very well how it can be done. Tree trunks, rope and people. Nothing very difficult there.'

'Apart from the fact we might have moved it a foot by mid-winter and have lost several toes, fingers and complete people in the process.'

'It's got to be this one,' Wulf was apologetic for all the work this was going to entail.

'When I say can't be done,' Hywel said in a very serious tone, 'I mean it won't be done. I am not diverting the entire village to moving this stone off the mountain.' He folded his arms.

'What else can we do then?' Wulf asked. 'The circle has to be built and this stone has to do it.' He was stating a fact of nature.

There was a silence while they all gave the problem some thought. Or at least looked like they were giving the problem some thought. Wulf and the Arch-Druid looked like they were waiting for Hywel to change his mind, while Hywel looked like he was waiting for them to change theirs.

It was the Arch-Druid who spoke first. And he had his persuading voice in peak condition. 'Just think Hywel. Just think what a magnificent sight it will be.'

Hywel clearly wasn't thinking magnificent.

'Covered in gold,' the Arch-Druid breathed.

This did get a small twitch in the corner of Hywel's mouth going. 'Tell you what,' he offered. 'I'll get the gold, you move the stone.'

'This needs the toil of men Hywel,' the Arch-Druid went on. 'That will be part of its magic. And others will come. Word of the great stone will spread. Pilgrims, travellers, people will be flocking here.'

'Oh great.' Hywel saw this as yet another problem.

'And of course they'll bring all their offerings.' The Arch-Druid leant the word "offerings" all the charm of conversation behind a grubby tent in the market with a man who keeps his very particular products hidden in a sack – so no one sees him and runs him out of town.

'Offerings?' Hywel asked, part question, part naked self-interest.

'Lots of offerings for the great stone I should think. Particularly if the Arch-Druid makes the expectation clear.'

'What sort of offerings?' Hywel's eyes had narrowed to arrow-slits.

'Anything you like, I should think.' The Arch-Druid sounded nonchalant although he looked anything but. 'Food for the work of the circle, precious stones for the Gods, more gold. The whole village would be ruined.'

'Ruined?'

'Yes.' The Arch-Druid shook his head in reluctant acceptance of the inevitable. 'The simple life would be gone. The place would be awash with wealth and the well-to-do. The person in charge of a village like that wouldn't have time to do any work, he'd have to be organizing everything. Giving instructions, talking to people, dealing with the great and the good. Making sure all the offerings were being distributed properly.'

'All the offerings?' Hywel's question was as loaded as a longbow.

'After the temple has taken its dues. Which would be modest of course.'

The thoughts in Hywel's head were shaded, but the light in his eyes was positively brazen. He took a long time to look from the Arch-Druid, to the still smiling Wulf, to the stone and back to the druid again. All the while, the light in his eyes was building an empire that would make the Romans look like the sons of old man Gruffydd and their rat collection.

'In fact,' the Arch-Druid was offering more. 'We could even say that those who moved the master stone, were excused all further work on the circle. Having done great service to the Gods and all.'

Hywel's eyebrows now climbed his forehead with alacrity. He counted the points off on his fingers, 'Gold, offerings, only moving one stone.' The Arch-Druid gave an imperceptible nod. Hywel's face contorted through his internal dispute. Eventually it cleared. 'So,' he concluded. 'Where exactly does this stone need to go? Not that I'm promising anything of course.'

'Naturally,' the Arch-Druid smiled. 'Wulf is our stone seer. He'll know the spot.'

'Aha, yes.' Wulf sprung up, 'I know just the place.'

'Not too far away, I hope,' Hywel found a scowl from somewhere.

'Oh no, erm, not far.' Wulf wanted to say more, but now didn't seem quite the right moment.

Hywel peered down the hill and appraised the route from where the stone was now, to where it would end up if it simply slid down the hill. Once the entire population had spent probably the best part of a week just getting the thing moving in the first place.

'I think we'll need to build something at the bottom as well,' he observed. 'Otherwise the thing could end up in that little stream. Gods know how we'd get it out of there.'

'Good idea,' the Arch-Druid encouraged, happy that Hywel appeared to be committed.

'And then where?' Hywel turned to Wulf. 'Where do we go after that? Are we going down the valley, or across? The people in the village will need to know so we can plan ahead.'

'Yes.' Wulf gave a false laugh and a sidewise glance at the Arch-Druid. He swallowed hard. 'About the village…,'

He was stopped from going further by the reappearance of Lypolix. The old seer seemed to drift out of the drizzle and he approached the stone with quiet reverence. Which Wulf actually found a bit off putting.

'Ah,' Lypolix breathed, without even a hint of a cackle. 'The great stone, the master. Yes, yes, I see it.'

'Me too,' Hywel muttered under his breath.

The old seer tapped and stroked the stone. Wulf wondered if he was going to wee on this as well, like some dog leaving a message. 'It is the one. It has the power. I feel its emanations and the smiles of the Gods falling upon it from the spirit world.'

They all looked a bit askance at Lypolix.

'Also,' the seer went on. 'It looks very heavy.'

'You don't need to tell me,' Hywel commented.

Lypolix nodded in satisfaction at the stone. 'It should kill the monk quite quickly.'

Wulf's looked as put out at this as the Arch Druid had

at mention of the gold. He was starting to get the idea that some things should not be said to some people.

'What monk?' Hywel asked in all seriousness.

'The monk we'll sacrifice for the master stone,' Lypolix explained brightly. 'He should die quite quickly when we drop it on him.'

Caput IX: The Fellowship Expands; Unfortunately.

ou worry too much, Hermitage,' Cwen stated the blindingly obvious. She patted the monk heartily on the shoulder when he shared his concerns that travelling as a large group would attract the attention of even larger groups who would think they had something to steal.

They had left the river at the point they needed to turn more northwards and formed a ragged band, rather light on enthusiasm.

The option of travelling alone was worse of course, and Hermitage couldn't immediately come up with the perfect number of travelling companions, when Cwen asked.

If there was a single reason why young Hermitage worried as much as he did, about everyone, everything and every situation which brought the two together, it was that he was usually right.

Through the short years of his life it would have been easy to wean himself from worry if things had not turned out so bad after all. If his fervent anticipation of being chased, attacked, robbed or caught up in some hideous situation involving all three, had been wrong, and nothing of the sort had come to pass, he would have become a different person all together.

But they hadn't. They always turned out just as bad as he'd expected. Except, of course, for those frequent occasions when they turned out worse.

He was an intelligent young man of course. He was

able to think his way through this philosophy and consider that perhaps it was his worrying which brought things to pass. If he constantly thought about being chased, attacked or robbed, didn't that make it more likely to happen? Wasn't he going to present himself as a target, exuding humors which signalled to all about that here was a man ready for chasing, robbery or attack?

But that didn't explain all the awful things that happened, which he hadn't managed to worry about at all. He could still be completely surprised by some act of ill-will or wrong-doing, which proved he wasn't the cause.

He was very satisfied with this reasoning, although not with the conclusion.

As he considered this latest topic for concern, he recalled that even his first meeting with Wat had come about as a result of his not anticipating being attacked at all.[5]

Cwen scoffed at his predictions of woe, although they were delivered with such certainty that seeds of doubt were sown in her mind. Hermitage had plenty to go round.

And of course at the conclusion of it all was Wales. The place where he would meet his end. If there was anything that deserved a good worry, that was it.

...

Up ahead, a group who knew nothing of Hermitage's reasoning, or of reasoning at all, but an awful lot about chasing, attacking and robbing, were preparing for another day's work.

---

[5] Which is told in *The Heretics of De'Ath* from the Funny Book Company – the set book if you are considering course H424;   Brother Hermitage, a Contextual Analysis.

To say that not everyone in England was overjoyed at the Norman invasion was taking the obvious to the top of a very high tower and hoisting it up a flag pole.

In many instances, this lack of joy was outwardly expressed – usually when there weren't any Normans about. In fact, the further away the Normans were, the more outward the expression. Thus, in the further reaches of the land, resistance to the new rulers took a very ordered form.

To the east, Hereward the Wake bravely fought the invaders from the flat lands of the fens – the bravery coming to the fore when Hereward the Wake was spotted hiding in a ditch.

To the west, Edric the Wild was busy getting resistance organised against Norman nobles who'd been in the country for years. William's attack at Hastings was a marvellous excuse to get the swords out.

Elsewhere, men who had spent the time prior to the invasion chasing, attacking or robbing anyone they came across, declared themselves freedom fighters, and continued to behave in exactly the same way.

When their victims suggested that surely they should limit their chasing, attacking or robbing to Normans now, the men would come up with sophisticated arguments that the Normans were miles away, and they had to make a living.

To the group ahead of Hermitage and his companions, sophistication meant putting your leggings on the right way round before you went chasing, attacking and robbing. Or putting them on at all.

There was only one man in this assembly who had ideals which transcended the revoltingly mundane, and he was their leader. It might be assumed that if the leader was motivated by more than plain greed, then the group would follow suit. This leader was also an intelligent man, and was well aware of what happened to the previous leader, when he had suggested that some of the booty be given to the poor.

The old leader had delivered a sincere and impassioned speech about all the good they could do, which had carried on all the way to the river, where his band held his head underwater until he stopped talking.

Thus, the new leader realised that transforming this band into anything other than a despicable rabble of reprehensible animals would be a slow process.

The sight of a ragged band travelling the road without an apparent care in the world, was the trigger for the group to start doling out the sort of cares-of-the-world that were their speciality.

...

The party negotiated a rare bend in the road, caused by the fact that a tree had grown in the old roadway, and rather than chop it down, or even weed it out when it was small, people had simply walked round, creating a new path. Emerging from the shadow of the tree, they saw a gang of six men, three of them armed.

The leader of the gang looked them over disparagingly. A scrawny beard on legs, one monk, a rather small girl, a man dressed like a travelling cloth merchant, one skinny type who did look like he could handle himself and a druid. A druid? They would be more than a match for this lot.

'Alright you lot, over here,' the leader called and beckoned with his sword.

Wat led the way, ambling along as if they were going this way anyway, and were certainly not responding to any summonses.

As they got near, John pointedly drew his sword, which was much bigger and in much better condition than the leader of the group's. He then took a sharp and shining dagger from his belt, which he gripped between his teeth. Finally he drew what was basically a long metal spike from the side of his leggings and spun it in his left hand. One more weapon and he'd out-match the entire band of attackers.

Cwen managed to look daggers, so that probably counted.

The druid stood at the back, trying to look aloof, while Hermitage stayed at Wat's side.

The gang of robbers appraised the situation and adopted the appropriate position. Behind their leader.

'Now then,' the leader called out for all to hear. 'No need for any trouble here. Just hand over your valuables and you can be on your way.'

'No,' Wat said. 'You hand over your valuables.'

'What?' the leader was clearly thrown by this response.

'That's right,' Wat confirmed, winking at Hermitage. 'Hand it all over and you can be on your way.'

'We're not on our way anywhere,' the leader protested. 'It's you who's on your way.'

'How do you know?' Wat demanded.

The leader looked to his band, as if one of them would explain what was going on. 'Because we're here and you just arrived.'

'Only from where you're standing.'

The leader's face said he was trying to make sense of this, and was failing.

'We're freedom fighters,' he tried another tack.

'Well, that's nice. We're just robbers.'

'No you're not.'

'Yes we are.'

'You aren't.' The leader wasn't taking that. 'You're a monk, a girl and a druid.' He pointed out the offending characters.

'That's only because we just robbed a monk, a girl and a druid.'

The leader paused to think about this, staring hard at Cwen to see whether she was real or not.

'Oh for goodness sake,' Wat's humour had run out, 'John, make yourself useful. See them off.'

John smiled a smile as thin as his knife, and advanced on the leader, crouching in a very effective-looking fighting stance.

This man, who was taller and bulkier than John, and so ought to have the advantage, held his weapon out in front of him, although he looked like he wanted to hand the thing over.

'What's that?' John asked through the dagger in his teeth, when he got within striking distance.

'My sword,' the leader replied with an attempt at a growl.

'That's not a sword,' John stood up straight and neatly spat the knife from his mouth, catching it in a hand that already held a sword. The robbers breathed an impressed sigh.

'Will you people stop it,' the leader demanded, his patience having run off with Wat's humour. 'We are a band of freedom fighters, and this is my sword. Now can we get on with it, please?'

'Still not a sword,' John huffed. 'Looks like a bit of shield edging. Hammered out straight and sharpened a bit.' He actually leant forward and ran his hand down the weapon. 'But only a bit. That thing's useless. Do you want to go and get something better?'

'I haven't got anything better,' the leader snapped. 'Where do you think you are? The King's armoury?'

'The King wouldn't use that to prop the doors open on his armoury,' John scoffed. 'I can lend you one if you like. I'll get it back later.'

The leader, who had been out of his depth since the encounter started, was wading ever deeper. He looked at John with his collection of well maintained, and probably professionally made weapons, and then he looked to his band. This group had taken several steps backwards as the engagement continued, and were now well placed to run away if any actual fighting started. Finally he looked at his sword, which he thought he had hammered pretty well – once he'd prised it off the old shield.

He drew himself up to his full height. 'You may pass,' he announced.

'We know,' Wat said as he strolled by, pushing More ahead of him.

Hermitage scampered after him, 'Wat,' he called. 'We can't leave these people here to rob unwary travellers. The next people who happen along may not be able to defend themselves.'

'Good thought Hermitage,' Wat nodded. 'You think we should let John kill them then?'

'What? Good heavens no.' Hermitage hadn't meant that at all. How could Wat even think he would contemplate such an evil deed? He looked to his friend and saw the grin.

'Take their weapons?' Wat suggested.

'Ah, yes, that would be good.'

John had passed the leader of the band now, the band

itself having lined up on the opposite side of the road, making sure they didn't get in the way.

Cwen passed by, snarling at the leader and the band, while the druid maintained an admirable level of aloofness.

When the last of them had gone by, the leader hurried over to his band and drew them into a huddle of conversation. The other two who had weapons, were holding them out of sight, probably for fear of John criticising their equipment.

The leader gestured to where the travellers were moving down the road, and was making pleading gestures to his men. There was some shaking of heads and some shrugs, as if the band could not come to an agreed strategy.

Eventually the leader broke out of the pack and walked after the departing backs. He gestured again, this time for the band to follow him, which they did, reluctantly and at a distance.

'Erm, excuse me?' the leader called after Wat 'I say!'

Hermitage looked round and saw their followers. 'Why are they following us?' he asked Wat. Surely they weren't thinking of attacking from behind. Their attack from the front had been so useless Hermitage didn't think the element of surprise would help this lot at all. Anyway, it's not much of a surprise attack if you shout out "excuse me" first.

'Because you're right. Everyone we come across has some overpowering urge to tag along. I reckon if we step on a dead badger it'll come back to life with a burning desire to visit Wales. Yes. What is it?' he called back to the leader of the pack.

'Erm,' the leader hesitated. 'Did I hear the monk call

you Wat by any chance?'

'Yes,' Wat said with profound resignation.

'With the look of a weaver about you sir, I don't suppose by any chance you'd be the Wat the weaver?'

'Only one I know.'

'Oh sir,' the leader of the band of dangerous freedom fighters dropped his weapon on the floor and rushed forward to grasp Wat's hand and shake it vigorously. 'It's an honour sire, a real honour. We're real enthusiasts for your work, me and the lads.' He gestured back to the rest of the band of dangerous freedom fighters, who were waving at Wat.

'I see,' Wat said with some embarrassment and a sideways glance at Hermitage. Hermitage was now applying his very best disappointed look.

'The bath house series sir, an absolute marvel.'

Hermitage added a grumble to his scowl.

'Aha, yes.' Wat clearly wanted to move on.

'Of course we wouldn't have interrupted your journey if we'd known.' The leader was fawningly obsequious. 'We'd be only too glad to help you on your way. Wouldn't we lads?' He called to the gang who confirmed their agreement with a collection of positive, if rather suggestive noises.

'Well, that's very kind, but I think we're alright now.'

'Oh, wouldn't hear of it sir. Not after our rudeness earlier on. Where is it you'd be going?'

'This way,' Wat gestured. He urged the rest of the party to move on.

'Then we shall accompany you,' the leader announced.

'Oh God,' Wat muttered, running and hand over his face.

'We shall protect you from the vagabonds who live in

these parts.'

'Of course you will,' John snorted.

Hermitage laid a hand on Wat's elbow, 'Are you sure this is a good idea?' he asked. While these men may be rather inept vagabonds, Hermitage would rather they stayed where they were.

'Sure about it?' Wat asked with some disbelief, 'of course I'm sure about it. And it's not my idea. I don't want them to come. That'll be a dozen of us. So much for a quick wander into Wales, look around and then straight out again. At this rate the druids will think we're an invasion force.'

'Can't we tell them not to come then?' Hermitage asked. Surely that was what you did. You asked someone to do, or not do something, and they did it. Or didn't.

'Of course we can,' Wat said brightly, although Hermitage detected that underlying hint of "Hermitage doesn't know what he's talking about again."

'Gentlemen,' Wat called to the ragged band who were now gathered close by.

They gave Wat their attention.

'On further discussion we have decided that we do not want you to accompany us.'

Well, thought Hermitage, that was very clear indeed. A bit rude perhaps, but it got the point across.

'But we shall do so in your service,' the leader smiled, obviously turning down Wat's polite suggestion that they might have better things to do with their time.

'No. Really.' Wat looked the leader in the eye. 'Do not come with us.'

'It's no trouble,' the leader was still smiling.

'It is to us,' Wat insisted.

'It's our pleasure,' the leader said, clearly very full of

pleasure.

'I insist.'

'No, I insist.'

'What's your name?' Wat asked the leader.

'Banley,' the leader announced with some pride.

'Look, Banley,' Wat gently ushered the man to one side to have a quiet and confidential discussion. He beckoned Hermitage to join them and the young monk was fascinated to hear what the weaver was going to say.

'I cannot tell you why we are travelling, or what it is we're going to do. What I can say is that your presence will be an obstruction. It will get in our way. It will actually prevent us achieving our aim. Not only do we not want you to come with us, you actually need not to.'

'I wouldn't hear of it,' said Banley with a smile.

Hermitage couldn't follow this. Surely it had been made comprehensively clear what Banley needed to do.

'I really mean it,' said Wat, in all seriousness. 'Please. Do not come with us.'

Hermitage looked at Banley. This could not be any clearer.

'Aha,' said Banley, in an overloud whisper that said he had now got the message.

Well, thought Hermitage, that was a relief.

'We shall follow discreetly.' Banley tapped the side of his nose.

'No,' Wat explained, quite loudly. 'Do not follow discreetly. Do not follow at all. Stay here and do whatever it is you do. Here. Not with us. Not following us, but right here.' He even pointed to the road.

'You want us to guard the road for your return?' Banley asked.

'If you like.'

'No need sir,' Banley beamed again. 'There's only us here, and if we're with you, the road will be safe.'

'Ahrgh,' Wat expostulated.

Hermitage realised there was no talking to this Banley. He had come across a number of obstinate people in his time, those who didn't listen to what he was saying and did what they wanted anyway. Churchmen who cut his very reasonable arguments short and insisted that they had perfect scriptural justification for taking the alms intended of the poor and spending them on a new saddle. He had never come across anyone who listened carefully to your arguments, acknowledged them, and even agreed with them, and then went and did exactly the opposite.

'Banley,' Wat took the man by the elbow and held his gaze, 'will you do something for me?'

'Of course,' Banley was proud to be asked.

'Stay here. Do not accompany us. Do not follow us. Simply stay here. Understood?'

'Oh, yes sir.' Banley nodded a very knowing nod.

Well, that was a direct order. Hermitage noted how the exchange had gone, and put Banley away in his expanding register of experiences. Perhaps that had been the point of Wat asking him to join the conversation. More of what Wat called Hermitage's education in the real world.

They left the man and joined Cwen, More, John and the Druid, all of whom had taken the opportunity of the discussion to sit down and rest their feet.

'Up everyone,' Wat called enthusiastically, 'we're off. Banley and his band are staying here.'

Everyone rose and brushed the dust of the track from their clothes. Hoisting packs and adjusting weight, they set off once more to the West.

After a few paces, Hermitage looked back over his shoulder. He turned to Wat. 'They're following,' he said in frank amazement.

'Of course they are,' Wat replied, without surprise.

'But,' Hermitage simply could not understand this. 'You told them not to.'

'That's right.'

'But they are.'

'Correct again.'

'Why?'

'Because they're just what we need on this quiet mission into a foreign land to steal gold from a bunch of mystic killers - six more idiots.'

Caput X: How to do a Sacrifice.

hat do you mean drop it on him?' It wasn't clear whether Hywel was more outraged at the thought of killing a monk, or of being expected to lift the stone up at all.

'Ha, ha,' Lypolix cackled in a full explanation.

Hywel turned his demanding look to the Arch-Druid and Wulf. 'What does he mean, drop it on him?'

The Arch-Druid was thoughtful. 'Not sure, exactly. It could be we just sort of hold the monk down and slide it over him, or it's possible he needs the whole thing lifting. He'll explain closer to the time.'

Hywel's mouth moved about as if it had some words inside, but they didn't want to come out. Eventually he spluttered it to working order. 'I don't mean the detailed process,' he shouted, 'I mean killing a monk at all. Killing anyone at all. Why is he suggesting we kill anyone at all?'

'Got to have a sacrifice to the Gods for the circle. And for the Grand Complication it would have to be something pretty special.' The Arch Druid nodded to himself.

'Are you serious?' Hywel was not coming down from the high plateau of excitement he had climbed. 'We do not sacrifice people to the Gods. We do not sacrifice anything to the Gods. You do the odd chicken, which we eat afterwards. Maybe a goat or a sheep for a special occasion but not people. And certainly not monks. For the Gods' sakes, you'll be suggesting virgins next. This isn't the dark ages you know.'

The Arch-Druid looked calm and disinterested, as if

this was just so much raving from the uninformed.

'He's, erm,' Wulf started, and then immediately thought he shouldn't have done.

'He's what?' Hywel snapped.

'I was only going to say that Lypolix has already done three stones.'

Hywel didn't need to say anything. It was enough that his face managed to simultaneously portray shock, horror, revulsion and the anticipation of real trouble on the way.

'He started the circle,' Wulf explained. 'The Grand Complication. He put the first three stones in place and I had to find the master.'

'And just who did he sacrifice for those?' Hywel demanded, looking hard at the old seer who was sitting cross legged on the ground, talking to a fern.

'Not sure,' Wulf confessed. He didn't really know how to ask the next question. 'Is, erm, is anyone missing?'

'Is? What? Who?' Poor Hywel looked like he was trying to turn round inside his own body.

'You know,' Wulf encouraged, 'sort of not around anymore?'

'I know what missing means,' the head of the village screeched in a most unleader-like manner. 'Are you suggesting that villagers have been killed for this circle?'

'Not at all,' Wulf tried to calm things. Things he had started in the first place. 'It's just that he won't tell us what he sacrificed. Says the Gods helped him. And there is a lot of blood on the stones.' He tried a shrug. It didn't help.

'Show me,' Hywel demanded, gesturing down the hill.

Wulf reluctantly shrugged and started to move. He didn't really want to leave the master stone now he'd found it but reasoned that it wasn't going to go anywhere.

Hywel followed, scowling intently with the Arch-Druid in his wake. Lypolix noticed the movement and got up from his conversation, skipping down the hill in front of them.

...

The ears on either side of the eyes at the back of the cave heard Hywel's outburst and emerged from behind their rock. The eyes saw the figures departing amidst gesticulation and shouting, as well as a bit of dancing from the old, mad one. This was too intriguing.

The cave was a happy place, peaceful and undisturbed but the eyes had been alone for a long time now. Snaring the odd rabbit and stealing bits of food from the village under cover of darkness was not what could be called a life, and now there was clearly something going on. Curiosity and the need for some human engagement – at a safe distance – was too much for the cave-dweller. He emerged from the mountain and made his way down the hill. Once the others were out of sight of course.

...

'This is not chicken blood,' Hywel announced as he examined the first stones of the Grand Complication. 'And before you ask again, no, there is no one missing. People don't go missing without other people mentioning it.'

The three of them stood by the stones, with Lypolix skipping from one monolith to the other, making sure they were comfortable.

'But the Gods,' Wulf began.

'Even if the Gods took someone away in the middle of the night in a shining mystical fog, someone else would notice. There aren't that many of us. You don't wake up in the morning and think, I'm sure I had a wife last night, wonder where she's gone.' Hywel was getting over excited again.

'You,' he called to Lypolix in a less than reverential manner. The Arch-Druid scowled at the impertinence but didn't interfere. 'What did you sacrifice here?'

The old seer looked up, at least that was progress of a sort.

'The Gods,' Lypolix nodded and gave a little laugh.

'You sacrificed the Gods?'

This got the seer into a positive laughing fit.

'Explain,' Hywel commanded.

Lypolix looked quite surprised, 'The Gods came from the clouds in their shining raiment and brought the sacrifice for the first stones from the other side of the sky.'

Well, there was a surprise. Wulf had never thought to simply tell Lypolix to explain himself. Perhaps it was a magic word.

The Arch-Druid looked positively alarmed, and a little envious.

'And what did this sacrifice look like?' Hywel pressed on.

'Strange,' Lypolix breathed the word.

'A stranger,' Hywel interpreted the seer's words quite literally.

Wulf thought it was hardly likely to be that simple.

'Aye, aye,' Lypolix agreed.

'You killed a stranger?' Hywel had run out of excitability. He had now moved to a dead calm of concern and fear. 'Three of them?' he asked in worried whisper, glancing at the stones. 'You killed three strangers?'

'More will come, even now they come.' Lypolix laughed and danced about a bit. 'We can gather more stones now and get them ready. Every stone will have one.'

Even Wulf felt himself turn cold at this. It was all very well talking about sacrifices for the stones, but Hywel was right, no one sacrificed people anymore. The ancient ones used to do it all the time of course, but then they were ancient and the people they sacrificed would have been dead by now anyway.

It was bad enough even discussing squashing some monk under the master stone, Lypolix now seemed to be suggesting one person would be sacrificed for each stone. He did a quick sum in his head. They'd need a lot more strangers from somewhere. No. It was unthinkable.

Wulf had done the odd chicken, but everyone killed chickens, druid or not. He looked at Lypolix, who had gone back to scittering among his stones. If three strangers had really been sacrificed for the first stones, Wulf wondered how the old seer had managed to do it. There were too many incongruities; Lypolix was a tiny old man, how could he control and sacrifice three strangers? If he had managed it, where were the bodies? And most alarming of all for these parts, where on earth had three strangers even come from?

Wulf realised that he was doubting the tale that the Gods had done it. Of course if the Gods had done it, it wouldn't have been a problem at all. The Gods could sacrifice a hundred people at once if they wanted to, big strangers or not. It was just that in all his experience under the Arch-Druid he had never seen them do anything so obvious. In fact, as he thought more about it, he'd never seen them perform the obvious at all. In an alarming step he found himself wondering if he'd ever seen the Gods actually do anything.

If anyone was asking to become a sacrifice it was Wulf with blasphemous thoughts like this. Of course he'd never seen the Gods do anything, he was an acolyte, not an Arch-Druid. And he was a stone seer. He'd had the vision Lypolix had planted in his head. How to explain that if not the Gods?

'If the Gods wanted three strangers sacrificed for the stones there wouldn't be much we could do about it.' He nodded to himself in satisfaction at this entirely proper explanation. He was grateful to see the Arch-Druids beard nod up and down in agreement.

'And if the Gods want a great stone moved down the mountain they can do that as well,' Hywel argued.

'Now that is ridiculous,' the Arch-Druid countered. 'The Gods may well do the sacrifices themselves but if they want us to move the stones, that's what we do. They can't do everything you know.' He tutted at Hywel's presumption.

The village head grumbled defiance, 'I thought that's exactly what they could do.'

'Now then Hywel, careful,' the Arch-Druid warned.

'Tell you what,' Hywel offered, 'if we get this rock down off the mountain, the Gods can lift it up and drop it on the monk. They sacrificed strangers for three tiddling little stones, the least they can do is a monk for the big one.'

'If the Gods,' the Arch-Druid began.

'I am not waiting for some monk to come wandering along the road for me to drop half a hillside on his head. If word got out to our Lord in his mighty castle that we were going round killing strangers, he'd have my guts. You know he gets to kill all the strangers himself.'

The Arch-Druid frowned at this mention of the bane of his life, the wretched Lord Bermo who kept staring at the gold all the time. The man wouldn't dare take it of course, but in a balancing act between the old Gods with their mighty powers in the spirit world, and Lord Bermo just down the road with a lot of big men, the Arch-Druid had to be careful.

'We shall wait until the monk is delivered to us,' the Arch-Druid sounded sage and reasonable.

Lypolix had wandered back into ear shot. 'We shall, we shall,' he sounded very certain. 'And when the monk arrives and the stone is ready, the Gods will squash him flat.'

Caput XI: The Doubtful Pilgrims.

'Wat,' Hermitage hissed into the weaver's ear. 'This is getting ridiculous.'

'Really?' Wat sounded as if he didn't have a clue what Hermitage was talking about.

Hermitage cast another look over his shoulder and appraised the entourage that now stretched down the road.

The three original members of the group were together, Wat leading as normal, Cwen scowling along slightly behind and Hermitage fretting backwards and forwards between them.

They had been walking for several hours along the old Roman road towards Silchester.

'The king and Le Pedvin gave the three of us instruction about Martel and the you-know-what in Wales.' Hermitage paused in thought for a moment. 'Well, actually he gave me instruction. Then he added you in, and I don't think they thought about Cwen at all.'

'That's right.' Wat still managed to ignore the rest of the party.

'Then we get John the mercenary forced upon us.'

'Hm,' Wat grunted.

'And then a druid of all things,' Hermitage went on. 'And a boat man, and now six more people who started off trying to rob us.'

'But not very well,' Wat said, as if that made a difference.

'I'm not sure that helps. We shouldn't have six people

following us at all. Even if they were very good robbers.'

Wat gave silent agreement to that.

'Well,' Hermitage drew his own resigned conclusion. 'I don't suppose we can make six robbers, a druid, a mercenary and a boat man disappear.'

'No, we can't.' Wat had the look that said he was thinking. Hermitage was always encouraged by that look. It usually meant the weaver had come up with some way out of whatever awful situation they found themselves in. Locked in a dungeon, pursued by Normans, standing accused of murder; all the things that had become run-of-mill to Hermitage were alleviated by that look.

Come to think of it, the awful things which were now run-of-the-mill only started when he met Wat. No. He would put that thought away for some other time.

...

As the outlying dwellings of Silchester came into sight, Hermitage didn't know whether to be encouraged or discouraged. Discouragement came more naturally and they were several steps closer to their goal. A goal he wanted nothing to do with. He absolutely did not believe in Druid prophecies. However, he absolutely did not believe in them just a little bit less with each step closer to Wales.

Wat assured him they were still miles away from Wales. After Silchester would be Speen and Baydon, as they headed north-west towards Gloucester and the river. But then over the river what lay in wait? Hermitage could only imagine. He had always been very good at imagining things lying in wait. They were usually big, scary things with no good intent. Many of them had given up lying and were now standing in wait.

He glanced again down the ragged band on the road, who, far from being an ordered column, had drifted apart as their interest and enthusiasm varied. The main protagonists were still to the fore, himself, Wat and Cwen with John and the Druid slightly behind. The erstwhile robbers straggled along at the back, with More hopefully boring them to death with his tales of the riverbank.

He counted them again, just to confirm his concern.

'Erm, Wat?' he asked as nonchalantly as he could.

'Hm?' Wat answered, his attention being on the road ahead.

'Where did the, er, extra people come from?'

Wat woke from his light daze and frowned at Hermitage. 'We picked them up when they tried to rob us,' he said with some worry. 'are you losing your mind Hermitage?'

'No,' Hermitage explained. 'Not those extras. The extra extras.' He nodded back down the line of the road.

Wat turned his head to look and his eyes widened.

If just one more person had joined the round dozen it might have been easy to miss, but there were now three complete strangers among the band, walking along without a care in the world.

Wat drew the march to a halt and waited for the newcomers to join him.

Each of them had a travelled look about them, as if their bodies had been used for great journeys through harsh weather. Although probably only a few years older than Wat, they were dark skinned, either because they had been exposed to sun and rain over many summers and winters, or because they hadn't washed for the last few years. Probably both. They were reasonably well dressed though. Sturdy boots and tied-down leggings over open jerkins and shirts that might once have been white – or a closely related shade. And they all looked pretty well fed and rather happy with their lot.

'Who the hell are you?' Wat asked quite bluntly.

'Just pilgrims,' the first of them announced in proud tones. 'I'm Elard, this is Lanson and that's Pord.'

The others nodded their smiling welcome to Wat.

'Pilgrims?' Wat's confusion made him look to Hermitage, as if the monk would be able to answer this.

All Hermitage could do was shrug. The men did have the look of the pilgrim about them, but then so did a lot of people who just spent time outdoors.

As if to prove their credentials they each produced a small shell from somewhere in their jerkins and held them up proudly.

Wat shied backwards, as if they were offering him diseased fish.

'Ah.' Hermitage nodded.

'Ah, what?' Wat asked. 'What does "ah" mean?'

'It's the symbol of the pilgrim,' Hermitage said, but noticed that this did not seem to be helping Wat. 'St John's body miraculously emerging from the waves covered in shells?' Surely everyone knew this.

'Did it?' Wat asked.

'Of course it did. In Santiago de Compostela, in Spain. Although I think they're supposed to be scallop shells.' Hermitage peered at the rather plain shells the pilgrims were holding up, which could have come from anywhere.

'Well, what are you doing following us?' Wat demanded. 'Why aren't you off pilgriming somewhere?'

'We are,' Elard explained. 'We're coming with you.'

Wat was in danger of getting angry he was so confused. 'Why are you coming with us?' he demanded. 'We're not pilgrims.' He held his arms wide to illustrate the lack of pilgrims in the party.

Elard grinned, and even gave Wat a light-hearted punch on the shoulder at this teasing. 'Yes, you are,' he said.

Wat's face looked ready to scream, 'What do you mean yes we are? We know what we are and what we aren't.' He stole a glance at More. 'Well, most of us,' he clarified. 'We are not pilgrims and you are not with us.'

'Oh, you are,' Elard confirmed, as if Wat was trying to hide the fact. 'We can tell a pilgrimage when we see one.' He looked the group of men up and down. 'Yours must be a good one, so many of you. And you've got a druid. Must be very important to have a druid with you. Are you taking him somewhere to have him converted?'

'What?' Wat seemed so far out of his depth he was in danger of drowning.

'Tricky job, druid conversion I'd have thought. Must need a lot of holiness to convert a druid. And you've got an armed guard.' The man nodded at John and the robbers. And her.' He tipped his head towards Cwen. 'She been rescued from the druids then? What was she? The sacrificial vir...' the word died on his lips as Cwen's piercing look did its job and dared him to go further. 'Where you off to?' The man smiled encouraging friendliness at Wat and tried not to look in Cwen's direction.

'We are not on a pilgrimage,' Wat ground out of his teeth.

'Oh I see.' Elard nodded very knowingly, clearly in on the secret, whatever it was. 'You can tell us though.'

'I just have.'

'Don't worry, it won't go any further.' Elard tapped the side of his nose. Lanson and Pord nodded their agreement. 'If you've got a new miraculous cure for being a druid somewhere, we won't breathe a word. Experienced pilgrims us. Done all the major routes. Holywell, Walsingham, Canterbury, Santiago.'

'You've really been to Santiago?' Hermitage was very impressed. 'All the way to Spain?' He knew of the place of course, and of the great sacrifice there was in making the pilgrimage. It was such a long way off. Over the sea, it was. Which sea, he had no idea.

He'd never even met anyone who'd actually been there.

'No, no,' the man scoffed at the suggestion. 'Spain?' He clearly thought Hermitage was some sort of idiot. 'Cornwall.'

'Cornwall?' Hermitage found his voice sounding like More. 'Santiago de Compostela isn't in Cornwall.'

'The one in Cornwall is.'

Hermitage's suspicion, which Wat was always encouraging him to use, brought some more questions to mind. 'So that's where you got the shells then? Cornwall? And which Holywell, Walsingham and Canterbury have you been to?'

'Oh, now you're asking.' Elard stroked his chin and gave his face an expression of deep thought. 'Holywell was down Oxford way. Walsingham is just this side of Cirencester and Canterbury's almost as far as Bath.'

Hermitage's shoulders sank. More frauds and liars, was he never going to meet anyone honest?

Wat joined in the questioning. 'I see.' it was his turn to sound very knowing and in on the secret. 'I expect people are always very generous to pilgrims, given that you're on a sacred mission and all.'

'Oh, yes,' Elard confirmed. 'Always keen to support the pilgrim on his way. One show of the shell and we're handsomely supplied.'

'You're not pilgrims.' Wat confronted the men with a bald truth. 'You're just a bunch of thieves walking about a lot. You carry some old shell and wave it in peoples' faces, and they think they have to give you alms or there'll be trouble.'

Hermitage simply stood by and tutted.

'We are pilgrims,' Elard protested, sounding very offended. 'We've pilgrimmed all over. I told you.'

'Well you've made pilgrimages to all the wrong places then,' Hermitage explained. 'Santiago is in Spain, despite your protests that it's in Cornwall. Canterbury is in Kent, Holywell, the one I know of, is in Wales somewhere and Walsingham is in the east. If you think you've achieved anything with these pilgrimages of yours, I'm afraid you're mistaken.'

'What would you know about it?' Elard snapped.

Wat looked at them in renewed shock, 'He is dressed as a monk,' the weaver pointed out.

'Ah, right.' Elard accepted this, reluctantly. 'Doesn't make any difference though, we still do what pilgrims do. Devote their lives to walking about and the like.'

'Pilgrims.' Hermitage scoffed, finding himself quite irritated with this sacrilege. He had a shameful urge to take it out on the false ones in front of him. The good book had an awful lot to say about the fate to be handed out to false prophets, he imagined false pilgrims wouldn't fare much better.

'Wandering around a small piece of England is not a pilgrimage,' he concluded. 'In fact to atone for your sins I think you should go on pilgrimage for real.' They looked very unhappy at this. 'Perhaps to Jerusalem,' Hermitage rubbed it in. 'Without any shoes.'

'We've done Jerusalem,' Elard said, although his confidence looked shaky.

'Oh, yes?' Hermitage asked. 'The one near Dorchester?'

'No,' Elard retorted, his voice heavy with contempt. 'The real one. Near Lincoln.'

'Ah.' Hermitage was on safe ground as that was his very neck of the woods. 'I know it well.'

That wiped the smile off Elard's face.

'Yes,' Hermitage went on. 'It's in the woods just off the old Roman road to the east. Put there so people didn't have to bother going all the way to the real Jerusalem, which,' Hermitage added with unfamiliar certainty and assertiveness, 'is miles away.'

'So.' Wat rubbed his hands. 'You are not pilgrims and neither are we. We'll carry on going our way and you can go in another direction completely.'

Elard did not look happy. 'We're going this way in any case,' he sniffed.

Wat looked at the band of fourteen people gathered around him waiting for a decision. He didn't seem to be weighing up conflicting arguments, rather he looked comprehensively stunned by the passage of events. 'Oh, please yourselves.' He threw his hands in the air and turned away. 'What's the point? Why do I bother? Let's see if we can round up a few more to join in. Perhaps once we get to fifty we can start our own village.'

He stomped off up the road, closely followed by Hermitage and Cwen.

'What do we want this lot for?' Cwen clearly thought

little of this development.'

Hermitage could see that once his face was turned from the band, Wat was smiling to himself. 'If they confuse us,' the weaver said with a wink, 'imagine what they'll do to Le Pedvin when the whole lot turn up in Derby.'

Hermitage was not so confident, 'I don't think killing three or fifteen will make much difference to King William.'

'Depends which one we say was carrying the gold when we left Wales.'

'Wat, you wouldn't,' Hermitage breathed in shock.

Cwen was nodding her head, 'Good plan,' she said.

Caput XII: Lord Bermo Rides Out.

Discussion of the gold was continuing in the courtyard of the castle Bermo, although courtyard is a generous description of the space bounded by the buildings that made up the Lord's fortress. Fortress is a not a word any self-respecting fortress builder would apply to this place either, and even buildings is pushing it a bit. It was an area on top of a hill with some things built on top which kept the rain out. Mostly.

Of course the lord's own chambers were solid and comfortable but there had been no need to extend such extravagance to anyone else.

On this particular morning the lord's forces were gathering for a mission none of them had been told about. Lord Bermo and his visitor had been engaged in such long and private conversations that it must be something pretty significant. Even now the two men were engaged in heated but whispered debate.

Lord Bermo's forces, all five of them, were used to not knowing what they were doing or why. Even after they'd done it. Their lord had ideas of his own which he certainly wasn't going to share, but which seemed to involve activities that made little sense to anyone. The forces just followed orders and got fed. What more was there to worry about?

The lord held the land for Gruffud ap Llewellyn and if summoned to battle would gather the fighting men from the hills and farms and rush to his king's side. In between times he had his core of fighting men to maintain control and he simply took the tithes that were his due.

The news that Gruffud ap Llewellyn had actually been dead for several years had not reached castle Bermo, or rather no one had bothered to send to this remote outpost. In fact Gruffud ap Llewellyn had had several wars and battles during his reign, but had never sent for the men of Bermo. Their reputation went before them, and he had never been quite that desperate.

There was an heir to the Bermo estates, but soon after his birth his mother had taken him from the castle to educate him in the ways of the world and prepare him for the role he would take on. She had also found that she quite liked the ways of the world herself, and had no intention of going anywhere near Bermo until the man's funeral.

Thus the lord and his guest discussed their quest in hushed and private tones. The stranger was encouraging the lord with assurances and promises that the appropriation of the druid gold would not rain terror on their heads. The lord was glancing out of the courtyard towards the woods, probably expecting the squirrel to jump out at any moment.

Eventually, Lord Bermo seemed to accept that they had better get on with it.

'We'll go there and see,' he agreed.

'Very well,' the stranger sighed.

'I'm not promising anything.'

'Of course not my Lord.' The stranger looked down at Bermo and bowed his head as he sat comfortably in his saddle.

He was quite a bit taller than the lord, and his horse was quite a bit taller than the lord's horse. It was also quite a lot more horse than the lord's horse. Lord Bermo's mount had been with him for many years, but what freak of nature had actually produced the thing in the first place did not bear thinking about. In fact several of Lord Bermo's forces speculated that there might be a bit of bear in there somewhere.

A cross between a bear and a horse would be a creature of myth. The act of crossing a bear with a horse was not something anyone was going to confess to.

The lord's forces had no mounts at all. It was their job to walk at their master's side, ready to fend off anyone who dared approach, be they man, woman, squirrel-god or jealous she-bear.

The stranger was also better equipped than lord Bermo. He wore solid leather with a light chain mail surcoat. He had a shining metal helmet on his head with a metal extension which sprang from the front to protect his nose. He wore thick gloves, the backs of the hands protected by more chain mail, and he carried a large sword at his side. And a short one at the other side. And a dagger at his belt. And a crossbow hung from the wooden saddle. He was the most heavily armed thing for miles around.

The Lord Bermo had a sword and his forces had sticks. Quite big and heavy sticks perfectly capable of inflicting damage, but sticks none the less. But then those they came up against didn't even have sticks.

Lord Bermo had made it clear that if the nature of their mission was disclosed to his men, they might rebel and run for the hills. The stranger kept to himself the thought that the mission might actually go better without them. He had seen ragged bands of ne'er-do-wells before, but never with quite so much ne'er or rag.

'Which direction is the nearest, erm, gathering?' the

stranger asked aloud.

'I think the village of Cwm a Pobl will do,' Lord Bermo said in exaggerated tones, largely for the benefit of his men.

'What a what?' the stranger asked.

'Cwm means valley and pobl means people,' Lord Bermo translated.

'Valley of people?' The stranger didn't seem to think much of this as a name.

'Accurate description, the lord confirmed. 'And quite a centre for the sort of activity we're looking for.' He said this quietly in case of his men were showing interest.

The men were not showing interest, nor any other tangible signs of intelligence. They all just seemed happy to be reunited with their sticks.

Lord Bermo beckoned his men to depart and the troop led off down the hill.

'Many of them?' the stranger asked now that they were out of earshot of the men.

'Who?' Lord Bermo looked at his men and then around to see if anyone else had joined them.

'Druids,' the stranger said pointedly, and with a sigh that he found he was using quite often in conversation with this man. 'Are there many druids?'

'Can be,' Bermo said, unhelpfully.

The stranger waited a moment for the explanation which he suspected was not going to come. It didn't. 'Explain,' he instructed.

Bermo looked slightly puzzled, but did go on. 'It seems to be a sort of centre for them. They have one of their circles there, and an old druid who teaches the young ones. Quite a few acolytes and the like come and go. Then they pass their initiations and go off to be druids somewhere else.'

'Hm.' The stranger thought deeply. 'So if there's a lot of them there'd be a lot of gold.'

'I suppose so.' Lord Bermo's nervousness at the plan was re-surfacing.

'And old druids have a lot more gold than the young ones.'

'Well, yes.'

'And if it's a centre for them, they're likely to have even more stashed away somewhere.' The stranger was warming to his task.

'But if there's a lot of them?' Bermo cast a worried glance at his men, who he clearly thought would not be up to the task of dealing with a crowd of druids.

'Won't be a problem.' The stranger was reassuring as he patted his sword.

'What about the king?' Bermo asked in a hurry, as if he'd only just remembered there was one.

'What about him?' the stranger asked, suddenly alert with suspicion.

'King Gruffyd isn't going to like it if any of his druids get, you know, damaged.'

'I think you'll find there's a new king on his way. Remember that William I mentioned? The one who likes gold?'

'William,' Bermo scoffed.

'Very, very fond of gold is William. You're a lot better off getting hold of it now, before he turns up.'

'He'll have to go through me and King Gruffyd first,' Bermo said with loyalty.

The stranger cast his eyes around the place and at the troop of men wandering along in front of them. 'That won't take long,' he muttered to himself.

The worried look had appeared on Bermo's face again, the one that had caused so much difficulty over the last few days.

'When we get to this village,' the stranger tried reassurance, even though it hadn't been much use so far, 'you and your men just hold back.'

Bermo seemed happier with that.

'Don't say anything, or do anything. Just let me do the killing.'

Caput XIII: Playing with the Rock.

Despite his own reservations, Hywel found that the people of People Valley were quite enthusiastic about moving the stone for the circle. He tried to point out how absolutely huge the thing was, and how it would be impossible to move, but they were still keen. He even suggested that some of them might die in the process, but they dismissed his concerns. They were used to dismissing Hywel's concerns and variously referred to him as a fuss-pot, and old nag and just plain boring.

He went on to explain what the druids had in mind for the stone and even threw in the outrageous suggestion that the Gods were going to descend from the sky and use the great rock to murder a monk.

The villagers thought this sounded absolutely marvellous and some of them asked if they'd be allowed to ride on the rock while the deed was done.

He then added, in the best discouraging tone he had, that there would be many stones in the circle and each one would have a sacrifice. The whole place would be running with blood.

This did cause several of the villagers to look askance at the druids. Lypolix happily cackled that the sacrifices would all be strangers, which cheered everyone enormously.

'They are coming to us even now,' the old seer rambled on. 'Brought they are. Brought to us.'

'Even now?' young Caradoc asked from the midst of the modest crowd. He was always the most easily impressed by druid mysteries. But then many aspects of daily life were mysteries to Caradoc.

'Aye.' Lypolix nodded.

'We'd better get a move on then.' Caradoc looked to his fellow villagers to encourage them to action.

The energy and commitment demonstrated by the villagers to the task of getting a massive rock off the mountain and dropping it on a monk was unlike anything Hywel or the druids had seen before.

Wulf started to worry that they might get a taste for this sort of thing, particularly when they'd done the twenty fifth and final stone – and presumably the twenty fifth and final sacrifice.

'You do remember Lord Bermo,' Hywel called at the departing villagers who scattered to collect tools. 'You know. Our Lord who likes to kill all the strangers himself?'

'Ah, but this is different. This is for the druids,' Caradoc called back. 'And anyway, the Gods are going to do the killing, not us.' He frowned in thought for a moment. 'I'd quite like to see a God do a sacrifice. Should be pretty spectacular.'

...

When Wulf arrived back at the master stone, just where he'd left it, the villagers went to their work with a will. There was none of the moaning and complaint of Hywel about how impossible the task was, and how unmovable the stone. There was some frowning and scratching of heads and chins but eventually they all settled on a plan.

Several of the group went to the back of the stone and

started digging out the ground around the sides, while a similar number attacked the top and bottom. Their thinking was that they would dig all around and underneath as far as they could and slide in some tree trunks as rollers. The stone would then be resting on an undug pillar of ground in the centre.

The Arch-Druid gave Hywel some seriously disappointed looks as the work took off at quite a speed.

The final part of the plan was, to use Hywel's words, as mad as a bee up a badger's bottom. Someone, it had not yet been agreed who, would climb under the stone and dig out the earthen pillar. At that point the stone would come to rest on the rollers, or it would snap the rollers and come to rest on the person doing the digging. As this was the chosen method for the sacrifice of the monk, there was little doubt the digger would be seeing the Gods before any of them.

Hywel made it perfectly clear that he would not be putting so much as a toe under the stone, let alone his whole body.

Someone suggested that the person who could achieve such a task would be strong, supple and excellent with a spade. If there was an accident, such a person would be a great loss to the village. Hywel, on the other hand, would hardly be missed at all as no one was sure what actual use he was anyway.

After much sniggering, Caradoc said that he was the person to do it. In fact he'd quite like to. It would be exciting, he said, which caused some worried glances. If he found a job like this exciting, what other completely stupid things was he prepared to do?

With the digging proceeding at a remarkable pace, helped by the soggy ground on which the rock lay, a smaller group was sent to fetch the tree trunks from the winter log pile.

These great lengths of pine had been felled two years ago and left to season. Hywel argued that they would be very dry and might not take the weight of the stone.

Caradoc reasoned that if that happened, at least they'd get the wood broken up for them, instead of having to chop it like normal.

Hywel thought about pointing out that if that happened, Caradoc would be flatter than a wood louse at the bottom of the heap. Perhaps the young idiot would figure it out when he heard the first splintering sound.

All of this frenetic activity was watched by the eyes in the cave, now safely back in the dark having wandered down and back up the hill as people came and went. He had no idea what they were up to, but wished they'd make up their mind where they were going to do it.

The whole village appeared to be trying to dig up a huge rock. Perhaps it was a special rock of some sort, or someone was trapped under it. He had seen that they had a thing about stones, particularly the ones in circles, so perhaps this was part of that.

He saw the party from the village coming back up the hill carrying tree trunks between them and quickly made the connection to rollers. They would have to be pretty careful about that. If they managed to get the stone onto rollers, the slope of the hill could carry the thing away at some speed. He imagined they'd thought of that. Have to be pretty stupid not to.

Then he remembered that he had seen one of their number trying to put the head back on a chicken after he'd chopped it off.

He stroked his chin with a worried frown on his face.

...

The roller party dragged their burdens up to the stone and tested them against the gap that had now been dug all round. A few more spade fulls and there was room to push one of the trunks under the front of the great stone and another under the back.

Some discussion around the stone now ensued, with several members of the team gesticulating down the slope away from the rock. They added mimes of a mighty rock plummeting down a hill, completely out of control, and smashing itself to bits at the bottom.

There was a suggestion that if they waited for this monk to arrive they could stand him at the bottom of the hill and let the rock do its thing.

In fact the rock was so big they could probably gather all the sacrifices together and do it in one go.

The observation that anyone standing at the bottom of a hill with a massive rock coming down it, would move out of the way, was countered with a plan to build a stockade of some sort, to keep the sacrifices together and in the right place.

They then recalled that the Gods were going to do this sacrifice and so they probably shouldn't interfere. If the Gods wanted a stockade they could knock one up in no time.

Perhaps it was the talk of the Gods that brought Lypolix into their midst. He cackled a lot and shook his head while the villagers all kept their distance.

'A hole,' the old seer either suggested, instructed or noticed, no one could tell.

'Yes,' one of the villagers confirmed loudly, nodding

extravagantly as one did to all dangerously mad people.

'Ha, ha.' The seer nodded back.

'I think he wants a hole,' Wulf observed, joining the strange conversation.

One of the villagers muttered something about giving Lypolix a hole but the Arch-Druid smacked the man round the head.

'A hole, a hole,' Lypolix confirmed that he did indeed want a hole.

'We put the stone in the hole?' Wulf asked. He could see that this would be required if the stone was to stand upright in its final position.

Lypolix did a little dance of confirmation. Or at least that's what it looked like to Wulf.

'I see.' Wulf nodded his understanding. He explained to the villagers. 'We need to dig a hole where the stone is to go. Then we move the stone to the right place and tip it up until it drops in the hole.' He smiled at the simplicity of the plan.

'Tip it up?' Hywel was aghast. 'You've seen the size of the thing. How on earth are we going to tip it up and drop it in a hole?'

'We could use Caradoc as a lever,' one of the villagers sniggered.

Caradoc didn't immediately see a problem with this.

'That's right.' Wulf saw how it could work. 'Not Caradoc though,' he added, quickly. 'We get it to the right place, dig out to get a tree trunk or two under one end and then lever it up.'

'The lever would sink into the ground,' Hywel dismissed the plan.

'Then we put a smaller rock on the ground to rest the levers on.' Wulf was quite excited by working all this out.

'Another rock?' Hywel scoffed.

'A smaller one,' Wulf explained with some irritation. 'Then, when we've levered it up a bit we stick some logs underneath to stop it falling back again. Then we move the small rock and the levers and do it again. See?'

'Never work,' was Hywel's considered analysis.

'When it gets to the right height it will drop into the hole,' Wulf concluded.

Several of the villagers nodded at this and seemed impressed.

Lypolix also appeared very happy with the plan. 'And the monk,' he added with a clap and a skip.

'Ah yes.' Wulf recalled the sacrifice of the monk, which gave him pause for thought. 'Once the stone is up I suppose the sacrifice comes next.'

The villagers nodded some more. They were clearly looking forward to that bit.

'No, no,' Lypolix dismissed the idea.

'No?' Wulf was surprised, but actually found himself quite relieved that they wouldn't be killing anyone after all.

Lypolix explained what would happen using mime, dance, some grunting and screaming noises and a final, very terminal-sounding gurgle.

'I see.' Wulf slowly translated for the villagers. 'We dig the hole. Tie the monk up and put him in the bottom of it, then we drop the stone on top.'

'Ah.' The villagers saw it now. What a clever plan.

'But I thought the Gods were going to come and do it?' Caradoc asked with disappointment.

'Perhaps the Gods will give the stone its final push,' Wulf observed with little pleasure.

'That's not very interesting,' Caradoc mumbled.

Wulf had a further thought which he was sure hadn't been taken into account. 'There will be one for every stone and every stone shall have one?' He checked Lypolix's sums.

'Aye, aye.' The seer was very happy.

'So.' Wulf thought it through. 'If three stones are already up and they've been done, there's twenty two to go. Twenty four for the main circle and then the master stone.'

Everyone nodded in appreciation at this display of advanced calculation. Druids really were clever people.

'Which means.' Wulf hoped someone else would get it as well, but they looked like they wouldn't get it if the stone fell on them. 'Leaving out the monk, who's tied up at the bottom of the hole, there's another twenty one people to be sacrificed.'

Lypolix rubbed his hands in glee at the prospect.

Wulf surveyed the small crowd which was the cream of the village crop. 'So the sacrifices will outnumber the villagers.'

Still no one picked up on the facts.

'Twenty one people, who probably aren't all that keen on being sacrificed in the first place, against a dozen villagers?'

Surprisingly it was Caradoc who saw that this might be a problem. 'Perhaps they're all small?' he offered.

Wulf looked to Lypolix.

The seer counted on his fingers, 'The monk, the artisan,'

Well, that didn't sound too bad.

'The warrior, the fearsome woman, the robbers,' Lypolix went on.

Wulf was gratified to see the faces fall.

'How are we supposed to manage that lot?' Needless to say, it was Hywel who voiced the difficulties.

'The Gods,' Lypolix laughed happily. 'The Gods will come and deal with them all.'

Caradoc was relieved. 'Oh, great,' he said, happy that there was going to be a God after all.

'Twenty one strangers,' Hywel mocked. 'Twenty one would-be sacrifices are going to wander into the village and just wait for us to drop rocks on them? They're not going to put up a fight at all?'

'Not if the Gods are with us,' Caradoc argued.

Hywel just snorted, which brought a scowl from the Arch-Druid.

'I shall be in my hut if you need me,' Hywel huffed, clearly intending that they wouldn't need him. Or rather they would when they saw he was right after all, and then he'd be able to say "I told you so".

Wulf held a hand up to stop Hywel, but the village leader was stomping off down the hill, leaving them to their digging and levers.

'Do you want him back?' The Arch-Druid asked, clearly prepared to drag Hywel by the hair if need be.

'I suppose not.' Wulf shrugged. 'We can tell him about the final location of the stone later.'

'Final location?'

'Yes. I didn't like to mention it before as he seemed so put out by the whole business. As well as the master stone, I can see exactly where it's got to go.'

'And that is?'

'Well, let's just say that his hut is a bit in the way.'

The Arch-Druid failed to hide a small smile at this.

'And so's his bed,' Wulf added.

The Arch-Druid sniggered. Just the one snigger and it

was gruff and reluctant, but Wulf had never seen the Arch-Druid snigger before.

He smiled, but then had an image of twenty one people tied up in the bottom of twenty one holes, with twenty one rocks about to be pushed on top of them. He couldn't see himself able to do it when push came to shove – which it would, as the stones would be pretty heavy. The Arch-Druid and Lypolix? He was sure they wouldn't have a problem at all. And most of the villagers seemed positively enthusiastic. He had another vision, quite a strong one this time, that this was not going to end at all well.

Caput XIV: And Now, Stragglers.

Fifteen people were making the best time they could towards the border with Wales. Wat seemed able to walk along as if he was on his own without a care in the world. Cwen walked as if annoyed by every step of the way, and by the shuffle of feet that followed. Hermitage couldn't keep his head still, his eyes darting about to try and force him to accept that there really were twelve complete strangers with them on a mission made for three.

He looked at John and almost felt as if the man was one of them. True, he had been foisted on them by Le Pedvin, but then Le Pedvin spent a lot of his time foisting things on Hermitage.

The Druid was still a total confusion. The man said nothing, just looked serene and confident – which annoyed Cwen no end.

The six robbers kept to themselves and seemed enormously content simply to be in a party led by the great Wat the Weaver. Their quiet conversation about tapestries brought out occasional bursts of laughter; very crude and lascivious laughter.

The three pilgrims were also happy with their lot. That might change when evening came and they found they would have to fend for themselves. There would be no free food and drink on this trip.

More scuttled backwards and forwards through the group, trying to find someone who was willing to engage in a conversation. As a conversation with More entailed a lot of listening and very little talking, he had no takers.

Not that that stopped him.

For a relatively secret mission given to three people, the road was positively crowded. As Hermitage passed his gaze over the assembly he had trouble understanding how this had all come to pass. Obviously he recalled each occasion someone had been added to their number, but the total now seemed beyond sense. How did they end up like this? And if they carried on, how many would they be as they crossed the border. Wat was right, someone might think they were invading.

Hermitage remembered what tended to happen when invaders turned up at someone's border. He swallowed and added death in battle to his collection of worries.

They were entering the town of Wanborough now, where the old road from the south joined their path towards Wales. Being of a sufficiently large number, they caused all the townsfolk to immediately adopt the normal procedure in these cases. They dropped whatever they were doing, ran inside and barred the doors.

The population of this place, if only they knew it, would be perfectly capable of seeing most of this rabble off with a selection of moderately offensive abuse.

But they didn't know that. For all they knew the monk was one of those who came collecting alms with a band of fourteen swordsmen at his back. Or he was the member of the band responsible for blessing the swordsmen before they started their rampaging.

Of course the town had its own militia, but they were only the farmers who could wield a big stick and shout louder than anyone else.

The pilgrims looked very disappointed as doors were slammed and shutters put up at windows. They had their shells ready and were probably looking forward to a good feed.

The robbers scowled about the place, unhappy that not so much as a spade had been left propped outside a hovel.

Wat just carried on walking.

'Oh, Wat.' Hermitage took in their welcome. 'This is awful.'

'What's awful about it?'

'These poor people are frightened of us,' Hermitage explained. 'And we're completely harmless. What has the land come to that a man must hide in his own dwelling at the passing of a stranger?'

'Wouldn't you? If fifteen strangers came wandering into your monastery.'

Hermitage tutted, 'No, of course not. I would welcome them with the hospitality commanded by our Lord.'

'Which could explain why you keep having to move monastery,' Wat observed with a wry smile.

Hermitage couldn't see the connection at all.

'We could always knock on a door or two,' Cwen suggested, sounding quite keen on the idea.

'To what end?' Hermitage asked. 'Instil more fear in these humble villagers?'

'Don't look very humble to me.' Cwen nodded towards the well-kept dwellings with their solid doors and windows. 'Should be good for some supplies to help us on our way.'

'I wouldn't hear of it.' Hermitage was surprised and disappointed. 'We must not sink to the level of those who come to take what we have. In fact,' he thought the situation through, 'we should probably ask the townsfolk if we have anything they need. Or if there is some service we can do them.'

Now Cwen looked surprised and disappointed. And very baffled, 'You're mad,' she concluded.

Hermitage shrugged and walked on. As the last of the band, which on this occasion was More, left the edge of the town, the first doors began to open again, and curious heads popped out. Probably curious to make sure that the strangers were really gone. And without burning anything to the ground. Wonders would never cease.

...

At the edge of the well-to-do town were the less well-to-do people. A collection of hovels crowded the road side, populated by those a lot less shy about keeping their doors closed. Probably because what was inside the doors would frighten most strangers away.

These people watched with naked interest as a larger group than they had seen for quite a while strolled past. The group didn't seem very coherent somehow, it took quite a while for the last one to go ambling by. And he was a grizzled old man who seemed to want to have a conversation with anyone who stood still too long. He was enough to make even some of these people want to go indoors and hide.

Once More had passed the last of the hovels Wat took a moment to check that his unwanted travelling companions were in some sort of order.

'Oh for goodness sake, now what?' the weaver cried out with a cross between despair, disbelief and hopeless resignation.

Hermitage turned to face back down the road and saw that a number of the hovel dwellers were outside their mud and stick constructions, probably to see the most exciting thing that had happened around here for years.

As More wandered on, Hermitage noticed that the hovel dwellers seemed to be wandering as well. They were definitely further away from their hovels than they had been.

Wat stopped and so the rest of the band stopped as well.

So did the population from the hovels.

Impatiently, Wat gestured to the band to join him down the road.

For perhaps the first time, Hermitage, Wat, Cwen, John, the druid, More, the pilgrims and the robbers got together in a reasonably tight bunch. They soon spread themselves out a bit.

The bunch was observed from a distance by the hovel owners, who didn't look like they wanted to get any closer.

With an abrupt gesture Wat moved his team several steps along the road away from the town.

The hovel people hesitated, but then moved as well.

'All right,' Wat cried out in frustration. 'Just what is going on?'

He strode back through his followers until he came face to face with one of the women from the hovels.

She showed no sign of retreating in the face of Wat's approach, and in fact folded her arms to wait for him.

Hermitage appraised the woman and saw that she was probably no older than Wat. That she was a lot less comfortable than Wat was blindingly obvious. Her clothes were rent with rips and snags, a long floor-length skirt dragged on the ground. Her top was a thick, ill-fitting jerkin and her hair was roughly cut.

'Who are you?' Wat asked. 'Camp followers?'

The woman looked horrified and slapped Wat's face.

The weaver didn't know what to do, so he stood still and looked shocked.

Cwen sniggered.

'How dare you.' The woman put her hands on her poorly clothed hips and glared at Wat. 'We are not camp followers.' She spat to give the statement extra emphasis. 'We are stragglers.'

Wat didn't look any less confused. 'Stragglers?'

'That's right. Stragglers and proud of it.'

Hermitage was as lost as Wat. He'd never heard of anyone actually calling themselves a straggler. Surely it was a failing of people who couldn't keep up. This woman made it sound like it was a profession.

'You, erm, straggle?' Wat tried, looking to Hermitage as if this some new sea of specialism, and he couldn't swim.

Hermitage wandered over to join the conversation.

'Of course.' The woman clearly thought that so much was obvious.

Hermitage didn't know what to ask in this situation. He had not a clue what was going on. But that was pretty normal so he just said the first thing that came into his head. He'd worry about consequences later.

'What do you straggle, exactly?'

'Anything of interest,' the woman confirmed.

'Aha.' The first thing in his head proved to be no use at all.

Helpfully, the woman continued. 'Militia, wagons, merchants. We've straggled them all. 'Course merchants are the best for straggling but militia aren't bad. Plenty of supplies.'

'So.' Hermitage thought the information through. 'You

straggle along behind people and live on what's cast aside or left over?'

Again the woman looked at Hermitage as if he was some sort of idiot. 'Don't know of any other sort of straggling.'

'Is it a good living?' Wat asked, seemingly bemused by the whole thing.

'Oh, this is a good spot, this is. Roads from east and west and from the south. Just the sort of place you need for really effective straggling. Course, it's been a bit quiet recently.'

'But if you straggle,' Hermitage couldn't help himself, 'surely you don't stay in one spot? You follow, sorry straggle along behind a group and go wherever they go?'

'Look.' The woman gave Hermitage a harsh stare. 'If you are going to carry on being insulting we shan't bother straggling you at all.'

'Suits me,' Wat mumbled.

'If we was to follow you, we'd be followers see? But we aren't. We're stragglers. So we straggle along a bit and then come home.'

'Well, we're going to Wales, and we aren't merchants or militia so if I was you I'd stay at home and straggle round your own hovel if I was you.' Wat folded his arms and glared at the stragglers, many of whom were looking the other way.

'Oh, it's been a bit quiet for a while now,' the woman explained. 'Don't know what's going on. We could do with a bit of a straggle up Cirencester way, might pick up someone useful.'

Wat did a quick appraisal of the group loitering on the road. None of them were any better dressed than the first woman and it was hard to tell which were male and which female. 'There are seven of you for goodness sake! There are only fifteen of us. What is it where there are half as many stragglers as the people they're straggling?'

Hermitage thought this was a fascinating question.

Wat clearly didn't.

'Free country,' the woman responded. 'We can go to Cirencester if we want. There's safety in numbers anyway.' She nodded to her group who took this as the signal to get ready for a good straggle.

Wat counted off the answers on his fingers. 'It is not a free country. The Normans have taken over, in case you hadn't noticed. Which probably accounts for the dearth of passers-by to be straggled at. And if you come with us I can assure there won't be safety in numbers. If robbers start picking you off, don't expect us to help.'

The woman snorted and gestured at Wat's gathered party. 'You've got the robbers with you.' She exchanged a wave with the leader of the robbers. 'Be much safer having them where you can see 'em.'

'Come on then,' Wat said with an enthusiasm that sounded completely out of place, and which made Hermitage look at him warily. 'Let's all go to Wales. Let's all go and find the druids together. Twenty two of us. That's a nice number. Twenty two people where there should have been three.' He gave a slightly hysterical laugh and walked away from the group.

Hermitage, left alone with the stragglers didn't know whether he was supposed to continue the discussion or follow Wat. The head straggler looked at him as if he needed to move away before she could start straggling. He did so, more confused than he had felt for quite some time.

Back at the front he joined Wat and Cwen.

'Twenty two?' Cwen was incredulous. 'Twenty two people walking along the road to Wales? I thought this was supposed to be a secret mission.'

'Well you try getting rid of them then,' Wat growled. 'We've tried telling them they're not wanted. We've tried telling them not to come. It's completely ridiculous. If I made a tapestry of this as a great quest, nobody would believe a thread of it.'

Cwen exchanged a hopeless look with Hermitage. His was much more hopeless.

'And it's not as if any of them are any use,' Wat went on as they walked on down the road. 'We've got John who can handle a sword and that's it. If a real enemy descended on us from the hills this lot would run a mile. More might talk them to death but the rest couldn't form a defensive circle if it was drawn on the ground for them.'

'Perhaps once they see we're really going into Wales they'll turn around,' Cwen suggested.

'Possible,' Wat grunted. 'After all, no one in their right mind would go there out of choice.'

This did nothing for Hermitage's confidence.

'Still,' Wat mused. 'If they do come with us into Wales it might solve the problem.'

'How?' Cwen asked.

'Twenty two people walking into a Welsh village uninvited? We'll probably all get slaughtered.'

Caput XV: Making Your Sacrifice Feel At Home.

still don't think twenty two people, one of them a monk, are just going to politely wait around while we put them in holes and drop stones on them.'

Wulf was continuing his argument with the Arch-Druid back at the temple. There was no point taking this up with Lypolix. Interpreting the various noises and movements was tiring and probably inaccurate.

'Will of the Gods,' the Arch-Druid confirmed to Wulf.

'Will of the Gods or not, I think they could put up a fight.'

The Arch-Druid looked puzzled, 'Why?'

'Why?' Wulf couldn't understand how this wasn't perfectly clear. 'Wouldn't you struggle a bit if someone was trying to sacrifice you?'

The Arch-Druid gave it serious thought. 'They're coming to be sacrifices, Lypolix has said so. Why would they cause trouble if that's the reason they're coming in the first place?'

'They might be coming, but I don't think he's said anything about them knowing why. Be a bit of a problem anywhere, finding twenty two willing sacrifices.'

The Arch-Druid frowned.

'Heathens,' Wulf added for completeness. 'Twenty two heathens, lining up by their stones?'

'Hm,' the Arch-Druid hummed. 'I suppose the heathen doesn't know he's going to the spirit world to be with the Gods.'

'Exactly.' Wulf was glad the man was seeing the problem. 'Heathens probably kick up an almighty stink if you try to sacrifice them. And with so many of them, we could end up in the holes ourselves.'

The Arch-Druid was thoughtful, 'What do you suggest?'

'I really don't know,' and Wulf really didn't. 'Can't we get Lypolix to organise them one at a time? You know, form a bit of a queue? Twenty two at once is a bit of a handful.'

'He's a seer,' the Arch-Druid pointed out with one his tutting noises. 'He sees things. He doesn't organise them.'

Wulf thought hard. 'I suppose if they did line up, the ones at the back of the queue would see what was going on at the front and decide not to stay. Or worse.'

The two men frowned and thought and tried to come up with ideas to control twenty two wouldn't-be sacrifices.

'The Gods will help,' the Arch-Druid offered, although he didn't sound very sure.

'From what Lypolix said, it doesn't sound like the Gods are going to play a terribly active role.'

They returned to thinking.

'Could we dig a pit?' Wulf suggested. 'You know, a great big hole large enough for all of them. Then we can pick them out one at a time when we're ready.'

'With that many people I don't think they'd fall into a pit in one go. The ones at the back would see the first ones go in and they'd hold back. Then they'd probably even help the first lot out again.' The Arch-Druid snorted at such uncooperative behaviour.

Wulf took to pacing up and down. 'If they didn't know

139

they were sacrifices they wouldn't run away or start a fight,' he reasoned.

'Bit hard to miss when you're in a hole with a rock on its way down.'

'Ah, but what if they didn't know until then?'

'They'd be pretty stupid.'

'No, no, think about it.' Wulf's idea was taking shape and he suddenly felt confident enough to give the Arch-Druid instructions. 'We welcome them all as guests, give them a feast even, make them comfortable.'

The Arch-Druid scowled at this generosity.

'Then, when they're all settled and off their guard, we grab the first one for the first stone and no one's any the wiser.' He held his arms out to demonstrate the conclusion of the plan.

'Until they ask where the missing one has gone.'

'Well, we don't know do we? People wander off all the time. Maybe he's gone home again?'

'And when half a dozen have disappeared and there's six new stones in the circle?'

'They're heathens,' Wulf dismissed the problem. 'And probably English as well. What do they know?'

The Arch-Druid gave a grudging acknowledgement that if anyone could be relied upon not to notice their companions being sacrificed, it would probably be an Englishman. What with their reputation and all.

'I'm not sure.' The Arch-Druid shook his head slowly.

'If Lypolix is right, twenty two people will be turning up here any moment. We either say "hello, have you come for the sacrifice? What size hole do you take?" or we settle them in nicely and bide our time. I don't see how we can do the first. This village isn't capable of dealing with a large group of anything. Hywel will run a mile and

Caradoc would probably use his head as a battering ram.'

The Arch-Druid seemed to be coming round. 'I suppose we don't have the holes and the stones for the circle ready yet anyway. And the master stone is going to take some moving.'

'In fact.' Wulf had another good idea. 'If we're very generous and feed them well, they might even help us dig the holes. Tell them it's a sacred duty and so on.'

'Dig their own holes?' the Arch-Druid gave a chuckle. Another one.

As they stood, satisfied that at least they had a plan, the sounds of shouting could be heard from over the mist-topped trees. These were followed by a loud splintering noise and an ominous silence.

'I don't think moving the master stone is going very well,' Wulf observed.

'Let's hope we haven't already had our first sacrifice.' The Arch-Druid raised an eyebrow. 'I'm not scraping Caradoc off the bottom of the master stone.'

...

In fact, moving the master stone had started quite satisfactorily. The technique of cutting out underneath and letting the rock come to rest on the rollers had been a surprising success. Surprising to everyone involved. Caradoc had even emerged unscathed from his excavation.

The first problem had been that the weight of the great master stone had immediately sunk the rollers up to their tops in the mud and soil. They weren't so much rollers as props.

The first suggestion had been to repeat the process

used for the stone; lever up the rollers and put more rollers underneath.

It was Wem the Strange who pointed out that the new timbers placed under the rollers would probably sink into the ground as well, if the stone didn't just fall off.

Wem the Strange was rightly named as he had a constant supply of strange ideas that meant he was always held at a distance in the village. It was Wem who suggested putting the very thin, flat grey slates that littered the hillsides onto the roofs of the huts to keep the rain out. Everyone knew earth was best for hut roofs. Wem was an idiot; as well as strange.

He was roundly castigated as a know-it-all, but the idea of an ever increasing stack of rollers was abandoned.

Wem hesitated to suggest that they use some flat rocks to rest the rollers on, instead of more timbers, but he did anyway. Flat rocks being less likely to sink. Everyone scowled at him and grumbled incoherent insults but went off to get some rocks anyway.

With the rocks prepared, the task of levering up one end of a front roller was a lot easier than lifting the whole stone. No one could figure that out, not even Wem.

Wem then suggested that if they did get the rocks under the rollers and the stone moved, the rollers would sink again once they rolled off their rocks.

Oh, yes, and what did he think they should do? The crowd was getting restless.

He thought they should build a small road of flat rocks under the rollers. This would stop the timber sinking into the ground and help the master stone move.

The assembly looked at the rocks and the timber and the soft earth. Without saying anything, they went to gather more rocks. At least there were plenty available, the mountain being made out of them.

With a solid path of flat rocks laying out the route down the hill, the villagers moved round to lever the remaining rollers out of the earth and slip their new surface underneath.

The other side of the front roller went easily into position and so they moved to the back. As they levered the first back roller up, the stone shifted slightly, which gave them great encouragement.

When they levered up the final roller and dropped it on its road, the stone departed.

The party watched with huge satisfaction as the great stone, the huge monolith which no one had thought even movable, set off down the hill.

The rollers were rolling, the stone was moving, it was all absolutely marvellous.

Trust Wem to point out that the stone appeared to be moving faster than the rollers. The great rock was sliding across the top of the timbers in such a manner that the tree trunks would soon be left behind.

'We should have had more tree trunks,' Wem pointed out.

Even Caradoc wasn't stupid enough to run down to the front of the stone to try and make it stop.

Screwed up faces watched the inexorable progress of the stone and saw that they were going to have to start the whole process all over again when the stone came off the end of its rollers and buried itself in the ground once more.

In fact, not only had they not got enough tree trunks for rollers, they hadn't realised that the tall pine tree which grew in the middle of their path was going to be a problem.

Before it came to the end of its rollers, the great master stone slammed into the innocent tree which gave way with an equally great splintering. It had stopped the stone, literally in its tracks.

There was much shouting and waving of arms as people tried to figure out whether what had just happened was good, or bad. They looked to Wem.

'At least we've got another tree trunk now,' the man observed. 'And we know what not to do next time.' He smiled.

It must be good, then.

'I think we'd better ask Wulf where he wants this stone before we build the track. If this road and rollers thing works, it could get there pretty quickly. And the Gods help anyone who gets in its way.'

'Hm,' Caradoc mused as he surveyed the wreckage of quite a sizeable tree. 'If it can do that to a tree trunk, think what a mess it's going to make of a monk.'

They all had a good laugh at the prospect as they went to get more wood and rocks.

Caput XVI: Over the Border.

'ight.' Wat held his arm out to direct everyone's attention to the bridge over the River Severn. 'This is the border with Wales, so you can all just bugger off.'

Hermitage still found it hard to believe all these people had followed them this far. Instead of finding someone else to straggle after in Cirencester, the stragglers had moaned about the paucity of travellers these days and tagged along.

More said he wanted to see the river, so he could spot if it was any different from the Thames. He showed signs of real disappointment that it wasn't flowing up hill, or didn't glow in the dark, or wasn't in mid-air. He summarised England's greatest river in five words. 'Well that's a bit dull,' he said.

The robbers simply wanted to go wherever Wat went and the pilgrims just did what everyone else did.

Wat tried a bit of passion. 'Who knows what evils lie over these waters? It is our mission to go there, but mayhap we will never return. Flee I tell you, flee before your lives are ripped from your bodies and your souls are cast into the dark depths.'

'Do what?' One of the robbers looked very puzzled at this bizarre outburst.

Hermitage and Cwen both gave him a rather hopeless look.

The entire party, which now took up quite a bit of the road, was silent, but clearly considered Wat had gone slightly mad.

Eventually, the silence was broken by Elard the pilgrim. He spoke as someone who'd been told a joke about a week ago, and had just got it. 'Ahaaaa,' he drawled out.

'Aha, what?' Wat said, disappointed that the whole group had not run for the hills.

'I see what you're up to,' Elard went on, knowingly.

'I doubt that,' Wat mumbled to himself.

'Relics.' Elard announced – although it sounded rather rude the way he said it.

'I beg your pardon?'

'You've got the relics.'

Wat checked himself over. 'No, still not with you.'

'That's why we're going to Wales. And why you've got a druid and a swordsman'

'Is it?'

'Oh, yes. Me and Lanson and Pord been thinking.'

'Well done,' Wat sounded suitably surprised.

'There's relics in Wales. Everyone knows that. You lot are going there to steal relics and bring them back to Christendom.'

'Are we?'

'Absolutely. There's lots of saints gone into Wales over the years. Most of 'em get killed or eaten or something.'

Hermitage pondered for a moment how someone could be killed or eaten. Surely if you were eaten...? He let the thought drop.

'And where you got a dead saint, you got a relic. Very valuable things relics. Very holy. You been given a secret mission to go into Wales and rescue the saints' relics from the heathens.' He folded his arms and smiled in triumph at Lanson and Pord. 'So we're coming with you.'

Wat's mouth hung open and he just looked at Cwen and Hermitage as if shocked by the idiocy. And surprised at being shocked.

'What a load of rubbish.' The leader of the stragglers spoke up.

Hermitage was rather ashamed that after all this time on the road he still didn't know her name. Mind you, they had been purposefully straggling behind everyone else so the opportunities for conversation were few and far between. He supposed that was the point of straggling, but it wasn't very sociable.

'You're joining the army.'

'The army?' Wat squeaked out. Surely anyone could see he would be the last person to join any army. And anyway, what army?

'What army?' he asked.

'I don't know do I?' the head straggler answered smartly, 'I'm just a straggler. I don't know what the great and the good get up to. What I do know is straggling. This many people do not go wandering about the country without a purpose. The usual purpose is an army and there's nothing like an army for a spot of good straggling. There you are. See.'

Hermitage did see and had to congratulate the woman on her argument. She had obviously applied her experience and her knowledge to her situation and had drawn a very reasonable conclusion.

She was completely wrong, but had taken a commendable route to get there.

'There should not be this many people,' Wat cried out in exasperation. 'There should only be three of us. Four at most if you count John.' He gestured at John, who acknowledged the recognition with a bow of the head. 'So there is no way we are going to join an army.' He shook his head at his own reasoning. 'Anyway, there isn't an army. King William's got the only army these days, and he's miles away.'

The straggler seemed a little crestfallen, 'Still have armies,' she mumbled.

'It ain't relics and it ain't armies,' Banley the lead robber announced from the back of the group. 'It's gold.'

That sent a shiver down Hermitage's back. How could the man know? None of them would have told him. Perhaps John? Maybe he had really had been told the purpose of the journey by Le Pedvin. That man lied about pretty much everything. Or the druid? The mysterious priest seemed to know a lot of what was going on.

The word "gold" had caught the attention of stragglers and pilgrims alike.

'Gold?' Wat sounded like it was the most ridiculous suggestion of the lot.

'Of course,' Banley went on. 'Stands to reason don't it? Everyone knows Wales is full of gold. Only the dragons stop anyone getting at it.'

If Hermitage had been quite pleased with the proposal from the stragglers, he could see that the robbers were not even starting well.

'Dragons,' Wat said in resignation that this was not going at all well.

'That's right. And what do you need to fend off a dragon?'

'Do tell.'

Banley stepped forward, struck a dramatic pose and pointed to one of the number. 'A druid.'

'Ahh,' the crowd sighed in recognition of this amazing revelation.

The druid looked rather disconcerted to be the centre

of attention.

'So,' Banley challenged Wat. 'You tell me that you are not going to Wales to get gold.'

Hermitage thought this was a real problem. Yes of course they weren't going to Wales to get gold from a dragon, but they were going to get gold. And Banley had challenged them to deny it. What would Wat do?

'Of course we're not.'

Ah yes, lie. That was Wat was going to do. It would never have occurred to Hermitage.

Wat held his arms out wide to get their attention. 'Pilgrims, robbers, stragglers,' he called out.

More put his hand up.

'Sorry, and Boatmen.'

More smiled and nodded to everyone so they would know he was the boatman.

'Let me make it perfectly clear. 'We are not going to Wales to recover relics.'

The look on the pilgrims' faces said they did not believe this for a moment.

'Neither are we going to join an army. And most certainly we are not going to get gold from a dragon.'

Each of the groups seemed still wedded to their own particular version of events and were still dismissing Wat's denials.

'Shall I tell you why we're going to Wales?' he asked.

The groups exchanged confused looks. Yes, they would like to know, but not if was going to contradict their own theories.

'Disease,' Wat announced.

Disease? Thought Hermitage. What disease? He did though notice that the crowd had taken half a step back. He glanced at Cwen who had a smile hidden on her face.

'Aye.' Wat pressed his advantage. 'Horrible, deadly disease.'

'Plague?' someone whispered in alarm.

'Plague isn't even close.' Wat's eyes widened.

The lead straggler was the first to start frowning. Hermitage thought she seemed quite intelligent. Wasted on straggling.

'You've got a disease, or you're going to get one?' she asked.

'We're going to look.'

'You're going to look at a disease? That's sounds a pretty stupid thing to do.'

'King William sent us to find out about the mysterious welsh disease.'

There was a pause while the group took this in.

'I've never heard of a welsh disease,' the straggler sounded unsure.

'That's because most people just drop dead when they get it.'

'So what good are you to King William if you drop dead as well?'

Hermitage would like to have a debate with this woman over some topic of mutual interest. Perhaps she had opinions on the post-Exodus prophets? If not, he could always tell her his.

'He's a cruel master,' Wat explained.

The group seemed to be pausing, like some animal that couldn't make up its mind whether the other animal it was about to jump on could kill it or not.

'Nah,' straggling woman had decided. 'Don't believe a word of it. It's an army and you just want to keep it to yourselves.'

'It's a relic, I tell you,' Elard the pilgrim held his

ground.

'You're all idiots,' Banley the robber dismissed the lot of them. 'It's gold. Who in their right mind is going to go into Wales for some relic or an army? An army I ask you? Things best kept away from if you ask me.'

'Don't know what you'd know about it,' the straggler woman countered. 'Very lucrative a good army. Bigger the better.'

'Not as good as a relic,' Elard piped up. 'One good relic and you're made for life.'

The various parties to the discussion now drew their fellows into the argument until the middle of the road was just a mess of arguing robbers, pilgrims and stragglers, each one as sure of his or her own position as anyone could be.

Even More was piling in, although he seemed able to swap sides with each argument, and was heading for the conclusion that there was an army of robber-pilgrims who carried gold in their relics.

No one could be sure, but it was probably one of the robbers who pushed first, robbers generally being the sort of people for pushing and shoving.

It seemed that stragglers could hold their own as well, and pretty soon the pushing and shoving had extended to everyone engaged in the debate. The roadway became a melee of bodies and first one, then another was either pushed over, or off the path altogether.

Voices were being raised and it wouldn't be long before someone reached for a rock.

The confusion continued for quite some time and caused a loud disturbance.

After a while, an official looking man wandered slowly up, perhaps he was the toll-man or bridge keeper, paid to keep this vital artery of the country clear and free for traffic. Whoever he was, he took one look at the size of the crowd scuffling on his doorstep and decided that watching them was his best course of action.

More wandered out of the crowd and joined him at the side of the road.

'It's all about the rowlocks.' More grinned and nodded.

'Is it?' The man looked as if he was just as worried about the boatman as he was about the fight.

'Oh, yis. It's the golden rowlocks that the army have given to the druids. You see the weaver and the monk have been sent by the king to find Martel. He was on my boat. Did I tell you about my boat?'

The man wandered away again. He'd come back in an hour or two and hope that this had all just gone away.

With no progress being made in the resolution of the debate, the group was starting to break up into sub-fights. In the course of the conflict some individuals had developed personal grudges and were intent on taking them out.

'Stop!' Pord the pilgrim held his arms above his head and shouted at the top of his voice. This stunned everyone as he had been quite quiet until then.

They all paused mid-argument and turned to the pilgrim.

'Where've they gone?' Pord asked, or rather demanded of his fellows.

Heads were turned and the road scanned.

There was no sign of Wat, Hermitage, Cwen, John or the druid.

'The bastards,' the lead straggler exclaimed. 'They've gone into Wales without us. After them!'

Forgetting their disagreement over the purpose of the

visit, the entire party ran to the bridge over the River Severn, and without a second glance, or any offer to pay their toll, they hurried to meet whatever fate had in store for them.

The official toll-man watched them go with resignation that there was no way he was equipped to deal with this sort of thing. At least he had a fairly good idea what sort of fate awaited them, and relaxed as he concluded that he would never be seeing any of them again.

Caput XVII: Meet the Locals.

his way.' The druid had found his voice, although it was a pretty terse instruction.

They had run over the bridge as soon as attention was off them, and quickly turned to follow the druid as he headed north on the Welsh side of the river and strode confidently along the path.

Once they were sure that they were away from the crowd they slowed to fast walking pace.

Hermitage did not feel confident at all. Here he was, in Wales. With the Welsh. Not in England anymore. Something bad was bound to happen very soon indeed. After all, everyone William sent to Wales came to a bad end, and here they were sent to Wales by William. And now they were here, the bad end was bound to be just around the corner.

Neither Wat nor Cwen seemed at all bothered about treading into this unknown land, but at least John had his hand on his sword.

Hermitage scanned the sky but couldn't see any huge, fire-breathing shapes descending on them. There didn't appear to be any druids hiding in the bushes and no savage killers leapt out into the roadway to gobble them up.

Still, they'd only just stepped off the bridge. It would take quite some time before Hermitage would be able to relax at all. Probably five or six years.

The druid led them on, which at least meant they wouldn't have to wander aimlessly about the place.

Only now did it occur to Hermitage to wonder

whether the druid actually knew anything at all about Martel. He had just assumed that a druid turning up in the middle of the night knowing they were going to Wales, was in on the secret. Perhaps his assumption was a dangerous one. Many of his assumptions were. This druid might want them for his own devices. Whatever they may be. The man could be leading them in entirely the wrong direction.

He was about to raise his thoughtful finger and bring the party to a halt to discuss the question, when he noticed a cart accompanied by three people coming down the road towards them.

It was a simple enough affair. A donkey pulled it, dragged reluctantly along by a man at its head. A woman sat in the cart among a load of what looked like weeds of some sort, and another man walked at the side.

The shivers it sent through Hermitage's body were far from simple. This was it. The cart probably had a dragon in it, the man at the front would turn out to be a killer and the other two would undoubtedly call for help from the horde that was hiding in the woods that bordered the track.

The cart drew closer and no one seemed to be doing anything. Why wasn't John getting his sword out? Why weren't Wat and Cwen stopping and getting ready for the attack? The druid would be happy with the situation of course, leading them into this deadly trap.

Who knew what horrors a Welsh cart could unleash? He tried to tell himself there couldn't be a dragon in there. Where was the smoke? And how could you carry a fire breathing animal in a wooden cart? The whole thing would burn to ash at the first exhale.

He had to remind himself he didn't believe in dragons

in the first place. As usual, he was taking a perfectly reasonable situation and spinning his own personal cataclysm.

As the cart drew closer he recalled just how many perfectly reasonable situations had wound up in a personal cataclysm of some sort. It was quite a lot.

Shying away as the cart drew level, Hermitage was fully prepared to run for the woods, or hide behind John.

The man at the front of the cart raised his hand, probably ready to hurl a knife.

'Bore da,' the man said as the cart walked on by.

'Arrgh,' Hermitage screamed and hid his face in his hands. 'We've been cursed, we've been cursed.'

When he cautiously drew his hands down again he saw that everyone was looking at him. The cart had stopped and the people with it looked the most puzzled of all.

'What is the matter with you?' Wat asked.

'He, he,' Hermitage found the strength to point a shaking hand at the cart man, but could explain no more.

'He said good day,' Wat explained with a disappointed look that Hermitage would have been proud of.

'Er?' Hermitage said, the onset of embarrassment at his foolishness sweeping over him.

'Bore da,' Wat repeated the fateful words. 'It means good day. Bore, good. Da, day. See?'

'You speak Welsh?' Hermitage was amazed, which helpfully took his mind off his reaction to a simple cart man saying hello.

'Only a word or two.'

'Is he all right?' the cart man now asked in perfect English, albeit with a lilting accent.

'Not really,' Cwen replied. 'Nervous type. You know.'

Hermitage thought that was a bit harsh. Mind you, he

had screamed when someone said good day.

'Oh, aye? What's he doing here then?'

'We're looking for someone,' Wat said. 'Been sent. Well three of us have. The others are, erm, keeping us company.'

'There's nice.' The man appraised John and noted the weapons and gave the druid a respectful nod. 'Who you looking for then?'

'Chap called Martel.'

Hermitage thought it really would be ridiculous if this fellow turned out to know Martel. He knew nothing about Wales but it clearly wasn't a small place.

'Funny name,' the Welshman observed.

'He's a Norman,' Cwen said.

'Poor feller.'

No,' Hermitage explained. 'It just means he's from Normandy.'

'Yes,' the cart man replied. 'I do know that. Poor feller. And he's supposed to be in Wales is he?'

'So we're told.'

'Can't say I've heard about any Normans round abouts. Not that they'd last long if they turned up.'

The woman in the back of the cart spoke up. 'There's a Mantel up Knighton way,' she said helpfully.

'Oh, funny people up there,' the second cart man put in.

The woman climbed down from the cart and the three welsh people gathered at the head of the donkey.

'My cousin Albric said he'd met a stranger walking on the hills over by Brecon,' the second man offered.

'Your cousin Albric's says he's seen a lot of things, and I don't believe half of them,' the lead man replied with a lift of his eyes.

'Always in his pot is Albric,' the woman added. 'Don't think he can see the inside of his own eyes sometimes.'

'Now, chwarae teg, be fair.' The cousin was defended. 'He's had a hard life, what with the injury and all. In constant pain, he is.'

'More like he is a constant pain.'

'You take that back.'

'I will not. You shouldn't be so quick to claim him as your cousin. He's a wrong un, he is.'

'He's a wrong un? What about that nephew of yours, now there's a wrong un if ever I saw one.'

'Nothing was ever proved, so if you go spreading gossip I'll have something so say about it.'

The cart man and the woman started shoving one another about and the second man stepped in to separate them.

Hermitage, Wat and Cwen just gazed at the developing conflict in despair. Was it them? They'd only just left one group fighting among themselves, and here it was, happening again.

'So, you don't know Martel?' Wat asked at the top of his voice.

The squabbling stopped instantly, and it was as if there had never been a cross word between these people.

''Fraid not.' The cart man shrugged.

Hermitage sighed, heavily.

'You could try Lord Bermo's place,' the woman suggested.

For some reason the other two sniggered at this.

Hermitage looked at them all to see what was going on. Even the druid was looking rather alarmed at the suggestion.

'And where would we find Lord Bermo's place?' Cwen

asked, clearly as suspicious of this as Hermitage.

'You're in it,' the woman told them with a snort. 'Stand still long enough and he'll find you.'

'Is it this way?' Hermitage pointed in the direction the druid was leading them.

'If you like.' There was more snorting.

The woman climbed back into the cart, shaking her head at something.

'Good luck,' the cart man called as they moved off. 'Give our regards to Lord Bermo.' There was much sniggering from the cart.

Hermitage suspected there was something going on that he wasn't being told about. But then he suspected that nearly all the time.

With the cart gone, the druid led them on up the road.

'This Lord Bermo then?' Wat asked the bearded one.

'We do not go to Lord Bermo,' the man said, without looking at any of them.

'Where do we go then?' Cwen demanded, moving round to stand in front of the druid and bar his path.

'This way,' the druid explained.

'And what's this way?' Cwen persisted. 'And don't say it's the way we're going.'

The druid had his mouth open to speak, but Cwen appeared to have stolen his response.

'We go to the village.' He was back to his old, intoning ways.

'Which one?' Wat asked brightly as if he knew them all.

'The village of the stones,' the druid half sang, half intoned.

'Stones eh?' Cwen said. 'They'll be handy for knocking that beard off your head if there's any trouble.'

The druid looked positively alarmed that Cwen should even think of such a thing.

She moved out of his way and the man tried to take a dignified step up the road.

Judging from the slight stumble, Hermitage thought that under the man's robes his knees were probably shaking.

'Just how far is this village of the stones?' Hermitage asked after they had walked quite a way up the track. He wasn't sure whether he wanted to be out in the open after dark, or in a welsh village. They both sounded pretty awful.

'It is far,' the druid said.

'That's clear then,' Wat snorted.

Hermitage whispered to Wat, 'How do we know if this is the right direction to find Martel?'

'How do we know it isn't?' Wat replied.

Hermitage thought there ought to be more to it than that, but couldn't immediately think what.

The druid paused and looked around, as if getting his bearings. 'This way.' He now beckoned them off the main roadway and into the woodland.

There was a track there, but only just. The thin line of trampled undergrowth was more like an animal trail than a proper path.

'Are you sure?' Cwen asked, clearly suspicious about being taken into the woods by a druid.

'This is the way.'

Even Wat and John were frowning at this development. They clearly thought that being in the woods was not a safe option. Obviously you could be attacked on the open road, but the woods made it easier for people to surprise you.

It all seemed quiet and Wat took some time to appraise their surroundings and judge the situation. There was not a sound, apart from the calling of distant birds, and the occasional haunting cry of a buzzard, circling high in the sky somewhere.

Wat looked back down the road they had travelled and squinted into the distance.

Hermitage followed his gaze and yes, he too saw a rising cloud of dust as some force moved on the path. From this distance it was hard to tell whether they were coming in their direction or moving away.

Wat picked a nearby tree and with a lithe jump and a grab of a limb, hauled himself several feet above the path.

'Quick,' he instructed as he sprang down again. 'Into the woods.' He waved everyone off the track and into the cover of the trees.

'Who is it?' Hermitage asked. 'This Lord Bermo's men.'

'Worse.'

'Worse?' Hermitage paled at the thought of what was coming.

'It's a bunch of robbers, pilgrims, stragglers and the mad boatman. I think we'd better get back on the path and move along it pretty quickly.'

...

The path through the woods was narrow but seemed well used. It wound around quite a lot but followed a steady direction to the west. The ground rose consistently and Hermitage could do nothing but conclude that he was heading into the deepest welsh hills. The ones from which he would probably not return.

He had no time to notice how pleasantly the wood presented itself. Birds sang, the sun glinted through the trees and the smell of centuries of fallen leaves perfumed the air.

Nobody jumped out on them. No hideous fate presented itself. No strange animals, or two-headed people appeared through the foliage. It was all quite normal really.

The only thing to disturb the peace, apart from Hermitage's worry, was the distant sound of a continuing argument as quite a large group trampled through the wood some way behind them, probably scaring the wildlife.

They had kept up quite a good pace, the noises from behind encouraging them to haste, but there was no doubt the pursuit was getting closer.

'What do we do when they catch up?' Hermitage asked. He thought that the group would probably be pretty cross at being left behind.

'What can we do?' Wat asked. 'They'll only want to follow us again.'

'But if we do find the you-know-what,' Hermitage dropped his voice to a whisper, 'there'll be complete chaos. They got into a fight over why we were going to Wales at all. Imagine what they'll be like when they see what we have come for.'

'We could be safer if they do catch up,' Cwen suggested.

Hermitage gave her one of his questioning looks.

'There's only five of us, and one is a druid. That leaves four to fight off a whole welsh village.'

'How do you know there'll be a fight?'

'There's always a fight,' Cwen's conclusion was simple.

'Strangers walk into your village, what are you going to do? Fight them off of course.'

'Not necessarily,' Hermitage said with weary resignation that there probably would be a fight. Or a simple capture of the strangers for hideous purposes.

'So with twenty-odd of us, we'll be more than a match.' Cwen was happy at the odds. She turned to the druid, 'Oy, You. How many people in this village of the stones?' The man looked mightily offended at being addressed in this manner.

'There are many.'

'Good. How many?'

'As many as are needful.'

'Oh, very helpful.' She spoke to Wat and Hermitage again, 'Place in the middle of Wales, up in the woods? I'd be surprised if there's a dozen. In fact.' A thoughtful look settled on her face. 'If we wait for our lot to catch up, we could probably take the village by surprise.'

'Take it by surprise?' Hermitage wondered why they'd want to surprise a whole village.

'Yes, of course. The robbers can handle themselves, and the stragglers look pretty handy. And we've got John. We could hide in the trees and get the measure of the place. Then, when we've picked our moment we attack and capture the lot of them.'

'Cwen!' Hermitage was outraged. 'What a terrible suggestion. How could you?'

'Hermitage,' Cwen sounded just as outraged. 'We are walking into a strange welsh village in the middle of the hills with a druid. What do you think might happen to us? We're supposed to be looking for Martel. Goodness knows what the beard in a robe has in mind.' She nodded disdainfully towards the druid.

This only wakened Hermitage's worry that the druid had his own devices. And several of them might be waiting for them in the village.

'What's the point of having the upper hand,' Cwen argued, 'if you can't drop it on people.'

Hermitage shook his head in disappointment. 'And when Lord Bermo hears that twenty-odd English people have captured one of his villages?'

This did make Cwen pause for thought.

'You think he might send a great force to finish us off?' Hermitage's military thinking was like a smile on the face of a Norman; non-existent. But even he could figure this one out.

Cwen looked to the ground in a sulky manner, 'He might.'

Hermitage said nothing.

'But that wouldn't be 'till later. And we don't know how many men he's got.' She looked to Wat for encouragement, but got none.

'Nice idea,' the weaver sounded placatory. 'But I'm not sure starting a war with the Welsh is the best plan. Particularly not with the army we've got following us. The robbers might be robbers but I suspect it's only against people who don't fight back.'

Cwen scowled at this defeatist thinking.

Hermitage nodded at the reasonable approach.

'But then again,' Wat went on. 'I'm not sure I fancy just the four of us walking into a Welsh village. Cwen's right, the druid is one of them, and there's only so much John can do. Not much point giving you a weapon Hermitage?'

'Absolutely not,' Hermitage confirmed in horror.

'Then I think, reluctantly, that we have to wait for our

followers to catch up.' He slung his pack from his back and lowered himself to sit with his back against a tree.

After a moment's thought, probably very different in each of their heads, Cwen and Hermitage followed suit.

'We must go, we must go,' the druid urged, seeing them all settling down.

'We're having a bit of a rest,' John said, taking out one of his daggers and giving it a friendly polish with a wet thumb.

'But,' the druid protested.

'A rest,' John repeated, choosing his own tree and arranging his weapons comfortably.

The druid looked at them all impatiently but it was clear there was nothing he could do. He sat uncomfortably on a fallen tree trunk and watched them all, looking ready to get up and leave at any moment.

...

'Hello,' it was More who found them first. The old man sounded as if he'd just stumbled upon long lost friends at the market. The idea that he had been tramping through welsh woods looking for them had clearly departed his head some time ago.

'Hello More,' Wat said with reluctant resignation. 'The others coming up?'

More had to think deeply about this for a while.

'The robbers, the pilgrims?' Wat prompted. 'Stragglers at the back I expect.'

'Oh, them?' More said in surprised recognition. 'Yis, they're coming. There's been a bit of trouble though.'

'Not at all surprised.'

It wasn't long before the next group arrived. There was

still some argument going on.

'I did not steal your wretched shell, you stupid man,' one of the robbers was explaining to a pilgrim. 'What would I want a shell for? I don't even know what you want them for. And even if I did want a shell I could pick one up anywhere.'

The pilgrim, who was smaller than the robbers, and heavily outnumbered, continued to pester and skip about. 'It was here a moment ago, and now it isn't. Where else has it gone?'

'You dropped it.'

'A pilgrim does not drop his shell,' the pilgrim, who Hermitage thought was called Lanson, protested. 'We guard them with our lives. I've had it for years and then I lose it just when there's a crowd of robbers about. What am I supposed to think?'

'That you're a dolt who can't look after his property.'

The discussion halted when they saw Hermitage and the others.

'Ha,' Banley said, gathering his band of robbers around him. 'Thought you could get the gold without the rest of us eh?'

Wat sighed and rested his face in his hands.

'You mean reach the relic before we can benefit,' the shell-less pilgrim corrected.

Noises down the track now indicated that the rest of the sorry band was not far behind.

Elard and Pord were next, proudly holding out Lanson's shell, which they'd found on the path.

The accused robber simply smacked the rather small and defenceless Lanson firmly round the head.

Finally, of course, the stragglers wandered in.

Hermitage did notice that at least everyone looked a

bit puzzled to be in the middle of a wood. There was clearly no army nearby and so perhaps their theory was wrong after all.

'Good,' the druid stood and surveyed the crowd. 'Perhaps now we can get on?'

Hermitage dragged himself up from the seat at his tree and looked around to make sure he had everything. As everything was only his habit and the small devotional volume he kept secure in an inside pocket, there wasn't much to check.

His scream was a quite a surprise to everyone.

It didn't seem to disturb the wizened old figure that clung to the tree like a fungus. A sentient, smiling fungus.

The shape detached itself from the bark and skipped into the middle of the path. It appraised them all and grinned and clapped and skipped about some more.

Hermitage, Wat and Cwen exchanged looks. They now had a madman of the woods. Was there anyone left to join their group?

The new arrival hopped over to the druid and patted him on the chest. The druid nodded acknowledgement and the little mad man rubbed his hands in glee for some reason.

'What?' Wat said in a mixture of enquiry, despair and confusion.

'You are here, you are here,' the old man cackled.

Hermitage thought that in another world, this new arrival could be More's brother. His much older and much, much madder brother.

'Yes, we are,' Wat confirmed.

The old man was pointing at them all one by one, as if recognising long lost friends. 'I have come, I have come.'

'Excellent,' Wat said. 'We are here and you have come.

Couldn't be better.'

'And I shall take you to your stones, Lypolix shall take you to your stones.'

Hermitage assumed the strange man was called Lypolix. Sounded like a druidic name, but this creature looked like no druid. The left overs of a druid, perhaps, after a horrible accident with a sickle and some mistletoe.

'The monk, the monk,' Lypolix almost shouted for glee, apparently noticing Hermitage for the first time. 'The greatest of them is here.' Lypolix skipped with even more fervour than seemed possible. Or decent.

'Looks like you're expected, Hermitage,' Wat observed.

Yes, thought Hermitage, his prophecy shining in his mind, it did, didn't it.

Caput XVIII: Happy Times Ahead?

For a creature of very little substance, Lypolix led the party through the woods as if brushing them aside. The group's own personal druid now took second place, and from the outside this must look like a very strange parade indeed. Not that there was room for anyone on the outside.

Lypolix had taken some time to place them all in what he considered the right order. The right order for what, did not bear thinking about. It was pretty clear that there wasn't a sensible thought in the old man's head.

Hermitage had to follow the druid, and Wat and Cwen followed him. Next came John, who did not take kindly to be given orders by a cross between a cast-off druid's robe and a hedge.

The stragglers were at the back, obviously, and the robbers and pilgrims came in front of them. That just left More.

If anyone had been paying attention, they might have quite looked forward to a conversation between Lypolix and More.

'Aha.' Lypolix skipped and danced. 'And who might you be?'

'More,' said More.

'And who might you be, my pretty fellow?"

Clearly mad.

'That's me name.' More sounded very proud of this.

'Well, well, master That. I can see you are of our number.'

'Eh?' It took a lot to confuse More, mainly because he

spent most of his time confusing other people.

'You shall have a stone, and it shall be named That. Down the ages people will visit and say "look at That stone."'

'No, not That. No one would be called That. That'd be stupid. I'm More.'

'More than That eh? You have another name? This is mysterious and I must think upon it.'

More opened his mouth to explain but clearly thought it was a waste of time. Being considered an idiot by More was high praise indeed.

...

The whole party tramped on through the hours and it became increasingly apparent that they were leaving the civilised world behind. Over hills, following streams, taking herders' trails and then setting off through the woods again, Hermitage just hoped this Lypolix really did know where they were going.

After one crossing of a stream on stepping stones, every one of which wobbled, the lead straggler appeared at the head of the parade. She ignored Hermitage and made for Wat.

'We've been having a bit of a think,' she announced.

'Remarkable,' Wat replied.

The straggler was hesitant in admitting a misjudgement, 'And it does seem that there might not actually be an army after all. As such.'

'No army eh?' Wat asked, looking around the completely wild countryside, apparently to see if he agreed with her. 'You know, I think you may be right.'

'So, erm, we're going to sort of head off now.' She waved vaguely back the way they had come. It would take them quite a while to get back into good straggling country.

Lypolix materialised between her and Wat and there was a look in his eyes that wasn't quite right.

'Oh, no,' he wailed, as if casting a magic spell. 'The stragglers shall not leave. They have stones.'

'That's right,' the straggler spoke loudly and clearly. 'We've got stones and we'll just pop back and get them.' She nodded exaggeratedly and gave the usual accommodating-a-madman look to Wat.

'You cannot leave.' Lypolix seemed to find the prospect hugely amusing.

'I think you'll find we can,' the straggler confirmed, a hint of forcefulness in her voice.

'No, no.' Lypolix laughed and skipped a bit.

'Yes,' the straggler said. All humour was gone now and she was a fierce looking woman, ready to bat the old man away if he tried to stop her.

'But,' Lypolix began.

'But nothing.' She pointed her finger. 'We're leaving.'

'You'll miss the feast,' Lypolix cackled.

That got her attention. 'Feast?'

'A great feast there shall be. The greatest.'

'Great feast?'

'Days and days shall the celebrations continue.'

The straggler was coming round. She carried the look of a woman who couldn't remember the last just plain feast she had had, never mind a great one. 'Days and days? And we'll be there?'

'It cannot happen without you.' Lypolix pointed a withered finger at her, which he then circled around everyone else. 'Once the stones are complete, the whole village will feast.'

'Ah, well.' The straggler had clearly been persuaded. 'If

there's going to be a feast, I expect we could stay.'

The pilgrim and the robbers had drifted over to lend an ear to this conversation. It seemed they too were having their doubts about continuing to tramp through the welsh woods.

Word of the great feast spread quickly and everyone was very satisfied with the prospect. Even if there was no gold or a decent relic at the end of it, they'd get a good feed.

The straggler had a second thought. 'How much further is this feast?' Even if the feast was magnificent, it might not be worth tramping across the whole country.

'Nearly there, nearly there,' Lypolix cackled as he beckoned them to follow further into the woods.

...

Further into the woods went on for several more hours and the day was starting to tip into evening before the trees started to thin and the ground rose more appreciably.

Lypolix led them up what seemed to be a sheep trail, probably frequented by just the one sheep, who was lost anyway. This trail led almost vertically up a steep incline and as usual, the first crest was a false one. Down a small dip, sparsely grassed but more well-trodden, and up the other side, the true peak of the hill was reached.

Hermitage, being in the position of honour at the front of the group was the first to gaze down upon their destination.

'The village,' Lypolix announced with a general waving of arms.

Hermitage could see a valley. Its floor was broad and flat as the side of the hill enclosing it fell quickly away. In front of him, the far side must be several miles away.

Trees paraded down this distant slope as if thinking about an invasion.

Off to his right the head of the valley collided into an even steeper hill which rose like a rampart. What was on the other side of that could only be a matter of conjecture. Probably more of the same.

To the left, the valley rolled down towards open ground, although more hills stood sentinel, as if guarding its entrance.

This was a well-protected spot. No one would be able to approach the place without being seen from some way off. If the routes over the other hills were the same as the one they had endured, it was unlikely anyone would bother anyway.

But protection also meant isolation. If these people didn't tell anyone they were here, they could missed completely.

As Hermitage looked over their destination he was sure he felt the same basic emotion as would anyone who had tramped all those hours to get here. Enormous disappointment.

Lypolix had used the word "village", but as far as Hermitage could see, someone had used this valley as a dumping ground for half-built huts. The ones that had been half built before their builder realised the whole job had gone horribly wrong and he was going to have to start again.

A passing peasant had then seen the discarded shavings of a hut builder and asked if he could have it. The builder was glad to get rid of the rubbish and probably assumed the fellow was going to use it for firewood, not to live in.

There was one building larger than the rest, and that

seemed in better order, but there was even something wrong with that one. He frowned as he struggled to discover what it was about this place that bothered him so intensely.

Organisation. Of course. Anything that wasn't organised gave Hermitage the most intense irritation that almost felt physical. Naturally, he never gave expression to it, but it still rankled.

This village showed no signs of organisation at all. The huts had been randomly distributed over the available space and even faced in different directions. He assumed that if you had all the space you needed there was no need to lay things out carefully. But really, if you wanted to talk to your neighbour in this place you would have to leave your hut and there was a good chance you'd get lost on the way.

Once darkness fell, the village would be impossible to navigate unless you'd been born there. Perhaps that was the point.

There were some people moving around down there, although even they didn't seem to be doing anything coordinated. A livestock pen was empty, the sheep doubtless out to summer grazing.

He couldn't imagine this place producing a great anything, let alone a feast.

The rest of the party had arrived at the hill top now and looked down upon the village with a silence that almost sighed its own despair. Had they really come all that way for this?

'Is this it?' One of the robbers asked, in blunt criticism.

'Aye, aye,' Lypolix cackled. 'See, see.' He held his arms out wide to encompass the magnificence of the view.

Looks on faces said that the others were having a bit of

a problem spotting the magnificence, hidden as it must be, behind this pretty rubbish village.

Well, they were here now, and there certainly wasn't anywhere else to go. Hermitage clapped his hands together, trying to encourage some enthusiasm in himself and the others. He looked to Lypolix to lead the way.

As he did so he saw some more shapes up the cliff at the far end of the valley.

'What are they doing?' he asked.

'The stones, the stones,' Lypolix answered.

Hermitage wondered if the man said everything twice for the benefit of others or because he might forget himself.

'Aha.'

'They shall bring the master to the village.'

'So the village has a master,' Hermitage nodded. 'I look forward to meeting him.'

'You shall, you shall,' Lypolix said with a quite enormous cackle which continued as he beckoned and led them down the hill.

Caput XIX: Strangers and Stranger Still.

Wulf was in the village when the party arrived down the hillside and all he could do was gape.

The Arch-Druid had stayed at the temple to brew a fresh batch of his magic recipe for broken fingers, which he thought the stone-movers were going to need. In fact all it did was knock the patient out of their senses while he re-set the bones.

Lypolix led the arrivals, skipping and dancing and cackling and gesturing all at once.

'You're here,' Wulf said in staggered surprise as Hermitage drew up with the rest of the band at his back.

'How do you do.' Hermitage held his hand out, hugely relieved that the man could speak English. And that he didn't breathe fire.

Wulf shook it in a daze. 'You're a monk,' he observed.

Oh dear, thought Hermitage, these people really were isolated. 'That's right,' he explained slowly. 'I'm a monk. You see this is the habit of my order…'

'And how many are you?' Wulf asked. He scanned the crowd, quickly trying to add up.

'Twenty two I'm afraid,' Hermitage only now realised that this was a terrible imposition on such a small place.

'Twenty two of you, and one a monk,' Wulf's disbelief was only fading slowly. 'It's unbelievable.' He scanned the crowd and noticed that one of the number was another druid, a stranger to him, but one of their own. So it couldn't be quite right that all the sacrifices had turned up.

'You doubt, you doubt.' Lypolix tapped the young

druid hard in the chest.

'Doubt what?' Hermitage asked.

'Oh, nothing,' Wulf said, quickly. 'It's, erm, just that Lypolix foresaw your coming.'

Hermitage frowned at such nonsense. 'He found us in the woods,' he pointed out. 'Not much foresight required.'

'No, ha ha, indeed.' Wulf rapidly moved on. 'You are all welcome of course.'

'Twenty two is quite a lot to manage,' Hermitage apologised.

'But you're expected.' Wulf thought he'd explained that. 'We're just getting ready for you.'

A frown deposited itself on Hermitage's face.

'Where's the feast?' the lead straggler demanded as she stepped forward and saw no signs of cooking.

'Feast?' Wulf asked.

'Yes, feast. Your little man here said there would be a feast. A great one.' She nodded towards Lypolix.

'Ah, yes, the feast. Of course. I shall talk to the village headman and we'll get things started now you're here. We didn't know exactly when you'd arrive.'

This worried Hermitage. How could these people really be expecting twenty two of them to arrive? Surely their travel here had been a secret? Then he realised that it had been anything but. And they'd caused such trouble at the river crossing that the whole of Wales probably knew they were coming. No mystery there then. Apart from the fact of the druid who had met them at the inn? He couldn't immediately work out how that had happened. But he would.

Wulf held his arms out and addressed the crowd. 'You are all welcome my friends and the feast can begin.'

There was a restrained cheer at this, although Hermitage caught a mumbled "relics" from somewhere in the group.

'Choose a hut to take your rest and we'll all get together later.' He beckoned that they could take their pick of the comfortable dwellings on offer. 'We are all expecting you, the villagers will give you our greatest hospitality.'

Hermitage chastised himself for thinking that this probably wouldn't be very great. Still, the chance for shelter and a sit down was most welcome.

The group cast their various glances around the huts nearby and wandered off in twos and threes, probably to look for something better.

More wandered off on his own, perhaps to look for a river.

Hermitage, Wat and Cwen made sure they stayed together, and that everyone else left them alone. They nodded an assurance to John that they weren't going to run away if he took his eyes off them.

'Did you see it?' Cwen hissed as soon as everyone else had gone.

Wat led them off into the village, he seemed to be making a bee line for the largest hut of all.

'See what?' Hermitage asked.

'The you-know-what,' Cwen replied, quietly.

'What you-know-what?' Hermitage was lost.

'The you-know-what we have come for,' Cwen growled at his stupidity.

'Martel?' Hermitage asked. Surely it was too much to hope for that they would find the Norman in the very first place they looked.

Cwen sighed her annoyance. 'We are not looking for

Martel. Remember?'

'Oh, yes.' It came back to Hermitage. He always found the deceits of others very hard to follow. His eyes widened. 'There was some you-know-what?' he had missed that completely.

Wat had found the largest hut and stuck his head in the door. 'This'll do,' he said.

'Young mister Wulf was wearing a large chunk of you-know-what round his neck,' Cwen explained.

'But,' Hermitage started. Then stopped.

'He had a gold torc round his neck,' Wat said.

'Really?' Hermitage thought he was usually quite observant, but he hadn't spotted that.

'Don't know what else it was.' Wat shrugged.

'Why didn't the robbers spot it?' Hermitage asked. After all, it was the one thing they'd come all this way for.

'Who knows? It was very small and buried in his robe. Or perhaps they're just idiots who wouldn't recognise gold if it stabbed them.' Wat led them into the hut.

This was not a dwelling place, and Hermitage thought that it was not really a sensible place to stay.

'This looks like their meeting room,' he observed. 'Shouldn't we find a home to go to?'

'Personally,' Wat reasoned, 'I'd rather stay as far away from people as possible. Our lot are trouble and this lot are up to goodness knows what.'

'What do you mean?' Surely Wat hadn't had time to get suspicious already? Hermitage knew he still had a lot to learn about suspicion; which seemed to be a bit of a drawback for an investigator.

'Think about it.' Wat prompted.

Hermitage could do that. He did.

'Why are a group of isolated villagers welcoming a

large band into their midst and feeding us, when they probably have barely enough for themselves?' He asked the question to the air.

'Because we outnumber them.' Cwen clearly thought this proved her point.

'They could have simply run off into the trees and hidden until we'd gone,' Hermitage countered. 'After all, there's very little here of value to make us loiter.'

'They want something,' Wat concluded.

'We haven't got much,' Cwen noted.

'Then it's something we haven't thought of.' Wat dropped his pack in a corner of the hut.

Hermitage contemplated this, but could come up with nothing. He looked at their surroundings and could not ignore the huge, round table which occupied most of the space.

'I say, look at this table.' He ran his hands over the surface. 'I've never seen anything like this before. What's it doing in a place like this?' He walked its circumference which must be enough to seat a huge number of people. 'It's very good quality. Looks quite old though.'

Wat and Cwen looked disinterested.

'I imagine this has some stories to tell.' Hermitage smiled to himself as he imagined who it might have been made for.

'Doesn't look very comfortable.' Cwen slapped the surface of the wood.

'You can't sleep on their table,' Hermitage protested.

'Don't fancy the floor much.' Cwen turned up her nose.

'I'm not even sure we should close our eyes,' Wat observed with a knowing expression.

'Wat,' Hermitage chided. 'That Wulf fellow is a young druid and the strange Lypolix is the only other person we've met.'

'Could be a village of druids then,' Cwen said. 'And we all know what they do.' She made a cutting motion across her throat and accompanied it with a strangled gurgle.

'Oh, really,' Hermitage huffed. 'That's a complete myth. Anyway, how is a small welsh village going to deal with twenty two of us?'

'The question is how did a small welsh village know twenty two of us were coming at all?' Wat asked.

Hermitage thought his answer would help, 'We've been making enough trouble across the countryside for anyone to spot us miles away. We even had a fight at the river which was more like a small battle. I'd be surprised if anyone round here didn't know we were coming. Probably the most exciting thing that's happened for years.'

'And the druid who came to get us?'

Hermitage had hoped that wouldn't come up. He hadn't thought it through yet. 'Perhaps he didn't come to get us.' The idea sprang into his head.

'He said he had,' Cwen noted.

'Well, he would, wouldn't he? Once he'd seen us. Could be that he'd come to get anyone, whoever happened to be passing by. What did he call us? The monk, the weaver and the child? Anyone could see that just from looking at us.'

Wat coughed, 'You mean this welsh village has sent druids out to collect strangers?'

'Could be.' Hermitage saw that his reasoning was sound, which was always a comfort. 'We've all heard of villages that simply run out of people. You know, the old die and there are no children.'

Wat and Cwen nodded. It did happen.

181

'Could be the village is searching for new people to join them.'

'By sending a druid?' Cwen clearly thought that was odd.

'If you've got a lot of spare druids, why not?' Hermitage suggested. 'We just happen to be the first people he found, so here we are. He was just lucky we were coming this way. For all we know there are others out all over the place trying to recruit new villagers.'

Hermitage put on his, there-you-are face.

Cwen scowled a bit but didn't seem to have an immediate response.

'They're going to be a bit disappointed when we don't stay,' she said. 'Never mind,' she observed brightly. 'We still outnumber them. Fight this lot off easy if they try anything funny.'

...

Wulf was nervous about taking the news of the great feast to Hywel. The man had been very difficult about everything so far. Mind you, he was usually very difficult about everything anyway. His normal response to enquiries was to say no first, and then ask what the question was.

At least Wulf had the upper hand. Twenty two people, one of them a monk, really had turned up in the village. He wouldn't have believed it himself if he hadn't seen it. He knew that would knock Hywel back a bit, perhaps just enough for him to deliver the news that the twenty two people, one of them a monk had been promised a great feast.

'A what?' Hywel squealed when given the news.

Wulf had been right. The village headman had been knocked back by news of the arrivals, but he soon found his old self when the feast was mentioned.

'Lypolix said there would be a great feast, apparently.' Wulf felt bad about blaming this on Lypolix. Not very bad, though.

'Well Lypolix can get the food and cook it then. There is no way I am using the village's supplies on a great feast for a bunch of strangers.'

'Bunch of sacrifices,' Wulf corrected, hoping that the link to the Gods would persuade Hywel.

'Whoever they are, they are not eating our food.' Hywel folded his arms and dared Wulf to say more.

'This is very difficult.'

'It is, isn't it.' Hywel was not budging.

'Yes,' Wulf went on. 'Twenty two people, one of them a monk, several of them robbers, one of them a very adept looking warrior with a fine selection of swords and knives, and all of them expecting a feast.'

Hywel started to look suspicious.

'Not going to go down very well when you tell them there's no feast.' Wulf shrugged as light heartedly as he could.

'Why do I have to tell them?'

'It's your decision. You're the village leader after all. Just the sort of thing the leader does.' Wulf tried to look as innocent as he could.

'A sword, you say?' Hywel checked.

'Quite a shiny one,' Wulf confirmed. 'Well used, by the look of it.'

'Why can't the Gods provide?' Hywel asked. It was a very good question.

'They are doing,' Wulf gave the standard response. 'They asked us to do it.' The lessons of the Arch-Druid were sinking in.

Hywel frowned and grumbled, still not convinced.

The door of Hywel's hut was thrown roughly aside and Caradoc appeared, breathless and excited.

'What is it?' Hywel snapped, having enough to deal with already.

'The stone,' Caradoc announced. 'The great master stone.'

'What about it?' Wulf was worried. Surely they couldn't have broken it.

'We was getting it back on the rollers, even installed some front uprights to hold it until we were ready.'

Wulf didn't have a clue what Caradoc was talking about, but it sounded like the movement of the stone was getting quite sophisticated.

'Yes, yes,' Hywel grumbled his impatience.

'But one of the bracing stanchions slipped against its anchor.'

Hywel and Wulf gazed at Caradoc as he spouted this gibberish. Caradoc frowned at them for not understanding a plain description. 'The Stone moved.'

'Well, good,' Wulf said, as he thought that was the plan.

'Not really,' Caradoc explained with a grimace. 'At least not if you were the sheep standing in front of it.'

'You killed a sheep?' Hywel was outraged.

'Erm,' Caradoc was clearly thinking about saying no. He was also clearly thinking there was no way of describing a small sheep hit by a very large rock as anything other than dead. 'Yes,' he confessed.

'There you are.' Wulf grinned. 'The Gods have provided.'

Caput XX: A Hearty Welcome.

The sun had vanished completely behind the surrounding hills, presumably quite pleased not to have to look at the village anymore, and darkness was filling the valley like some inexorable flood.

The stragglers were now happy as the smell of cooking wafted around the village. Hywel had suggested preserving the sheep for the long winter months but was overruled by the large group of people occupying his village, all of whom were looking forward to the feast.

The sheep-killing stone movers had come down from the hillside, laying what appeared to be a path of flat rocks as they came. After a whispered conversation with Wulf, Wem instructed his men to terminate the roadway just outside Hywel's hut. The village elder was too distracted seeing a perfectly good sheep vanish in one meal to ask what on earth was going on.

Hermitage, Wat and Cwen found themselves inexorably drawn from their hut by the delicious odour, and wandered towards what seemed to be roughly the middle of the village to find all their companions ready and waiting.

Everyone was gathered round a fire pit, watching with slavering anticipation as a sheep did what sheep do best. It was still going to be hours before the thing was ready, but some outer slices might be available early. It always paid to be at the front of the queue.

Hermitage looked over the crowd with disappointment. He appreciated that this group was naturally light on dignity and self-control but you would think they'd never seen food before. He had spent so much of his life starving hungry that he considered it normal. In any event, his charitable nature meant that he would always let others go first. Which was mainly why he spent so much of his life starving hungry.

He appraised the assembly and realised he should have expected no different. Then he frowned and turned to Cwen.

'Where's More?' he asked.

Cwen turned from her own internal slavering. 'Eh?'

'Where's More?'

'Where's More?'

'Yes.' Hermitage held his arms wide to cover the multitude. 'Where is More?'

Cwen looked rapidly over the crowd, searching for the unpleasant shape of the diminutive boatman.

Villagers and new arrivals were mixing quite well now. At first there had been a lot of suspicion, but when it became apparent there was going to be fresh meat, and it was all because of the visitors, cautious friendship broke out. There must have been thirty-odd people around the cooking now. More would be hard to spot.

'He could be sitting in the fire,' Cwen said. 'You know, waiting for the very first slice.'

'Cwen, really.'

'What does it matter where he is? He's old enough to look after himself. He's old enough to do anything.'

'Why wouldn't he be here?' Hermitage didn't like things out of place. 'Meat cooking on the spit, everyone else gathered round. But no More.'

'Don't worry about it.' Cwen should have known this was entirely the wrong thing to say to Hermitage.

He wandered off into the crowd and looked down by

the fire, round the nearby huts and even at each group of two or three people who had broken up into separate conversations. More was nowhere to be seen. Had he wandered off and got lost? He returned to the fire as that was the most likely spot.

He looked for the young druid, Wulf, he seemed to be in charge and might know where More had last been seen.

He spotted the white robe of the druid emerging from the woods off towards the back of the village. The bizarre Lypolix was there as well, along with the druid who had joined them at the inn. It was getting to be quite a druid gathering. And there was another.

This new arrival was as strikingly a druid as anyone Hermitage had ever seen. A huge beard with a man attached strode at the head of the small group and Wulf was clearly the junior. This new man had enough shining metal around his neck that even from this distance Hermitage could see it was gold. Much gold. There was no chance of the robbers not spotting that lot.

The villagers moved to make way for the new arrivals.

Hermitage looked, but they were not accompanied by the figure of More. Where had the man got to?

The druidic threesome made straight for the fire, the press of people breaking like a wave.

Hermitage stood his ground as the druids came up.

'Ah,' the great druid said on seeing Hermitage. 'The monk.'

'Actually, there are several monks in the world,' Hermitage pointed out. Perhaps this man had been so isolated he didn't know that monks were quite numerous.

'You were expected,' the great druid boomed.

'So we've been told.' Hermitage tried not to be rude,

but really. All this talk of foresight and expectation was just plain ridiculous. Of course the Old Testament prophets foresaw the coming of the Messiah, but that was different. They were right.

'This is the Arch-Druid,' Wulf introduced his master. 'And this is Master Hermitage. A monk.'

'It's Brother, actually,' Hermitage corrected.

'Master Hermitage brother.' Wulf nodded.

'Just Brother Hermitage.'

'Ah.' Wulf understood but didn't look like it made any sense to him.

'The feast has begun?' the Arch-Druid asked as he cast his eyes around the village, 'I thought we were saving that until after the stones?' He looked at Wulf and Lypolix.

The old seer cackled into life, 'We shall have another feast once the stones are in place.'

Hywel brushed past, fussing over something or other, 'Oh no you won't,' he said. 'I'm not letting another sheep go to waste.'

'A whole sheep?' the Arch-Druid was clearly surprised at such largesse.

'Your wretched master stone ran the thing over.' Hywel grumbled.

This delighted Lypolix, 'Killed by the stone. It has come to life and struck down a magnificent sacrifice.'

'It slipped off a bit of wood and squashed a sheep,' Hywel corrected. 'And now we're eating it,' he added, with a sigh at the extravagance. 'All of it.'

'Talking of eating,' Hermitage said. 'You haven't seen one of our number about the place have you? Small old man called More?'

'You want to eat him?' the Arch-Druid turned up his nose.

'No, no,' Hermitage said quickly. Good heavens, what were these people like? Perhaps the stories were true. 'It's just that with a feast about to begin I'd expect More to be here.'

'No,' Lypolix leapt in with a spontaneous cackle. 'Not seen him, not seen him.'

Hermitage frowned. The strange old druid seemed very quick to deny seeing More. 'He hadn't wandered off into the woods?' He nodded in the direction the druids had come from.

'No one wanders off into those woods,' Wulf pointed out. 'Those are the sacred woods.'

'Ah, yes. I see.' Sacred woods! What a load of nonsense.

'I'm sure he'll turn up somewhere.' Wulf sounded encouraging.

'The stone, the next stone.' Lypolix skittered about for no apparently good reason.

'You don't have a river nearby do you?' Hermitage asked.

'A river?' Wulf seemed thrown by the question. 'We've got quite a big stream and a small lake.'

'More is a boatman you see, he might have gone to look at your boats.'

The druids exchanged looks that said dealing with this strange idiot-monk was becoming trying.

'No, no boats.' Wulf nodded and smiled politely. 'We had a coracle once for fishing in the lake, but the things we caught didn't look quite right, so we gave that up.'

'I'd better go and look for him then,' Hermitage concluded.

The druids smiled a smile that said they'd be quite glad if he just went away.

Hermitage left the druids and didn't really know why he was worried about More. After all, he hadn't wanted the boatman to join them in the first place. Now he was missing he should be glad. But they were in a strange land with strange people. Very strange people. This was his mission and he felt some unwanted sense of duty towards those who accompanied him.

All this talk of sacred woods and stones that sacrificed sheep was giving him a feeling of foreboding. He suddenly felt that they were a very long way from the safe world he knew. Well, he would have to admit that the world he knew wasn't actually very safe, but at least it was familiar. Everything around him now was wrong. The druids in their robes, the language people spoke amongst themselves, the shape of the hills, the colour of the rocks. All wrong.

Eventually, Hermitage re-joined Wat and Cwen, having circumnavigated the entire village. He had even taken a cautious step or two into the sacred woods. When the druids weren't looking. Not that he believed for a moment that they were sacred. Just a normal wood with normal trees. Except they weren't like the trees at home. When something rustled in the undergrowth he left the sacred woods quite quickly.

'He's not here,' he announced, holding his arms out to demonstrate just how far he had searched.

'He'll turn up,' Cwen reassured. 'As soon as the actual eating starts. You wait and see.'

'Why would he go off?' Hermitage fretted.

'Why does he do any of the things he does?' Wat asked with little interest. 'He's an old man, he can take care of himself. He's survived this long without anything bad happening to him, which must count as a miracle in its own right.'

'I suppose so.' Hermitage scowled at the borderline blasphemy. 'But he is an old man, so he may have fallen somewhere.'

'Why are you worried?' Cwen asked. 'We've got far too many people with us on this task anyway. One less is a good thing surely?'

'I don't know.' Hermitage was thoughtful and serious. 'I've just got a sense that something's not quite right. There's a feeling about this situation that's nagging at the back of my mind and I can't put my finger on it.'

'Really?' Wat asked. 'Being in a village in the middle of Wales with a group of druids. Eating a sheep that's apparently been murdered by a rock? What's odd about that?'

Hermitage looked at Wat with surprise. He saw that the weaver was being sarcastic, which Hermitage always found trying. He had studied the form of the Greek sarkasmos in some ancient writings an old abbot had kept in his private chamber. The old abbot had a lot of material in his private chamber that Hermitage did not approve of.

...

More did not appear when the eating started. It was easy to see everyone as the entire population, villager and visitor alike, sat in silence on the ground concentrating hard on what was probably the largest meal many had ever had.

Only Hywel wandered about, making sure there was no undue indulgence or waste. The whole business with the mead had been bad enough. Now they were devouring a whole sheep. And the bread that was going with it was simply unthinkable. It would take months to recover from this. Lord Bermo might as well have marched his entire army through their village for all the damage this one feast was doing.

Hermitage noticed that only the druids were showing any restraint.

Perhaps they were holy men after all, not indulging in the pleasures of the ordinary man in order to keep their spirits pure.

Or maybe they were like those awful brothers at the monastery in De'Ath's Dingle.[6] The ones who stuffed themselves with a secret supply of food and wine while everyone else was starving.

More likely they were being put off their meal by Banley, the lead robber who sat very close to the Arch-Druid and was staring at the gold as if his eyes were stuck to it.

After a while, the druids got up and wandered off, back to their so-called "sacred woods", making it perfectly clear that no, Banley could not come with them just to have a look around. Before they departed, the Arch-Druid leaned close and whispered something in Banley's ear. He returned to his fellow robbers, eyes wide, muttering something about druid curses.

This really gave Hermitage the wobbles. Perhaps this really was the place that cursed Le Pedvin's messenger to death? Or it could just be a normal community of druids who cursed people as a way of life.

With all this worry swimming about his head, he really didn't feel like eating. His stomach soon told his head to

---

[6] Those awful brothers are fully exposed in The Heretics of De'Ath, the very first Chronicle of Brother Hermitage and an essential volume in any collection.

stop being so stupid.

Just a few moments later, he was concentrating on extracting the last morsel from a particularly troublesome bone when a question from another group of feasters caught his ear.

Those who had attacked their meal with vigour had already finished their allotted portion and were relaxing with groans of pleasurable discomfort. Each group of people had returned to their companions for the actual eating. Pilgrims sat with pilgrims and robbers with robbers. It was as if they trusted strangers with many things, but not with their food.

The question arose from the group of stragglers, which surprised Hermitage.

'Where's Leon?' one of them asked in a loud voice.

As a topic of after dinner conversation it was interesting, but Hermitage puzzled over what possible discussion could have led to this being asked.

There was no reply from the assembly and so Hermitage offered the best information he had.

'I believe it's a Kingdom many miles away,' he called. 'Over the sea, beyond Normandy.'

'What?' the voice of the straggler sounded angry at the answer. Which was odd.

'I said I think it's a Kingdom,' Hermitage started.

'What's that got to do with anything?' The lead straggler was standing now. 'I asked where Leon was.' She sounded rather snappy and irritated with Hermitage for some reason.

'And I was giving you the best information I have,' Hermitage defended himself.

'You're an idiot,' the straggler announced, which was entirely uncalled for.

Hermitage looked to Wat and Cwen who seemed equally confused by the straggler's outburst.

'He's missing,' the straggler said in a very pointed manner.

'He?' Hermitage was lost. Why would anyone call a Kingdom over the seas a he, and how could it be missing anyway? Ah, now he got it. 'One of your number is called Leon and he is missing.'

'Well obviously.' The straggler stepped through the seated crowd and came over to Hermitage in a very purposeful manner which did nothing for his digestion.

'We don't know any of your names,' Hermitage pointed out. He thought this was a very reasonable argument, but it didn't seem to placate the straggler. 'I don't even know yours,' he added. 'I can't just call you straggler.'

The woman scowled at him. 'I'm Ellen,' she said, as if it was an accusation.

'Ellen,' Hermitage repeated. 'And you say one of your number is missing?' He asked the question lightly, but worry soon followed.

'That's right,' she snapped, as if Hermitage was obviously hiding the missing straggler somewhere. 'He was here at the start of the feast and now he's not.'

'Perhaps he's just gone to relieve himself?' Hermitage suggested cautiously. Partly cautious because this Ellen seemed a terribly aggressive woman and partly cautious because he didn't like to talk about such things.

'He did that ages ago,' Ellen explained. 'Then he came back and now he's gone.' She glared at Hermitage, Wat and Cwen in turn.

'Well we don't know where he is.' Cwen gave a stare to match Ellen. 'If you can't look after your own stragglers it's hardly our fault.'

'Where is he?' Ellen demanded, apparently now convinced that they had this Leon.

'We don't know,' Cwen said slowly and clearly and aggressively. 'Perhaps he straggled off again?'

'Don't you get smart with me girl,' Ellen instructed.

'Even the sheep's smart compared to you.' Cwen popped a piece of the animal in her mouth.

Ellen took a decisive step forward but Wat leapt to his feet and held his arms wide to stop a fight.

'We really don't know where Leon is,' he explained calmly.

Hermitage got up as well. He was pretty sure he didn't want to get caught between Cwen and Ellen but he felt he should support Wat.

Ellen scowled at them both and tried to look over Wat's shoulder to give Cwen a withering glance.

'Perhaps he's gone with More,' Cwen offered, showing no interest in Ellen's impending attack.

'More what?' Ellen snapped.

'Our, erm, friend.' Hermitage couldn't think of a better word. 'Our friend More is missing as well. Don't know where he's gone.' As he said this he felt his familiar sinking feeling plumb new depths. He turned to Wat and Cwen. 'We've only been here a few hours and two people are missing.'

'They've just wandered off.' Cwen dismissed his worry. 'We're in the middle of nowhere, they're hardly likely to just vanish.'

'Unless they've been taken.' Ellen's words were less suggestion than accusation.

'Who'd take More?' Cwen scoffed. 'And once they'd taken him what would they do with him?' What would anyone do with him?'

'I don't know do I?' Ellen snapped. 'If you can't look after one old man, it's hardly my fault.'

The glares between the two women could have lit the whole valley.

'We've only just got here,' Wat pointed out. 'Who's going to start taking people? And in this place? There's hardly enough of them to bother a flock of sheep, let alone start stealing strangers.'

Hermitage's sinking feeling was trying leave his body by the lowermost exit. 'We were expected,' he croaked out.

'Beg pardon?'

'We were expected. The villagers were expecting us. The druids were expecting us. All of us. Especially a monk.'

'So?'

'So perhaps they were expecting us because they were going to steal us away?'

'Twenty two of us?' Wat clearly thought the idea was ridiculous. 'And one of the twenty two is a druid anyway. They're hardly likely to start stealing other druids. And what could they possibly do with twenty two people? Cwen's right, we outnumber them.'

'Not if they keep stealing us.'

'It's ridiculous.' Wat waved the whole idea away. 'It's dark. We're in a strange place. More and Leon probably just wandered off and got lost. Nothing more to it.'

Hermitage mumbled a bit.

'Anyway,' Wat said brightly, 'if people really are being stolen away we've got the perfect answer.'

'What's that?' Hermitage asked, feeling encouraged by Wat.

'A King's Investigator. He can sort out what's going on.'

Oh yes, thought Hermitage. Then he remembered that was him.

Caput XXI: Surprise, Surprise.

If eyes could slaver they would be doing so right now. The odours of the feast had drifted up the valley until they reached the bottom of the cliff. Here, the heat of the cooking and the wood smoke forced them to climb until they located the cave. They wandered into the depths and found a nose which hadn't smelt anything similar for what felt like years.

The comforting scent of burning pine, and the appalling insult of roasting meat produced a groan from the figure in the cave, who came to the entrance to look down and see what was going on.

From this high vantage point the village and the valley were laid out like a tapestry. The glow from the fire was clear and one or two lamps bobbed about the place. The figure could tell that people were eating, he could almost taste the meal and feel the chewing and swallowing. How dare they?

He had planned to survive in his cave by finding some berries and snaring the odd rabbit. The berries around these parts did the most appalling things to his stomach and the rabbits were very odd indeed. More like deformed mice. He had come rely on stealing left-overs and cast-offs from the village. And this village positively parsimonious in its leaving-over and casting-off.

This feast, whatever the reason for it, would give him plenty of material to work with. He was already imagining a magnificent broth of mutton bone. The only snag was that this feast seemed to involve an awful lot more people than was normal.

On the worst of his days and nights he had considered walking down to the village to introduce himself. The villagers were few in number, and while they might react badly to a stranger in their midst, it had to be better than starving to death in a cave.

But then there were druids. The place seemed to be swarming with them, and he had not had good experiences with druids. He found it hard to understand why such a small place, with so few people, needed quite so many of them. Just the sight of a white robe was enough to send him scurrying to the recesses of his dismal dwelling.

The old druid, the serious one with the beard and the staff was something from a nightmare. There was no way he was going anywhere near a village with a man like that in it. Perhaps they'd all go away at some point.

But they hadn't. And they'd had horrible pagan ceremonies at that awful stone circle of theirs. He hadn't seen any virgin sacrifices yet, but imagined it was only a matter of time. Sacrificing strangers was probably a regular occurrence.

Still, at least they'd all got drunk and he'd managed to gather some cast-off mead, which had warmed him a bit.

And now the place looked like it was preparing for war. Where had all these people come from? He knew he was in the middle of nowhere. It had taken him so long to get here that he couldn't be anywhere else. How had the village suddenly doubled in size?

Perhaps it really was war? Or maybe the neighbours had just come over for a visit? Whatever the reason it disturbed him, and he did not handle disturbance well.

As if the Gods of this place wanted to ram the point

home, there was another disturbance a lot closer down the hill somewhere. The scree was moving as feet trod its treacherous surface. He could tell the difference between human and animal climbing his hill, and this was human. A human treading lightly by the sound of it. Which probably meant someone sneaking up here who shouldn't. Or someone with a nefarious purpose.

Nefarious purposes up welsh hills at night could only mean trouble. He retreated further into the cave.

The clattering of falling rock did not diminish as the person climbing clearly thought there was something up here worth the effort. Perhaps the cave dweller had been spotted. Maybe the wretched villagers had left him up here on purpose, until they were ready. Ready for what, he didn't know, but it would be horrible.

At least it was only one pair of feet. He might be able to defeat his attacker and escape. Escape to where, he had not a clue. He couldn't conceive of anywhere worse than this place.

The cowering in the cave and the clattering up the hill drew closer and closer together until the dark mouth of his home fell into even deeper shadow as a figure appeared.

He waited for the inevitable and steeled himself as best he could.

'Excuse me,' a voice called from the cave-mouth. 'Is this the way to the village?'

He stood up from behind his rock and wandered to the front of the cave in a daze. He looked at the man who had asked the question with a slack jaw. 'Good God,' he said. 'It's you.'

Caput XXII: Attrition of the Fellowship.

'People do not go missing from the middle of nowhere,' Wat reasoned. 'Where is there to go when you're already there?'

Hermitage tutted his frustration at such poor thinking.

The morning had arrived and there was still no sign of More or Leon, the missing straggler.

Cwen had made some very amusing comments about stragglers who went missing. Well, she thought they were amusing but Hermitage suspected they were intended to antagonise Ellen. Which they did very well indeed. But then the straggler did seem the sort of person who kept her antagonism close at hand.

'All we have to do is look,' Wat went on. 'And we don't even need to do that very hard.'

Ellen gave him a hard stare.

Hermitage thought that for all her talk about the wonders of straggling, she didn't seem to enjoy it very much.

'We just get everyone who's here to gather in one spot and then have a look around.' Wat explained the process he was thinking about. 'We should be able to spot More and Leon if they're up the valley or over by the woods. After all, it's not a very big place.'

Hermitage shook his head. 'What if they're in the woods?' He gestured to show where the woods were. 'Or they've gone back up the track out of the village?' He indicated where that was for those who might have forgotten.

'Why would they do that when the feast was only just starting?' Ellen demanded. 'Hardly likely to wander off when there's a free feed in the offing.'

'They could have already eaten. Or they grabbed some food and went off with it. Probably still asleep somewhere.' Wat clearly wasn't worrying about them. 'What's the fuss anyway? We can manage perfectly well without More.'

Ellen stopped glaring at them all and looked down at the ground. 'Leon can get a bit carried away sometimes.'

'What do you mean, carried away?' Hermitage couldn't make any sense of this.

'If someone wanted his food, or started an argument, he might have taken it the wrong way.'

'Ha,' Cwen snorted. 'You mean if he thinks anyone's looking at him funny, he starts a fight.'

'Not at all,' Ellen answered back smartly. 'People don't understand him, that's all. You just got to be soft and gentle with him.'

'Don't look at him. Don't touch his stuff. Don't talk behind his back. I know the sort,' Cwen wasn't giving up. 'He thinks everyone hates him so he starts trouble all the time. And that's why everyone hates him.'

'I'll start some trouble with you in a minute,' Ellen offered.

'Chances are he had a go at one of the locals. Got thumped on the head for his trouble and is now lying in a ditch somewhere.'

'Perhaps More annoyed him,' Wat suggested lightly. 'He annoys everyone else. Could be they're both in the same ditch.'

'Then we look in the ditches,' Hermitage offered,

wishing the simmering fight between Cwen and Ellen would go away.

'What's this about ditches?' Hywel walked up to the group, rubbing the sleep from his eyes and the look of disgust at the state of his village from his face.

'Oh, good, it's you,' Wat said. 'Wwhat's for breakfast?'

'Nothing,' Hywel replied, unhappily. 'You've eaten all the food we were going to have this week.'

Hermitage felt very bad about that.

'And what's wrong with our ditches?'

'They might some of our people in them,' Hermitage explained.

'Not surprised, the way some of them was behaving last night.' Hywel tutted a tut Hermitage would be proud of.

'There are two missing,' Hermitage went on. 'More and Leon. Don't suppose you've seen them.'

'Wouldn't know if I had. I expect they'll turn up. There's nowhere else to go.'

'See.' Wat saw his explanation vindicated.

'We'll just go and look in the woods then,' Ellen announced. 'They're obviously not here.'

'You most certainly will not.' Hywel looked at her in absolute horror. She might as well have said she was going to dig up the dead and see if the missing had climbed in the graves by mistake.

'Why not?' Hermitage didn't think it was such an odd suggestion.

'Those are the sacred woods,' Hywel almost shouted as if even idiots from out of the valley should know that.

'Sacred woods?' Hermitage tried to make it sound as if the very idea was nonsense.

'Yes, sacred woods,' Hywel said, making it clear the

idea was not nonsense at all. 'And there is no way any strangers are going into our woods.'

'You go and look then,' Ellen suggested, quite reasonably.

'I can't do that.' Hywel was getting quite agitated now. 'Sacred woods,' he repeated. 'Meaning that the woods are sacred and we don't just go into them for a look round.'

'Where do you get your wood then?' Wat asked, nodding his head towards the still smoking timbers of the village fire. 'They don't look very sacred.'

'The druids tell us which trees we can take. And of course some just fall down.'

'The non-sacred ones.' Wat nodded sombre understanding.

'And not all the woods are sacred,' Hywel tutted again at these strangers who didn't know anything. 'But the woods by here are. Very sacred.'

'Let's ask the druids then.' Ellen was not giving up.

Hywel almost sat down in shock.

'That young Wulf seemed quite pleased to see us, I'm sure he'd help.'

'You are not going into the woods, and you are not asking the druids anything.' Hywel was insistent. 'You can look around here for your friends and if you can't find them, that's that. I'm not wasting any more time with you.' He turned to leave.

'Oy, you!' Banley the robber called before Hywel could get away.

'What now?' Hywel cried out, but quietly when he saw the rough looking man who was striding toward him.

'Where's Stropit?'

'What?' Hywel didn't know what was going on.

'Stropit. Where is he?'

'What's a Stropit?' Hywel asked in bemusement.

'Not a what. A who. Stropit. My man Stropit. What've you done with him?'

'I haven't done anything with your Stropit.' Hywel was clearly very frustrated. 'What is the matter with you people? You come wandering into my village, eat all my food and then complain when your own people get lost.'

'You mean he's missing?' Hermitage asked Banley. This really was getting odd.

'Well, he's not here and he never strays far, does Stropit.'

Hermitage had a burning question in his head, and burning questions in Hermitage's head tended to set fire to everything close by. He restrained himself admirably, realising that now was not the time for a discussion on why the man was called Stropit.

'There you are,' Ellen was triumphant as she confronted Hywel. 'That's More, Leon and Stropit all gone now. And they only went and got gone when we come here.'

Hermitage paused while he got his head round this sentence. 'It could be they did go into the woods,' he offered, gently. 'Not knowing they were sacred.'

'Then their fate is their own,' Hywel replied. 'I can't be held responsible if people go walking where they shouldn't.'

'This is ridiculous.' Cwen stepped forward in that determined manner she had. 'We go and look in the woods, sacred or not.' She considered the men gathered around her as if they weren't capable of finding a tree in a forest. She looked at Ellen as if she were a tree. A rotten one, not even good for a fire.

Hywel looked at her as if the doom of Gods would fall

on her head. 'The doom of the Gods will fall on your head,' he explained.

'I'll cope.' Cwen had dismissed bigger irritations than a pantheon of ancient gods.

She stood and purposefully led the way to the edges of the wood, where the village ended and a path wound its way between the trees.

The others seemed to take courage from her decisive action and followed, albeit some of them at a bit of a distance. Ellen didn't seem worried about the doom of the gods but Banley looked decidedly shaky.

Hywel held back, clearly happy to leave these strangers to their awful fate.

'There you are,' Cwen said in some triumph when they arrived. 'There's even a path. Can't be very sacred if there's a path.

She stepped onto the path and past the first pine tree.

'Yes?'

She was a woman of calm control, not to be put out by the unexpected or by the foolishness of others, but even those at a distance could tell that every morsel of her body had jumped half an inch when the druid appeared.

The white robe seemed to be exhaled from the trunk of one of the trees and stood on the path before her.

If it had been a simple man who had jumped out from behind a tree she would have given him a simple punch in the face and moved on. This though was a druid. A man in a white robe who seemed to have been hiding inside a solid tree. She paused.

'Yes?' the druid repeated.

And worse than it being a simple druid emerging from a tree, this was the little wizened one, Lypolix. The one who would look quite unpleasant in a gathering of the unpleasant and wizened.

Cwen recovered herself with a couple of quick breaths. 'Where are our friends?' she demanded of the wizened one. Attack always being the best option.

'Aha,' Lypolix cackled.

Cwen gestured into the woods behind the druid, 'We want to go and look for our missing people. We think they may have wandered into the woods.'

Lypolix cackled again, pretty much in exactly the way he had only just cackled, which added very little by way of explanation of anything.

'Oh, for goodness sake.' Cwen made to brush the little inconvenience aside when a second shape appeared. At least this one walked down the path like a normal person. It also had two other druids at its shoulders.

'What is it?' The Arch-Druid asked as he joined Lypolix. Wulf and the still unnamed druid from their journey stood respectfully behind.

'I was just explaining to your tree-sprite here.' Cwen beckoned at Lypolix who seemed to like the title. 'We are looking for some missing people who may have gone into the woods.'

'Not into our woods,' the Arch-Druid explained with slow authority, 'they are..'

'Sacred, yes, we were told. Doesn't mean they couldn't wander in here. Them being woods and all.' Cwen's impatience was in full flight. 'And the people involved probably not being able to spot the sacredness in the dark.'

The Arch-Druid smiled magnanimously. 'We would know.' He nodded beard and head authoritatively.

'And now we'd like to know,' Cwen was not giving up.

'It is quite simple.' The Arch-Druid's languorous

speech forced Cwen to slow down. 'The woods are sacred and you may not enter. Not until invited.'

'Well, invite us then.'

'Now is not the time.'

'And when, exactly, will the time be?'

'Soon.'

'That's not very exact.'

The Arch-Druid held out his hand to demonstrate that this was the best he could do.

'This is ridiculous,' Cwen snapped out of the druid's gaze. 'We'll just go round.' She waved her arms about to instruct those accompanying her to go round the large druid.

No one moved.

She turned to see John had separated himself from the group, and was offering support to the Arch-Druid's instruction by pointing his best sword at everyone.

'What are you doing?' she demanded.

'You can't disobey the druid,' John explained as if the very idea was unthinkable.

'I was doing quite well.'

'If he says we may not enter, then we may not enter.'

'There's an awful lot more of us than there are of them,' Cwen reasoned with a prominent threat in her voice. She looked to Hermitage and Wat for support.

Wat shrugged. 'The man with the big sword says he'd really rather we didn't go into the woods.'

Cwen tutted at his lack of gumption.

Hermitage put on one of his hangdog looks. 'If the people really believe the woods are sacred, perhaps we should wait until we're invited? I mean, obviously they're wrong,' he hastily added, 'and will be held before the Lord to account for their evil ways.'

'But there's a man with a sword,' Cwen commented with contempt for everyone.

Even Ellen and Banley were keeping their distance from John and seemed a lot less interested in finding their missing companions now.

Cwen sighed her sigh of defeat. It was more a sigh of "I'll get you later", but it was the only one she had. 'What are they hiding?' she demanded with a backwards glance at the gathering of druids.

'I'm sure they just want to protect that which they hold most dear,' Hermitage argued, although he didn't really believe a word of it. After all, how on earth could a wood be sacred? Unless it was a thorn bush of course. Or a piece of the true cross. But that was different. These were real, big trees. The whole thing was ridiculous.

'We're hardly likely to burn down a whole forest, just looking for some missing people,' Cwen persisted. 'And what if they've been stolen away by these druids and hidden in the sacred woods. That would be a good reason for not letting us go and look, wouldn't it?'

Hermitage admitted that yes that would be a very good reason indeed. But why on earth would druids steal a robber, a straggler and More of all people?

The Arch-Druid laughed a light yet booming chuckle at the suggestion. 'We are not saying that you may not enter the woods, just that now is not the time. When the time comes, you may enter. In fact you will be welcomed with open arms.'

Cwen scowled her scowl at them.

'It's just that we're not quite ready yet,' Wulf offered with a smile. For which he got his own scowl from the Arch-Druid. 'Won't be long,' Wulf tailed off into silence.

'Well I don't like it,' Cwen concluded with a final hard

look at all of them.

Everyone seemed to accept that that was the end of it for now and began to move away.

'Just a minute,' Cwen called out with a very suspicious, extra heavy glare at Lypolix.

The old druid skittered about in reply.

Cwen pointed very deliberately at Lypolix, who pointed back as if it was a pointing game.

'Is that blood?' Cwen demanded, looking at a very particular part of Lypolix's robe.

They all looked at Lypolix now, who seemed quite happy with the attention. Hermitage gazed at the robe.

Being Hermitage, his immediate question was how much of a robe had to be missing before you stopped calling it a robe. There was the underlying foundation of a garment in there somewhere, but it had long since vanished beneath the years of accumulated detritus. Most of it dirty detritus.

Hermitage had never felt the inclination to give the old druid his detailed attention, and now he did, he could see that that had been very wise.

There were Things. Some of them appeared to have been deliberately attached to the druid's clothing, others looked like they'd been squashed against him in some horrible accident.

The colour of the ensemble was not white. It was not even an approximation to white. Neither was it a simple opposite. It was more like white's evil enemy.

There were rents and tears and holes, and the whole was coated with a grubbiness which seemed to have its own aura.

Like the Things, Bits of the woodland were scatted about the place, some attached by twine, some perhaps innocently caught up as the horrible train passed by.

But Cwen was right. There was something down the right hand side of the garment. It was only obvious because it had a freshness which was completely out of place.

'Well?' Cwen demanded of the Arch-Druid, not expecting to get anything sensible out of Lypolix. 'Is it blood?'

'Quite probably,' the lead druid replied in an off-hand manner. 'I dare say Lypolix has cut himself somewhere. He is rather careless.'

'I don't see any cuts,' Cwen pressed,

'Ah, but you wouldn't,' the Arch-Druid explained, quite reasonably. A simple gesture to Lypolix's grimy body demonstrated that you probably couldn't see if the man was bleeding to death.

'Cut himself on what?' Cwen asked.

'Could be anything. He's always finding things of interest in the woods. If he wants to keep one he cuts it off. Or stabs it. Always having little accidents.'

'Doesn't look like a little accident.' Cwen pointed at the large stain which overwrote the others on Lypolix's cloth.

'Be that as it may.' The Arch-Druid waved the question away. 'As Wulf says, we are not ready for you yet, but it won't be long. We will send word and you can all join us.'

Cwen still didn't look convinced.

'In fact we're actually looking forward to it,' the Arch-Druid offered in a tone which gave Hermitage a little worry.

Hermitage had far too many worries to notice another one, and with John still warding everyone off the druid, the group gave up and wandered back towards the village.

'I don't like it,' Cwen said to Hermitage and Wat when they were back among the huts. 'They're up to something. And what's John doing standing with them and waving his sword about at us? It should be the other way round.'

'Maybe they're preparing another feast,' Banley suggested brightly.

'Yes,' Cwen replied thoughtfully, 'with us as the main course.'

Caput XXIII: Secrets of Some Sacred Wood.

'See,' said Hywel when they returned looking disconsolate, and no more numerous than they'd been when they set off. 'I told you. Sacred wood I said. Didn't I say? I did, I said so, Sacred wood, I said.' At least he hadn't started his speech with "now I don't want to say I told you so, but…"

'Yes, yes,' Cwen waved him away. 'A sacred wood. Very good. And a sacred wood full of blood-stained druids who won't answer a straight question.'

'Ah, well.' Hywel sounded as if blood-stained druids were coming out of the woods all the time.

'I still say we go into the sacred woods and look for ourselves,' she grumbled, but mostly to herself.

Banley and Ellen were grumbling to themselves at the unsatisfactory conclusion as well. There didn't seem anything to do about it though, so they wandered off, looking for the missing among the left-overs of the night before.

Hermitage subtly beckoned for Wat and Cwen to join him. 'I think there's something going on,' he whispered when he was sure they wouldn't be overheard.

'Really?' Cwen sounded very surprised. 'Three people missing. A wood we aren't allowed to go in, and a druid drenched in blood? It's a good job you're the King's investigator Hermitage, I'd never have spotted that.'

He looked at Cwen with a frown. 'I think drenched is going a bit far,' he noted. 'Stained, perhaps.'

'All right stained, perhaps,' she acknowledged with hissing outrage. 'It is blindingly obvious there is something going on. We have got to find out what it is.'

'Ah,' Hermitage realised she had been sarcastic again. He would really have to look out for it more. 'What can we do? No one is willing to go with us so we can hardly storm the place.'

'We can sneak in, when they're not looking. After all, it's a bit difficult to guard a whole wood.'

Hermitage swallowed, 'Sneak into the sacred woods. The ones full of blood stained druids.'

'We don't know they're full. We've only seen four druids, and only one of those was blood stained.' Cwen smiled.

Before Hermitage could start to voice a number of concerns he was working on, there was a commotion around the huts towards the head of the valley and a number of the men of the village seemed to be gathering around one in particular.

'Now what's going on?' Wat asked. 'Perhaps they've found the missing men.'

'I do hope they're all right,' Hermitage said plaintively. He really did think that being called King's Investigator was a bit of a curse, not that he believed in curses. Wherever he went, horrible things happened and he ended up having to sort them out.

They made their way towards the gathering, which was not at the village hut they had spent the night in, but one very nearby. Hywel was there again, but as village headman, he probably had a say in everything that went on.

When Hermitage, Wat and Cwen arrived there was quite a heated discussion going on between Hywel and a small crowd of the village men, all of whom had tools in their hands. It looked as though they were on their way to till the fields.

'And I don't care what Wulf says,' Hywel was raising his voice. 'You are not bringing the bloody thing into the middle of the village.

The men were about to argue back, but when they saw Hermitage's party arrive they fell silent – apart from a few quiet whispers between themselves.

When it was clear that Hermitage had nothing to contribute, other than to watch, the villagers got back to business.

'That's not for us to say,' one of them, who seemed to be sort of in charge of the working party, answered back. 'If Wulf says it's got to come here then it's got to come here, hasn't it? Stands to reason. If you want it put somewhere else, you'll have to talk to Wulf and the Arch-Druid and get them to tell us to put it somewhere else.'

The other workmen nodded that this was undoubtedly the way to resolve whatever problem it was they were working on.

'Well, you just see if I don't,' Hywel challenged them. 'I'm not having this, I shall go and see him straight away.'

'Erm,' Cwen put in. 'You can't see Wulf now.'

'What?' Hywel barked at her, 'I can see him whenever I want.'

'I don't think so. He's in the sacred woods you see? And we're not allowed in.' She put her hands on her hips and gave Hywel one of her best stares.

Whether it was that, or the situation with the workmen wasn't clear, but Hywel stomped off across the village anyway. 'I'm the village headman,' he called back. 'I can wait by the woods if I want to.'

'Right then lads,' the leader of the workmen instructed.

'Caradoc, you, Daffydd and the others start getting the rest of the road stones laid out, I'll mark out the hole.'

Hermitage watched in fascination as the men went about their tasks. Several of them headed back off up the slope of the valley towards the cliff face at the end, while their leader approached a single hut. He didn't go in this, but rather walked around it a couple of times, crouching and squinting now and again as if judging its size.

There was only so much of this Hermitage could stand before he had to know what was going on.

'This looks interesting,' he said to the workman while Wat and Cwen looked on, clearly not finding it interesting at all.

'Oh, yes,' the workman nodded, without giving anything away.

'Some work going on then,' Hermitage observed.

'That's right.' The man looked up from his work and seemed to register that Hermitage was there. 'Aha,' he said, as if Hermitage was holding just the tool he needed. 'It's the monk.'

'Er, yes.' Hermitage couldn't think that this required much in the way of confirmation.

'Just the chap I need.' The workman stood from his task, whatever it was, and came over to the group.

Hermitage beamed. Perhaps he was going to be able to assist this fellow with some fine points of planning or calculation. He had heard that building involved calculation and it was a topic he had promised himself he would study, if he ever got five minutes to himself.

'Come over here would you.' The man beckoned him to join him by the hut.

Hermitage did so, glancing regularly at Wat and Cwen to assure them he was all right. They didn't seem to need much assurance as they had started talking in low whispers.

'Now,' the builder began.

'Brother Hermitage,' Hermitage introduced himself.

'What is?'

'I am.'

'Oh, right. I see. Brother Hermitage.' The man tried the sound out. 'Funny name for a monk,' he commented.

'A lot of people say that,' Hermitage acknowledged with a shrug.

'Well, I'm Wem.'

'Wem the builder eh?' Hermitage nodded. 'I knew a builder once. Chap called Chirk, don't suppose you know him?'[7]

'Er, no.' Wem started to look very confused.

'No, I suppose not,' Hermitage agreed. 'He wasn't a very good builder anyway.'

'Ah. Right.' Wem seemed to be having trouble keeping on topic.

'And of course he's miles away. Over Lincoln way. I don't suppose…'

'No.' Wem was emphatic. 'I have never been to Lincoln. Now. If you could do me a favour it would be a big help.'

'Of course, yes,' Hermitage smiled. He was always keen to help other people and do favours. Wat said that if he didn't sort that out he'd end up in real trouble one day.

'Could you just come and lie down in the hut,' Wem asked.

Hermitage looked at Wem. Wem beckoned Hermitage towards the hut. Wat and Cwen stopped

---

[7] You can find out all about Chirk the builder if you buy The Heretics of De'Ath – and then read it.

their whispering and looked on in interest.

'Lie, erm, lie down in the hut?' Hermitage knew that Chirk the builder had been a pretty strange sort of chap, but this really was too much.

The request took him back to the time Brother Amard had asked him to lie down in his cot, just to see how soft and comfortable it was. He had stood up again pretty sharpish when he discovered what Brother Amard's idea of comfortable was.

'It's for the stone,' Wem explained quickly.

'I need to lie down in the hut for the stone.' Hermitage was not convinced. 'How much building have you actually done?' he asked.

'Oh, none,' Wem explained cheerfully. 'I'm not really a builder at all.'

'Not really a builder at all,' Hermitage repeated as he stepped slowly backwards.

'That's right. Wulf and the druids want their stone moving and I'm the only one who seems to have the first idea how to go about it.'

'I'm not sure lying down in the hut will help,' Hermitage suggested.

'Oh, it will.' Wem nodded encouragement. 'It's for the size you see.'

'The size?'

'That's right. If I can measure you against the floor of the hut we can get the hole the right size.'

Relief flooded through Hermitage although Wat and Cwen still looked pretty suspicious.

'Oh, I see,' he said. 'You think I'm about the right size for the hole.'

'Well, obviously.' Wem sounded as if Hermitage should know that. 'We lie you down in the hut, dig the hole, run the stone down the hill and there you are, see?'

'The stone goes in the hole.' Hermitage could see what was planned, he just didn't know why.

'Course it does. That's my plan anyway.' Wem rubbed his hands and spoke to Hermitage full of enthusiasm. 'You see, I reckon if we have the hole dug first, and the stone is on the rollers, we can drive it straight in. Caradoc reckoned we should bring the stone and then dig the hole. But that way we'd have to lift the stone from stationary. My way, we just let it roll on right into the hole. Good isn't it?'

'I suppose it is.' Hermitage couldn't for the life of him see why anyone wanted a stone in a hole, but if you did, this might be the way to go about it. 'And the idea is that the stone ends up sticking out of the hole?'

'That's right.' Wem was very pleased that Hermitage was getting the idea. 'Just like the stone circles.' Wem paused for thought. 'Except, of course, the Gods threw the stones into the ground in the olden days. Now we have to do it. Apparently.'

'It must be a very big stone if it's about the size of me,' Hermitage noted.

'Well, of course it is.' Wem frowned at Hermitage. 'It's your stone. It would have to be the same size as you, wouldn't it? How else would it work?'

Now Hermitage was completely lost. He spent a lot of the time not really knowing what was going on, but just now and then a set of circumstances occurred which made him think he'd popped into the wrong body for a moment, and was in somebody else's situation altogether.

'I don't understand,' Wat asked, stepping into the conversation. 'What do you mean, it's Hermitage's stone?'

Wem looked at them all as if they were idiots. 'It's the

monk's stone. The master stone. And he's the monk. What's to understand?'

'I haven't got a stone,' Hermitage was very lost indeed.

'You will have.' Wem smiled.

'I'm being given a stone?' Hermitage looked at Wat, Cwen, Wem and the hut, hoping that one of them might explain.

'You certainly are.' Wem looked very happy at the prospect. 'The most important of them all.'

'There's more than one?'

Now Wem looked puzzled. 'How can you have a circle made up of one stone?'

Hermitage thought that was a very interesting question. Just not for now.

'Let me get this straight,' Hermitage said, hoping that saying it out loud might force it to make sense. 'You are putting together a stone circle.'

'Yes,' Wem stated the obvious.

'And the master stone is going here, in this hut.'

'In Hywel's hut, yes.'

'I can see why he wasn't happy,' Cwen muttered.

'And it's about the same size as me.'

'Exactly the same,' Wem confirmed.

'So where are the other stones? Where does the rest of the circle go?'

'From here off into the woods,' Wem nodded in the right direction.

'The sacred woods,' Cwen confirmed.

'That's right.' Wem nodded happily. 'There's a stone for everyone, and everyone shall have a stone,' he quoted.

'Very nice.' Hermitage was suddenly thinking it might not be very nice at all.

'When you say everyone,' Wat enquired very slowly.

'You mean Hermitage and me and Cwen and the other new arrivals?'

'That's it.' Wem was clearly thinking they would all be delighted.

'Including More and Leon and Stropit, who are now missing.'

'Really?' Wem enquired with interest. 'Perhaps they've been done already.'

'Done already?' Cwen made no attempt at all to remain calm. 'What do you mean they've been done already? What exactly is going to happen when you give this master stone thing to Hermitage?'

Wem sighed the sigh of a builder being asked to explain how to put one brick on top of another. 'We dig the monk-sized hole in the bottom of the hut and then bring the master stone down the hill on the rollers.'

'Rollers?'

'Very clever they are. We started off getting it a bit wrong but think we've got the hang of it now. Run along sweet as anything they do.'

'I'm sure.'

'So we put the flat stones down for the rollers to run on and lead them right up to the edge of the hole.'

'Go on,' Wat said, carefully.

'Stone comes down rollers, gets to edge of hole, tips up, falls in. Easy.' Wem held his arms out to illustrate the brilliant simplicity of his plan.

Wat asked the next question very carefully. 'And where exactly is Hermitage, the monk,' he used one hand to point out the monk. 'When the stone gets to the edge of the hole, tips up and falls in?'

'At the bottom of course.'

'The bottom of the hole,' Wat confirmed.

'Where else?'

'Eeek,' Hermitage couldn't think what else to say.

'Where else would you be?' Wem demanded. 'Not going to be a very effective sacrifice if you're standing at the top watching, is it?'

'I told you,' Cwen said. 'I told you they were going to sacrifice us.'

'You're all mad,' Wat concluded, stepping back from the hut. 'Come on.' He spoke to Hermitage and Cwen. 'We're getting out of here.'

The three hurriedly strode away from Wem and his hut/hole.

'Where are you going?' Wem called out, not understanding why the sacrifices were running away.

'We find John and Banley and the robbers, gather whatever weapons we can and get out of this place,' Wat shouted as they now ran back to the centre of the village. 'If John will even come with us and hasn't gone over to the druids.'

'What about More, Leon and Stropit?' Hermitage asked.

'Too late for them,' Cwen said.

'Cwen, really,' Hermitage chided.

'Well, what do you want to do? Scrape them off the bottom of a stone and take the bits home?'

Hermitage felt quite nauseous.

There was no sign of the robbers or John, but Ellen came running across the village to meet them.

'Where are the men?' Wat asked, 'John, Banley, that lot?'

'I was coming to ask you,' Ellen replied, and she sounded worried. 'They've all gone missing.'

Caput XXIV: The Sacrifices Object.

'Oh, hellfire and tiny fleas,' Wat swore.

'Now then, Wat,' Hermitage admonished.

'Don't tell me this is not the time for profanity. This is exactly the time for profanity. What the hell are we doing to do?'

'We get out of here,' Cwen confirmed the original plan.

'What is going on?' Ellen demanded.

Wat turned to her and looked right into her eyes. 'The whole village is mad. They have brought us here to sacrifice us to their stone circle. They're digging a special hole just for Hermitage. More, Leon and Stropit have probably already gone. Now the rest of the men are missing I can imagine what's happened.'

'Sacrificed?' Ellen was in such a state of shock at the word that she could hardly speak.

'Well, they put you in the bottom of a hole and drop a massive stone on you, if that'll do.'

The look in Ellen's eyes, said yes, that would do it.

'So, we gather what we can save and head back over the hills,' Wat explained. 'We used to outnumber them, but not anymore.'

The whole group now comprised three women left in the group of stragglers, Hermitage, Wat and Cwen. Even the pilgrims had gone. Hermitage knew that if there was to be a battle to escape the village their chances would not be good. Evaluating the little band he reckoned their best chance would be to give the best weapons to Ellen, Cwen and Wat. Except of course they didn't have any best weapons. They didn't have any weapons at all.

'But, the others?' Ellen asked, plaintively.

'I don't think there's anything we can do for them,' Wat shook his head sadly.

'We can't go,' Hermitage said plainly, having thought it through.

'Eh, what?' Wat and Cwen couldn't understand what he was saying.

'We can't go,' Hermitage repeated. 'We cannot run away and leave all those people to their fate.'

'They've already had their fate,' Cwen pointed out.

'We don't know that,' Hermitage was insistent. 'It is our Christian duty to stay and find out what has happened.

'We know what's happened,' Cwen went on. 'That mad builder told us what happened. Holes. Stones. Squashed. Remember?'

'No,' Hermitage corrected, 'Wem told us what was going to happen. To me. It seems very likely the same thing is planned for everyone else but we most certainly do not know it's happened already. In fact if I'm the one who gets the master stone, they might be saving me for last. The others could still be held captive in the woods.'

'No wonder they wouldn't let us in,' Cwen snarled.

'So what do you suggest Hermitage?' Wat asked. 'The seven of us storm the druid stronghold, the one in the middle of the sacred woods, the one full of druids that want us all underground? And then we release the prisoners?'

'Could we?' Hermitage asked, as if being invited to a tour of a cathedral.

'No, we couldn't' Wat half shouted. 'We'd get

slaughtered.'

'I think that's the plan anyway,' Hermitage observed.

'If we leave, we won't get slaughtered at all,' Wat said. 'And of all the options, I think that's my preference. And don't give me that look.'

Hermitage was giving Wat the look that said the weaver knew perfectly well what the right thing to do was. He just wasn't planning to do it.

'Yes, we could run away.' Hermitage gave the words "run away" their own peculiar character, a frankly cowardly and disgraceful character. 'But that might not work. As you said yourself, we're in the middle of nowhere, we could easily be captured again.'

Wat glared.

'And no one seems to be paying us any attention,' Hermitage observed.

That was true. No one in the village was paying them the slightest notice. It was as if large groups of sacrifices turned up every day of the week. Perhaps they did.

There were only one or two people wandering about, and even Wem had stayed at the hut, presumably to get on with digging Hermitage's grave.

'All we need to do is go over to the woods and see if we can find out what's happened,' Hermitage explained.

'And if they're all lying around in holes with stones on their heads?'

'Then we can leave,' Hermitage granted.

'Oh no we can't,' Ellen growled from somewhere very deep inside. 'If harm has come to a hair of their heads it will be a day of druid disaster.'

The others looked at her with newfound admiration, if tinged with a bit of fear.

'We can't take them all on.' Surprisingly, it was Cwen

who spoke up to soothe Ellen's temper.

'You don't have to,' Ellen replied. 'But I shall take as many of them with me as I can.'

'Leon,' Cwen said, reaching a conclusion.

'My son,' Ellen confirmed. 'Thick as a barn door and thinks with his fists, but if a druid hand has been laid on him, look for the druid with no hands.'

Wat looked hopelessly at them all, and longingly at the path over the hills that led out of the village. Hermitage looked at him pleadingly, urging him to search his conscience and consider whether leaving was really the right thing to do.

Cwen and Ellen glared at him, urging him to consider whether he'd still be able to leave the village if they chopped his toes off.

'Oh, bloody hell,' he cried aloud and headed for the woods.

...

Their entry to the sacred forest was not hindered this time, and the much reduced band made its way into the depths of the trees. Wat led the way. Hermitage suspected this was so he could prevent Cwen and Ellen diving head first into the first druid they came across.

Paths criss-crossed between the trees but the party followed what appeared to be the most well-trodden way. This was clear of leaves as if it had been swept religiously. Which seemed to be a good sign that they were heading in the right direction.

After a while there was a smell to follow as well. It was a sweet, sickly odour, with an undercurrent of bitterness that said the cooking involved bits of the forest.

Without warning, the wood stepped aside and deposited a clearing at their feet. It was quite a sight.

Hermitage gaped at the stone circle that was laid out in neat and well maintained order. The thing must be a hundred feet across and some of the stones were pretty massive. As he gazed upon the construction he wondered why the villagers wanted another circle when they already had this one. Perhaps one doubled the power of the other. Not that stone circles had power, that was ridiculous. It was just that these people were ignorant pagans who were about to double their cursedness.

'Look.' Ellen gave a sharp command and point of her finger.

Across the circle, buried somewhere in the trees at the back, was the fire from which the smell was coming. Smoke wound up into the cloudy sky and hints of a wooden wall could be made out between the foliage.

Leading them round the circle, (Hermitage thought walking straight across it would be most sensible but it didn't feel polite somehow), Wat brought the group to sight of the druid temple. The sight which knocked them back and drove all plans from their heads.

In the middle of the space in front of the temple was a large cauldron on a stand with fire crackling beneath. At the lip of the cauldron stood the Arch-Druid, stirring the contents with a large wooden spoon. Every now and again Lypolix would skip out of the undergrowth and throw something new in the pot. Wulf and the other druid sat nearby in relaxed conversation.

Scattered about at the feet of the cauldron, chatting amiably, or leaning against a tree trunk with eyes closed were the pilgrims, John and the rest of the stragglers. Leon, More and whoever Stropit was, were still missing. As was the entire band of robbers.

'What the devil is going on here?' Ellen demanded.

'Welcome, welcome,' the Arch-Druid called, pausing in his stirring for a moment. 'I said we would welcome you when the time was right. And now it is. It is indeed.'

'Where's Leon?' Ellen demanded.

'Leon?' The Arch-Druid looked to his fellows for some explanation. Wulf and the spare druid shrugged.

'My son,' Ellen pressed. 'One of the stragglers.'

'Ah,' the druid nodded acknowledgement. 'I don't know I'm afraid. I think there are some people off in the woods, but they'll come back in due course, no doubt.'

Hermitage couldn't quite take this in. There was a whole village preparing to sacrifice them, him in particular, and now the Arch-Druid seemed to be hosting some sort of gathering.

'What about the stones?' Hermitage asked.

'What about them?'

'You're going to sacrifice us all to the stones. I even have my own special stone, the master. You're going to put me in the ground and squash me with it.'

The Arch-Druid burst out laughing. 'Who told you that?'

'Well, er, Wem the builder,' Hermitage explained, suddenly doubting his own memory. 'He was bringing the stone down to Hywel's hut especially for the purpose.'

'My goodness me,' the old Druid chuckled. 'The things people come up with when they're left on their own.'

Wat stepped forward and looked at the Arch-Druid as if he was trying to see what was underneath. 'What is going on then? You are building a stone circle.'

'That's true,' the man explained. 'We have discovered that young Wulf here is a stone seer. Very rare thing, a stone seer. Only a seer can build a circle, so that's what we're doing.'

'And the sacrifices?'

'For heaven's sake, we aren't primitives. We don't really sacrifice people anymore. Is that what you thought?'

Hermitage thought that yes that was what he'd thought. And he'd also had good reason as people kept telling him it was going to happen.

'No, no, no,' the Arch-Druid protested. 'We have a purely symbolic ceremony of blessing the stones.'

'But Wem was most insistent there was going to be a sacrifice,' Hermitage said. 'Of me.'

The Arch-Druid leant in close, away from Hywel's hearing. 'Do you think he'd have lugged a massive stone all the way down the mountain if he thought all we were going to do was sprinkle it with berry juice? These are simple people, you have to give them something of a sensation to stir them to action. We spun them a yarn about great sacrifices to get the stone circle going and so they started work.'

'That's rather dishonest isn't it?' Hermitage chided.

'Better than squashing real monks with real rocks,' the Arch-Druid observed.

'So all this business about us being the chosen ones and summoned here across Wales was nonsense?'

'Oh, not quite,' the Arch-Druid confessed. 'The locals are well known to the stones and so strangers were needed for the ceremony. You just happened to be the first ones we found.'

'Well known to the stones,' Hermitage muttered at such nonsense.

'That still doesn't explain where my Leon has got to,' Ellen piped up.

'Or More, or Stropit,' Cwen added.

'Or all the robbers,' Wat noted.

'It is a big place my friends.' The Arch-Druid held his arms out to demonstrate just how large. 'I expect they've just wandered off and will be back shortly. We're not holding anyone captive after all.'

Cwen and Ellen still looked suspicious at this tale but the evidence was hard to deny. There was no one under threat. The missing people were just missing and the Arch-Druid seemed to be most concerned about his cooking pot.

Hermitage wasn't sure he could stand much more of this. First they tramp through the countryside, then they're going to be sacrificed, then they're not. He just wished everything would settle down and he could get back to normal. Whatever that was now.

The whole situation was completely bizarre, never mind whether there was going to be any actual death or not. And they were still no closer to completing their mission. There was no sign of Martel. Yes, there was some druid gold, quite a bit of it draped around the Arch-Druid, but there was no way they were going to be able to get away with any of it for the king. Not that Hermitage would dream of stealing someone else's gold anyway.

'I don't suppose you've seen a fellow called Martel have you?' he asked the Arch-Druid. 'A Norman. Came here some months ago, probably.'

'No,' the Arch-Druid boomed happily. 'As you now know, we get very few strangers in these parts. We tend to make a song and dance of it when any do turn up.'

'Hywel didn't seem very happy at having to supply a feast,' Hermitage pointed out.

'Ah, well,' the Arch-Druid explained. 'Hywel is never very happy about anything.'

Hermitage felt rather deflated. He didn't want to be sacrificed under a big rock of course, but he had been prepared to put up some sort of fight. Now it didn't seem to be needed.

'What now then?' he asked the Arch-Druid.

'It's ready,' the man announced, stepping back from his cauldron. 'We all have the ceremonial libation, then we move on to the blessing of the stones. Then you can all do whatever you want.'

Hermitage looked very suspiciously at the cauldron full of ceremonial libation.

'Oh, don't worry,' the druid reassured him. 'It isn't poisoned or anything. Look. I'll take the first portion.'

He dipped a small ladle into the cauldron, extracted a full measure and blew across it to cool it. He took a cautious sip, as anyone would of a boiling hot potion that you were about to stick in your mouth. Then, when satisfied it wasn't going to burn him, he drank the lot.

'Ah,' he smacked his lips in pleasure. 'May not be to everyone's taste, but I love it. Here you go.' He held the ladle out for the monk.

Hermitage and the others still held back but then the other druid, Wulf and Lypolix all queued up for their drink.

Perhaps Hermitage would try a sip. Just to be polite. He did wonder about the point of being polite to people who he had been assured were planning to sacrifice him under a rock. But if that really was wrong he ought not to hold it against them. It could be that Wem was a fanciful chap who made up ridiculous tales. He had come across people like him often enough. Most often they were his fellow monks.

After the druids had had their fill he took a small

mouthful of the frankly foul distillation. If this was what druids drank he wasn't surprised they were dying out.

No one else volunteered to taste what came out of a druid's cauldron, so the Arch-Druid went amongst them with his ladle, doling out small mouthfuls. The universal conclusion about this creation of the woods, with its secret recipe of natural ingredients, freshly plucked from the floor and walls of the forest, was that it was revolting.

People spat and did what they could to clear their mouths of stuff that seemed determined to cling to their teeth. Perhaps chewing a nettle would take the taste away.

Hermitage thought that he would need to have a long discussion with a devout abbot or bishop after all of this, just to sort out what was sinful and what he needed to do penance for. If he could find a devout abbot or bishop that was.

This thought was still in his head when he realised that he was falling to the ground. He seemed to be at one remove from the body of the monk that was now collapsing onto the ground in front of the cauldron. He could watch it, as if from a great distance, and note with interest what a body looked like when it fell senseless.

As consciousness fled, his final thought was to wonder if this might have anything to do with the druid's potion he'd just drunk.

Caput XXV: Tied and Ready.

As Hermitage's senses slowly wormed their way back into his brain, he noticed that his body was having a hard time keeping up. He felt stiff and uncomfortable, with the distinct impression that if he gave his muscles an instruction they would disobey.

He managed to move his head from the slumped position it had fallen into, and sucked up some of the dribble that had run down his chin. Even that still tasted of the foul brew.

He managed to blink his eyes open and at least his reason was still intact, even if his vision had a strange swimming quality about it. The druid potion must have been very strong stuff. He was not used to drinking at all. Certainly not the strong spirits the ordinary man and woman indulged in. He had never seen the attraction of ale, apart from it being safer to drink than water, and wine had never been offered.

He tried shaking his head lightly, which turned out not to be a good idea at all as it felt like the inside of his head stayed still while the rest of him moved around.

He let a little groan escape his mouth.

'Ah, master monk,' the voice of the Arch-Druid boomed into his head in unnecessarily booming manner.

Hermitage groaned again and tried to move his arms. Unsurprisingly, he found that he couldn't. He swore would never drink again. Druid potion was unlikely to come his way, but even the ale would be approached with caution.

He blinked more life into his head and tried again. His

arms still wouldn't move.

As sense returned in more force he detected that the reason he couldn't move his arms was that they were tied up. How had that happened?

Sight came back into order and he looked about him. They were still in the area of the cauldron and the others were still with him. Wat, Cwen, the stragglers and the pilgrims. And they were all tied up. That was very odd.

Perhaps they'd had to be restrained for their safety. It could be the drink had driven them into wild thrashings and shakings which could have injured them and the druids had kindly tied them up.

He recalled one of Wat's most insistent lessons. More like an instruction really. Stop thinking the best of people all the time and have a look at the worst.

The worst would mean that the druids had poisoned them after all; had tied them up to stop them getting away, and were really going to sacrifice them to the stones. Wem had been telling the truth and the Arch-Druid had been lying. Honestly. You couldn't trust anyone.

That had been one of Wat's instructions as well.

'What's going on?' he managed to croak out through a potion ravaged throat.

'Everything according to plan.' The Arch-Druid smiled broadly and walked over to crouch in front of Hermitage. 'Everything is exactly as it should be.'

'The stones,' Hermitage got out, half statement, half question.

'And the sacrifices,' the druid added. 'All proceeding very well indeed, thank you.'

'The drink.,' Hermitage was finding it very difficult to make his thoughts come out of his head in the right order.

'Good, isn't it?' the Arch-Druid replied. 'One my best, I think. Very effective and very fast. Just the job. Of course the right mushrooms aren't always available but the Gods provided.'

'But, we, you.' Hermitage knew exactly what question he wanted to ask. He knew what words he had sent to his mouth, but these were the only ones that worked.

'How come we all drank the potion but only you succumbed?' The Arch-Druid prompted.

Hermitage nodded.

The Arch-Druid shrugged, 'We're used to it. Lypolix and I haven't been druids for years without developing a certain resilience.'

Hermitage was now able to look around the clearing.

'In fact, I'm a bit concerned that Lypolix has been taking the stuff regularly, in secret.' The Arch-Druid tapped the side of his head with one finger. 'Can't be good for you.'

'And.'

The Arch-Druid followed Hermitage's gaze.

'Ah, yes,' the Arch-Druid nodded. 'That probably does seem a bit odd.'

Hermitage could see all of those he knew were tied up as he was and now knew why. He didn't know why the young druid, Wulf, was tied up as well. The other druid was tied next to him.

'He's the stone seer you see,' the Arch-Druid smiled, 'got to sacrifice a stone seer or the circle wouldn't work at all.' He paused in thought, 'Or so Lypolix says.' He looked at the cauldron with a frown. 'And the other druid isn't from round here. Probably best to tie him up anyway. Just to be on the safe side.'

A shape moved across Hermitage's vision and he

looked up. He was surprised again. But then this was a generally surprising situation.

John was prowling about the ground, sword in hand.

'Turns out John is one of our most loyal servants. Handy sort of man to have around if there might be trouble.'

Hermitage had so many questions but his brain was still so addled that he gave up on them and slumped in despair.

The Arch-Druid stood and looked down from his great height at Hermitage. 'Won't take long to get everything going.' The man rubbed his hands in happy anticipation. 'The master stone is ready to roll down the hill so we'll do you first, if you don't mind. Then we'll get on with the rest of the circle. Few days and the whole thing will be done.' The druid strode away, chuckling and humming happily.

Hermitage had a very long list of things he minded about. He minded about them very much indeed. As soon as his head was working properly he would present all his arguments to the Arch-Druid and get this ridiculous situation sorted out.

In the meantime he was tied up in a remote welsh village with a group of druids who wanted to sacrifice him under a large stone. 'Wat!' he hissed as loudly as he dare.

The weaver was tied up nearby but hadn't shown any sign of life. He now rolled over, wide awake, and looked at Hermitage as if all of this was his fault.

'The druids,' Hermitage started.

'I heard.' Wat's tone was rather fierce.

Hermitage rolled his head around and brought some more sense to bear. 'I expect you think we should have left when we could,' he said.

'Er,' Wat seemed to think about it for a moment. 'Yes.'

'What are we going to do?' Hermitage asked. Wat was the one who got them out of situations like this. Well, not exactly like this, obviously, but similar.

'What do you suggest?' the weaver did not sound happy.

'We need to escape.' Hermitage thought perhaps the potion was still effecting Wat.

'Good,' Wat said. 'Let's do that then.'

'How?'

'I don't know, Hermitage,' Wat ground the words out. 'I've been tied up by a mad druid who wants to drop a stone on my head.'

The others were all coming round now, and there were cries of surprise and complaint as they realised their condition.

'Untie me this minute,' a voice screamed across the forest. Cwen was awake then.

The Arch-Druid strode into the middle of his definitively captive audience and held up his hands.

'Friends, friends,' he said, calmingly.

There were some rather rude responses to this.

'I do apologise for the inconvenience. We'll get on with things as quickly as we can but in the meantime make yourselves as comfortable as possible.'

Now there were some suggestions of what people were going to do to the Arch-Druid once they were free. Suggestions what Cwen was going to do, mainly.

'Master?' Wulf's voice sounded more puzzled than fearful.

'Ah, young Wulf. Our stone seer.' The Arch-Druid walked over to his acolyte. 'It is just as I said, I always knew there was something special about you. Might have been best to stick to the priesthood after all, or a bard.'

'What are you doing?'

'The sacrifices to the circle.' The Arch-Druid sounded very disappointed that Wulf hadn't got this. 'The Grand Complication needs very special sacrifices. The monk is for the master stone, and the stone seer lies opposite.'

'What?' Now Wulf sounded angry.

'That's what Lypolix says.'

'And you believe that old loon?' Wulf was letting himself go.

The Arch-Druid stepped forward and clipped Wulf round the ear.

'Ow. Well he is. He is a mad, decrepit, off with the owls, full strength loon. He couldn't seer his own toes. All he does is cackle and skip about and pick things up off the floor. If he wasn't a druid we'd have chased him out of the village by now.'

The Arch-Druid was looking shocked at this tirade.

'And you're going to sacrifice me on his say so?'

'You were quite prepared to sacrifice us,' Cwen shouted out.

'That's different,' Wulf responded. 'You're heathens.'

'We're not the heathens,' Hermitage pointed out. 'It's you who are the heathens.'

'How can we be heathens?' Wulf retorted.

'Can we stop arguing about who's most heathen,' Wat interjected. 'The big druid here wants to kill us all. Perhaps we should concentrate on that?'

'It will all be sorted out when the circle is complete,' the Arch-Druid tried to calm the argument down. He looked quite surprised that his captives were arguing amongst themselves.

'And if the circle doesn't work?' Wulf challenged. 'If

Lypolix really is as cuckoo as I say?'

The Arch-Druid adopted a masterful stance, 'Then I am prepared to admit I was wrong.'

'But we'll still be dead,' Wat pointed out.

'Never mind.' The Arch-Druid strode off to the temple. He did cast his eye back at Wulf, and frowned as he went.

People struggled against their bonds but were held firm. Cwen and Ellen got positively frantic trying to shake their ties loose but to no avail. The druids must have done this sort of thing before.

John simply stood by and watched them all. Probably ready to stick his sword in anyone who really managed to escape.

'I thought you were supposed to keep us safe,' Wat demanded.

'You're safe aren't you?' John noted.

'Until we get stones put on top of us. Le Pedvin gave you specific orders.'

'Le Pedvin,' John spat on the ground. 'Why would I do anything to help the cursed invaders?'

Hermitage sighed to himself. Wasn't there anyone here who had told the truth? About anything? It was all very disappointing.

'We're pilgrims,' Elard called out, sounding very plaintive. 'You can't sacrifice pilgrims. It's not allowed.'

'I think you'll find a druid who wants to build a stone circle on top of you can do whatever he likes,' John shouted back.

'But God protects his pilgrims.' Elard was getting desperate.

'Then he will do,' John said. 'Except of course the druid Gods are the real gods and you aren't real pilgrims anyway. The monk said so.'

'Arguing over who is who is beside the point,' Hermitage had to speak up. 'Burying people under stone circles in the expectation that they will perform some sort of magic is just wrong.'

'We'll find out, won't we.' John wandered around among the captives to make sure they were all secure.

'Wulf,' Hermitage called. 'You're a druid. Do you think this is right?'

'Well,' Wulf drawled out very slowly. 'In principle of course, a blood sacrifice to power a stone circle is perfectly reasonable. In principle.'

'But in practice?' Wat took up the argument. 'And when it's your blood? In practise.'

'Erm,' Wulf didn't seem to have an answer he was prepared to share.

'And your friend there? Our mysterious druid companion whose name we don't even know? What does he think about the whole stone, sacrifice situation?'

'My name is Gardle,' the druid said in a calm and serene voice. 'And if the Gods will it, so mote it be.'

'What?'

'I said my name is Gardle..,'

'Yes, I heard that bit. What did you say after that?'

'So mote it be.'

'And what does that mean?' Wat asked with some irritation.

'Er.' Gardle was taken back by the challenge. 'It means so may it be.'

Wat coughed in contempt. 'So you're happy to have a rock put on top of you until you're dead.'

'Actually,' Gardle sounded confident, 'I don't think I'll be needed for the actual sacrifice, 'I think they've got enough.'

'Oh, very convenient.'

'It'll be all right,' Ellen called across from her resting place. 'Soon as my Leon gets back, he'll have this lot for breakfast. We'll be sticking them under stones before the day is out.'

John walked over and gave her a light tap with the flat of his sword. 'As soon as your Leon comes back, he'll be tied up like everyone else.'

Hermitage whispered to Wat, 'At least that means they don't have him.' He took some encouragement from this. 'And maybe Banley and the robbers are free as well, we could still be rescued. After all, they're a half reasonable fighting force.' His enthusiasm started to wane as he remembered how effective the robbers had been the last time they faced John.

Wat's snort indicated that he did not share Hermitage's confidence. 'At least they like me. If I offer them a tapestry they might help. The druids can't possibly have anything that would persuade Banley to go along with this.'

'And now for the gold,' the Arch-Druid announced as he strode out of the temple bearing armfuls of the stuff.

'Oh, bloody hell,' Wat said.

Caput XXVI: Ah, the Gold.

All eyes were on the Arch-Druid. Or rather they were on the nice shiny things he was carrying in his arms.

The expression "a king's ransom" was often bandied about to indicate so much wealth that actually trying to enumerate it was beyond the wit of mortal man or woman.

The assembled mortal men and women now knew what a king's ransom actually looked like. It looked very nice indeed. Virtually every mind in the place turned to how they might be able to leave this place with all the gold. Even people tied up and ready to be sacrificed could suddenly imagine a turn of events that left everyone else dead, or lost, and them escaping alone over the hills carrying more gold than they could carry.

'I've been discussing this with Lypolix,' the Arch-Druid explained. 'And rather than put the gold on the stones, where it might be stolen, we've decided to bury it with you.'

Several of the minds now thought that being put in a hole with a rock on top wasn't really so bad if you got big piece of gold all to yourself.

'That way, each stone will have its own gold and of course we don't have to go to the trouble of melting it down.'

The original triumvirate who had set off on the mission from Le Pedvin had varying reactions to the arrival of the treasure. The treasure they had been sent to find in the first place.

Hermitage was interested in the gold at an intellectual level. He considered it fascinating that these pagan people, in the middle of nowhere, had managed to accumulate and keep such a quantity of wealth. He also feared for their safety when William found out that he was right; Wales was full of gold. He thought it would be extremely satisfying if he could now find Martel and complete the set.

Cwen was considering which piece of gold in the Arch-Druid's arms, a big, heavy torc, a large plate or a simple lump of un-fashioned metal, would make the best weapon with which to knock out an Arch-Druid's brains.

Wat was dribbling.

'Gold,' the weaver breathed and drooled at the same time. 'So much gold.'

'And death,' Hermitage pointed out. 'Gold and death.' He thought it had a nice ring to it as a warning to the avaricious.

'Gold and death,' Wat repeated, as if it was an invitation. And a nicely balanced one at that.

'Let's see.' The Arch-Druid deposited his treasury on the floor and surveyed it casually. 'I think the monk and the stone seer should probably have the most significant pieces.

He selected pieces of such significance as was fitting, and of such significance that they could have bought a small town.

He took a massive, embossed gold plate and laid it by Hermitage. Then he deposited a torc big enough for a cow at Wulf's feet.

'Where did all this come from?' Wulf asked in awe. 'I've never seen any of it before.'

'And so you shouldn't young Wulf. This is the

Arch-Druid's treasury. Gifts to the druids over the years have been accumulated and kept safe for just such a purpose as this.'

'Killing druids,' Wulf was contemptuous.

'Sacrificing, Wulf,' the Arch-Druid corrected. 'Sacrificing. How many times have I told you? You'll have the honour of a place with the Gods.'

Wulf did not look like he thought it much of an honour.

As the Arch-Druid got on with distributing the gold among the soon-to-be foundations, the various faces around the horde of gold were getting over their awe at the sight of such wealth. Minds returned to the subjects of stones and holes and sacrifices. The reality of being a sacrifice, even a rich one, was dawning.

The Arch-Druid was pottering about, putting a piece of gold here, placing another one there, not quite liking it and then moving it back again. He was even humming merrily as he went.

With the last bit of gold distributed, the old man surveyed his achievements and noticed that he was still several treasures short of a full circle. He tutted mild annoyance that some people might not be put to death quite properly, and scuttled back to the temple, beckoning John to follow him and help with the load.

The swordsman appeared to be overwhelmed by the honour of this, put his sword, away and followed.

...

Other faces looked upon the scene from their place of hiding and were not in the least concerned about being a sacrifice - because they weren't tied up waiting to become one. They were quite taken with the rich bit though. And the route to becoming rich seemed pretty straightforward just now. It would be even easier if all the people who were tied up ready to be sacrificed, went ahead and got on with it.

One of the watchers was ready to leap forward immediately and start the harvest, but was held back.

'The gold,' the leaper-forward breathed.

'Wait,' the one who seemed to be in charge commanded. He seemed to be very much in charge and so the enthusiast waited.

'But they're going to bury it under rocks,' the first protested.

'Then we'll know where it is, won't we,' the second hissed and followed this up with a cuff round the head. A cuff round the head that sent the first man reeling as the cuffs were on the end of solid metal, armoured gloves.

...

And yet more faces watched the scene. It was a good job this area was so heavily wooded. The secrecy of the various parties would have been severely hindered if they kept bumping into one another.

'Look at all that gold,' one of these observers breathed.

'I say,' the other was impressed as well.

'We could get some.' A grin erupted which would make the god of avarice tut in distaste.

'Do you think we should?'

'It's there for the taking.'

'I'm not sure. I think it belongs to the druids. You see the big chap with the beard? I don't think they'd like it.'

'We don't have to ask.'

'But they've got all those other people tied up. If a couple of druids can do that, even to other druids, what chance do we stand?'

'Tell you what, we'll sneak in, free the people who are tied up, and then we'll outnumber the druids.' The head nodded at this cunning and daring plan.

'Do you think we should?'

'Oh come on,' the first said as he made sneaking movements through the undergrowth. 'You've been in that cave too long.'

...

Oh lord, thought Hermitage, as he heard a very distinctive hissing sound, there's that snake of the druids. He had told Wat there was a snake involved.

'Hissss.'

He waited, fully anticipating the sharp pain of fangs striking his vulnerable parts. Druid fangs, probably poisoned. He tightened his body and screwed up his face, perhaps in the forlorn hope that poisoned, druid snakes didn't bite people with screwed up faces.

He was so tense, he couldn't even shout out when there was indeed a sharp pain at his wrist. All he could do was let out a strangled gurgle as he anticipated the awful, slow death that was to come.

'Oh, sorry,' More spoke in his ear. 'Missed the rope.'

Hermitage felt the twine at his wrists tugged as a knife slid across his binding and started to saw at it.

'More?' Hermitage managed to breathe – when he had started breathing again.

'Yis.' More sawed away.

'Where have you been?' As he asked it, Hermitage

thought that this was probably not the right question for this particular situation.

'I went for a walk.' More seemed happy to start a normal conversation.

'A walk?' Hermitage let his annoyance slip out. 'We're tied up, about to be sacrificed by some mad druids and you went for a walk?'

'You weren't being sacrificed when I went for a walk,' More pointed out quite reasonably. 'And I sort of got a bit lost.'

Hermitage couldn't think of anything to say. Which was unusual in itself.

'Good job I did, eh?' More tugged and pulled at the rope which he was nearly through.

'I suppose it is,' Hermitage whispered. 'You haven't seen anyone else have you? We lost one of the stragglers - Leon, and all the robbers.'

'Oh,' More sounded very interested. 'Been busy then.'

Hermitage breathed deeply as he felt his wrists come free, but held them still, in case anyone spotted that he had been released.

There was no sign of Lypolix, so Hermitage took his chance and pulled himself up to a squatting position. Wat and Cwen looked at him with naked surprise.

He turned to face More. He should at least thank the old man for his rescue. The mad boatman, who he had not wanted on the mission at all, might have turned out to be the one who saved them all. It just taught him not to judge people.

'Oh,' he exclaimed, as he saw there was someone else with More.

The figure was more like a hermit than most hermits Hermitage had ever seen. He had been tempted to the isolated life himself, and even directed to it on one or two occasions. The problem had always been that the hermits he met seemed to have no gainful employment outside of starving and begging. They never considered great arguments. They never studied illuminating texts. They just sat in caves and thought. Apparently. He'd never even come across the results of any hermit's thinking.

As far as he could tell from this individual, he had really got the hang of the starving bit. His clothes seemed of good quality, but far too big. He was dirty and wrinkled and his hair would only be rescued by complete removal.

The other held his hand out, 'How do you do,' he said in a loud whisper. He sounded much more intelligent that he looked. 'Martel, Giles Martel. Pleased to meet you.'

'Giles Martel?' Hermitage was stunned. 'King William's looking for you.'

'Oh dear,' Martel said. And he sounded like he meant it.

'I found him hiding in a cave,' More explained.

'Living,' Martel corrected. 'Living in a cave.'

'Hm.' More was not giving Martel the benefit of the doubt on that one.

'In fact,' Hermitage added. 'The king sent us to find you.'

'Oh dear, oh dear.' Martel looked like he wanted to get back to his cave.

'Hermitage!' Wat's whispered shout crossed the clearing.

Hermitage turned to look at the weaver.

'Perhaps now is not the time for a conversation.' Wat made wriggling movements, indicating that he was still firmly tied up.

'Ah, quite.'

Crouching low, as if that would stop them being spotted if the Arch-Druid reappeared, Hermitage, More and Martel hurried over to Wat. The knife did its job and Wat moved on to release the others.

When he came to Wulf and Gardle, he paused.

'Not sure I should release you,' he said, thoughtfully.

'I would if I were you.' Wulf sounded very serious.

'Oh, yes? Going to join your master and put us all in holes in the ground?'

'I shall join my master to the nearest oak tree,' Wulf growled. 'With a sickle through his sensitive bits. And that prancing idiot Lypolix along with him.'

Gardle looked at his companion in some surprise at this challenge to authority. He didn't object though.

Wat was impressed by the venom in the young man's voice and so cut them free.

As soon as everyone's ties were cut and they were able to escape the horror of a druid sacrifice, they acted with one accord. Without exception they stooped to pick up their piece of gold and stash it somewhere safe.

'What?' Cwen demanded as Hermitage gave her a disappointed look. 'We don't want to leave it with the druids. Look what they do with it. That must be sinful.'

Hermitage thought this was a fine time for Cwen to start worrying about what was sinful and what wasn't.

'In fact, if you don't want your bit?' she asked.

Hermitage shook his head in despair, but did glance over to where he had been tied.

There was no sign of the large gold plate. More was standing there, smiling, with a large plate-shaped bulge under his jerkin.

'Oh, really,' Hermitage huffed at the entire assembly. 'Do you value gold more highly than your own lives?'

Ellen, the straggler shrugged, 'We can have both now,' she said.

'Unless the druids come back,' Hermitage pointed out.

'What's one old man, and an even older, mad one going to do against all of us?' Ellen asked, putting her hands on her hips, gold chalices firmly clasped in each. 'We've even got druids on our side now,' she pointed out Wulf and Gardle.

'And the rest of the village?' Hermitage asked. 'We should leave all this here and make good our escape. The gold will only hold us back.'

'The rest of the village are nowhere to be seen,' Ellen pointed out. 'We still haven't found Leon so we're not going anywhere. And no one's asking you to carry any gold.' She seemed to think she had finished with Hermitage.

He had no satisfactory answer. 'This will not end well,' he warned. 'The gold will be a division between us. Wars have been fought over less.'

'Then the further apart we are after this, the better,' Ellen concluded.

'What's going on?' the voice of the Arch-Druid boomed over the woodland.

They all turned to face the man who did not look happy, even though he had an arm full of fresh gold.

Lypolix was now with the bearded one, and hopped about in his shadow, still grinning for some reason or other. Or most likely for no reason at all – or the complete absence of reason.

John stood at his side, sword freshly in hand

'Get back to your places,' the Arch-Druid commanded.

No one moved.

'Now!' he brought this instruction from the very depths of his massive frame.

'No.' It was Wulf who spoke up in defiance. A voice which seemed to give the Arch-Druid a shock.

'Wulf Barelock,' the Arch-Druid corrected a mere acolyte who dared to speak up.

'It is Wulf Barelock and I am not going to my death on the say-so of that.' He pointed at Lypolix, who seemed not to notice. 'I am the stone seer. I am the one who saw the great circle and the fact that it demanded gold. I did not see any sacrifices. I never saw any sacrifices. I don't think there need to be any sacrifices at all, never mind a list of specific people. It's only Lypolix who's said there should be any at all. And I never believe most of the things he says anyway.'

Hermitage could see that young Wulf was trembling at this outburst. It must have taken considerable courage to speak out against his master like that. Hermitage recalled speaking out against one of his own masters once. That man had been so profoundly wrong about an interpretation of scripture that his error had to be pointed out.

The man had asked Hermitage if he was stupid or just impudent. While he'd been thinking about it, the master had hit him anyway, so there didn't seem much point in asking the question in the first place.

The poor Arch-Druid didn't seem to know what to do about this situation. John still stood at his side and could probably take care of everyone in pretty short order but didn't know where to start. Wulf and Gardle were off to one side of the clearing, Hermitage, Wat and Cwen were in the middle and the remainder of the stragglers were to the other side. By the time John attacked any of them, the rest could run away.

'The Gods,' Lypolix cackled at the top of his voice.

'Yes,' the Arch-Druid leapt on the explanation. 'The Gods have dictated the sacrifices. If they want Wulf Barelock crushed under a rock, that's what they'll get.'

'The Gods,' Wulf was dismissive. 'We've only got Lypolix's word that any of that is true.'

'No,' Lypolix cackled on. 'The Gods.' He was pointing towards the woods behind Hermitage's head.

Everyone swung round to see the Gods come out of the trees.

Hermitage knew perfectly well that there was only one God and he was hardly likely to appear in some Welsh woods. Of course, he could if he wanted to, but this seemed to be such a local issue it wouldn't be worth his trouble. Anyway, his days of direct miraculous appearance had tapered off after the Old Testament. He acted in a much more mysterious way now. Hardly likely to come marching out of the trees demanding sacrifices. This druid was clearly and absolutely wrong.

He still had to look though.

They all had to look.

Breath could be heard being drawn in as a large figure stepped out from between two trees and looked left and right across the clearing.

It had a head of shining glory with piercing eyes that took in all they surveyed. It had a mighty sword of vengeance in its right hand and a shield of justice in its left. Its front was a blazing lion which roared its anger at them all and its feet bestrode the ground as if growing from the earth itself.

There was silence in the clearing as eyes widened in

252

alarm at the sight.

Apart from one set of eyes.

'That's not a god,' said Giles Martel, in disappointment, 'That's Hector de Boise.'

Caput XXVII: Now Who's Lying?

hat?' the Arch-Druid demanded.

'Hector de Boise,' Martel repeated. 'It's Hector de Boise. I'd recognise his arms anywhere.'

'His arms?' Hermitage enquired, wondering how anyone recognised someone from their arms.

'He means his coat of arms, Hermitage,' Wat explained.

'Ah.' Hermitage nodded, content that that had been cleared up. It was obvious that the man before them was just a normal Norman Noble. He had Norman helmet, armour and weapons. He hadn't for a moment thought the man was god at all. Not really.

'He knew my father,' Martel went on.

The Arch-Druid turned to give Lypolix a very questioning look.

'The Gods,' Lypolix confirmed with a nod. 'The Gods.' He gestured towards the armoured figure as if it should be obvious.

The Arch-Druid wiped his face with his hands. 'Is this the God who gave you the instructions about the sacrifices?' He suddenly sounded very old and weary and not all in charge of things anymore.

'The Gods,' Lypolix cackled and nodded happily.

'See,' Wulf said in some triumph. 'One perfectly normal man,' he held out his arm towards de Boise. 'And one loon,' he gestured to Lypolix.

'Ah.' de Boise spoke from under the nose piece of his helmet. 'My sacrifices all gathered together. Marvellous. And you brought the gold.' He smiled a smile at the

Arch-Druid that gave Hermitage the shivers. Even though it had only grazed him as it passed by.

De Boise gestured imperiously with his sword and the clearing seemed instantly flooded with men.

Hermitage recognised Banley and the robbers, and Ellen clearly recognised Leon.

John seemed to recognise when he was outnumbered and faded away from the back of the Arch-Druid, disappearing towards the temple.

Hanging back rather, were six others. Five were local looking men, carrying sticks as if they really wanted to do something with them. The sixth was sitting on a mount that bore an alarming resemblance to the distant relation of a horse.

'Leon,' Ellen demanded in rather aggressive manner, considering she'd been fretting over him for hours. 'What do you think you're doing?'

'I've joined the Normans,' Leon explained, proudly.

He was a full grown man, but still young. His beard had not yet come but he was clearly built for strength. There was a certain vacancy in his face that said when the strength wasn't required he could sit and stare at water for entertainment.

'You've done no such thing my lad,' Ellen made clear. She strode across the clearing, heedless of the large Norman warrior. She grabbed Leon by the ear.

'Ow, mum,' Leon whined. 'Not in front of the Norman.'

'You're a straggler,' Ellen insisted. 'You were born a straggler and you'll die a straggler. And all the time in between you'll be a straggler. Ow!' Ellen cried out as de Boise reached out a mailed hand, grabbed her by the hair and propelled her back into the clearing.

'Leave my men alone, witch,' he rumbled.

'Who are you calling a witch?' Ellen demanded.

Cwen hurried over and held Ellen back from launching herself into a fully armed Norman noble almost twice her size. With more than twice as many weapons.

'My Lord de Boise,' Hermitage stepped forward and bowed his head. He could tell that this man was a fairly typical Norman noble. The type who didn't so much kill first and ask questions later, as kill first then ask who to kill next. However, something the man had said was bothering him.

'Ah.' de Boise cast his glare at Hermitage. 'The monk eh?'

Hermitage restrained himself from asking why this needed confirmation. 'That's right my Lord.' He bowed again. 'His majesty the king will be delighted to hear you are still alive. He thought you dead. We are of course grateful for you rescuing us from the druids.'

'Rescue?' de Boise sounded puzzled, which worried Hermitage further.

'Er, yes, that's right. But you mentioned "your sacrifices"?'

'Did I?'

'You did, my lord.' Hermitage bowed again.

'That must be right then,' de Boise nodded to himself.

'But now the druids are vanquished there is no need for the sacrifices.' Hermitage tried to make it sound like a commanding statement. It came out like a timid question.

'Oh, no.' de Boise beamed at them all. 'Got to go ahead with the sacrifices. I promised the funny little one.' He pointed in Lypolix's direction.

Hermitage didn't know whether the next thing he said was going to lead to instant resolution of all their problems, or make things an awful lot worse. He dropped his voice and spoke in what he imagined was a conspiratorial manner.

'We are here on a mission, my lord.'

'A mission?' de Boise sounded very interested.

'Yes, my lord. A mission. A mission from..,' he looked left and right to make sure de Boise understood the importance of this. 'Directly from King William himself.' He stood back and tried to look significant.

De Boise now looked left and right and beckoned Hermitage to come closer. He looked the monk in the eye and said, 'I know.'

Hermitage felt relief flood through him.

De Boise stood back and addressed the whole field. 'All the more reason to sacrifice you.'

Of course. It had turned out an awful lot worse. He should have known.

'But, but,' Hermitage spluttered. 'Le Pedvin.'

'Le Pedvin,' de Boise roared. 'Another good reason to sacrifice you.'

'I don't understand.' Hermitage was telling the truth. He was also rather annoyed that he didn't understand. It had to be quite simple, surely.

De Boise gave a short laugh, 'Ha,' he said. 'Not much of an investigator then.'

That really stumped Hermitage. If this noble knew they had come from the king and that Hermitage was the investigator, what was all this about sacrifices?

'You, er, know that I'm the King's Investigator?' Hermitage kept his voice down in case anyone else heard and took the information badly.

'Of course I do. And this is the one who weaves.' He gestured at Wat, who gave a little nod of acknowledgement.

'And I'm Cwen,' Cwen said with feeling.

De Boise looked at her, clearly puzzled as to why the woman was announcing herself.

'But if you know, my lord?' Hermitage tried to reason this through but wasn't having much success.

'I think..,' Wat took a cautious step forward. 'I think Lord de Boise's interests and the king's are no longer in quite such close harmony.'

'Eh, what?' Hermitage couldn't see how that comment helped at all.

'One way of putting it,' de Boise confirmed, with a grunt.

'The king sent you to find Martel,' Hermitage protested, his head bobbing backwards and forwards from de Boise to Martel.

'And now I have.' de Boise nodded at Martel. 'Although I suspect he's been avoiding me. Typical Martel tactic.'

Martel had found something interesting to look at in the trees.

'It's no good gaping master investigator,' de Boise addressed Hermitage. 'If you can't work it out for yourself I am under no obligation to explain it for you. You will go to your grave not knowing what on earth is going on. Ha.' The noble seemed to think this was quite amusing.

Hermitage had no intention of going to his grave not knowing what was going on. He intended to know pretty much everything by the time he went to his grave.

'You really intend to let these pagans sacrifice us?' he asked in honest disbelief.

'If they like. They seem very keen on the idea.'

Hermitage cast a glance at Lypolix and saw the connection from false god to strange druid. 'Probably because you gave it to them.'

De Boise shrugged. 'Tie them up again,' he commanded.

The assembled men, including the new arrivals stepped up to their task and started securing the sacrifices once more.

Wulf and Gardle tried to demonstrate that they were druids and so were excused tying up. One look from the Arch-Druid confirmed that this was not the case.

Leon started to approach his own mother but almost immediately handed the rope to someone else.

'You can't believe that sacrificing us in this manner is going to make some stone circle magical,' Hermitage protested to de Boise as his wrists were rebound.

'Of course not,' de Boise confirmed, snorting at the very idea. 'I'm not a savage you know. It will make you dead though, which is the general idea.'

Hermitage found himself bound next to Wat and Cwen now, as if de Boise was starting a collection. He watched in bewilderment as the Norman instructed his men to go round gathering up all the gold. It was taken from jerkins and leggings, from boots and from gloves. Some was even taken from one place Hermitage had never dreamed anyone could hide anything - or would want to.

He watched as the treasure was piled into quite a significant heap, over which de Boise stood guard.

When the gathering had been concluded, the Arch-Druid left his position near the temple, and walked over to de Boise. There was some gesturing and quiet conversation - and an awful lot of pointing at the gold and at the captives. De Boise appeared to dismiss whatever it was the Arch-Druid was saying and dismissed the man with a wave of a heavy metal hand.

The Arch-Druid stomped back to the temple, all the while looking over his shoulder at de Boise.

Hermitage let the events swirl around in his head. There had to be some explanation that would cover everything that was going on, it was just that he hadn't thought of it yet. If he let his various ideas wander round on their own for a bit, it wouldn't be long before two or three banged together and the whole thing would make sense.

He couldn't force this to happen, that was the sure-fire way to make the process slow down. He had to think of something else. That way his ideas would think he wasn't watching them anymore and would sort themselves out.

He took his mind off the problem by thinking about the gold. He had never in his life seen so much in one place. He had been in some bishop's palaces that boasted great wealth, but even they weren't a patch on the pile of precious metal that was lying around in these woods. He also knew several of the bishops who would drop a baby in the font to get their hands on it.

'The gold,' he said as his revelation came. 'de Boise wants the gold for himself.'

'Well done Hermitage,' Wat said. 'Knew you'd get there in the end.'

'And he wants to kill us so no one will know he's got it.' Hermitage was appalled at such a senseless waste of human life. Particularly his own.

'Not quite, I suspect.' Wat was , thoughtful.

'Really?'

'Yes. I think he wants to kill us so that everyone does

know he's got it.'

'Er,' Hermitage was lost again, and he had been doing so well.

'Or rather, he particularly wants to kill you and me so the king knows he's got it.'

Hermitage let his ideas off the leash again. It was probably going to take them quite a while to work this one out.

Caput XXVIII: A Few Revelations.

'ell.' de Boise brought Hermitage out of a reverie which hadn't got him anywhere at all. 'Time for the sacrifices then. I think we're ready.'

They were unceremoniously hauled to their feet and pushed off, back towards the village.

The only one complaining about their treatment was Ellen, but she was doing enough complaining for everyone.

'Leon,' she snapped at her son, who was, perhaps wisely, keeping his distance. 'If you sacrifice me I shall be absolutely furious.'

'Yes, mother,' Leon sighed.

'I shall haunt you,' Ellen cried.

Leon's mumbled reply could only be heard by those close by. 'She's haunted me for the last twenty years, why should being dead stop her?'

'Woman," de Boise called across the field. 'If we drop a rock on your head, will you shut up?'

Ellen shut up.

'Better. Now look,' he addressed the assembly. 'There's no need for any excitement. We only need to sacrifice the monk and the weaver.'

'Oh, that's a relief,' More piped up.

'And perhaps the two druids who are probably going to be trouble. After that you can all be released, if you behave. And if you don't behave I promise I won't sacrifice you. I'll just kill you in the normal manner.'

The Arch-Druid approached de Boise again, this time with Lypolix hopping at his heels. There was a more heated discussion this time, but once again the druid was waved away.

'Why just us?' Hermitage asked.

'It'll send a message.'

'We can't send a message if we're under a rock,' Hermitage pointed out.

'You don't have to deliver it in person,' de Boise sighed at Hermitage. 'Well, not a whole person. You know, I really don't understand what the king sees in you.'

At the word "king" Hermitage's ideas came home to roost. This de Boise spoke about the king as if he knew him personally. Hermitage drew on his experience to conclude that any Norman who knew the king personally was likely to be a dangerous madman. And dangerous madmen tended to do dangerous, mad things.

Now, what would be dangerous and mad that a Norman could do in Wales?   Something involving a lot of gold that the king wanted. And messages involving dead investigators and weavers?

'You're challenging William,' Hermitage said, now sure that he was right. How much more dangerous and mad could you get?

'At last,' de Boise raised his eyebrows as high as they would go.

'You knew about the gold and didn't volunteer to go and look for Martel. You decided to come and take it for yourself.'

'Quick, isn't he,' de Boise commented to Wat. 'As soon as Martel sent word of the gold, the king kept going on about getting hold of it but insisted on going north instead. I reasoned that if he knew the gold was under threat he'd come personally to deal with the problem. He'd probably come without his main force which would make it easier to deal with him.'

'Yes,' Wat said to Martel. 'Why did you send word to the king? Why on earth would you do that?'

Martel shrugged, 'It seemed like a good idea at the time. I thought the king would be happy and might let me come home.' He let out a little sob, 'It's horrible here. You don't know the things that go on. I've had to hide in a cave for the last six months. I even had to hide from hiding in a cave when de Boise arrived.'

'You knew he was here?' Wat was appalled.

'Er,' Martel had clearly said too much. 'I only saw him briefly,' he excused himself. 'He occupied the cave for a few days and I thought it best not to bother him. He's always been a most difficult man. Then, when I saw him chase someone into a lake and kill them, I kept right out of his way. After his time in the cave, he moved on.'

'Where exactly did you hide when all that was going on?' Wat asked, quite rudely.

'In a bush.'

'So this is all your fault,' Cwen said, clearly intending to do something about it.

Martel said nothing.

'And the bits,' Hermitage said, still on track.

'What bits?' Cwen asked while looking at Martel in a very unhealthy manner.

'The bits that the king received. He thought they were de Boise's and that one of his knights had been killed.'

'And even that didn't bring him,' de Boise huffed his discontent. 'You'd think, wouldn't you? You'd think if you were a king and someone sent you bits of one of your knights, you'd immediately set off seeking revenge?'

'Er,' Hermitage really didn't have an opinion on this.

'Well, I would,' de Boise confirmed.

'They were the bits of the first messenger,' Hermitage concluded. 'The one you killed.' He threw the accusation at de Boise. He had found the killer of the poor messenger. In his mind the mission had been a success. Of course he might have known it would be a Norman. He could have stayed at home and come to that conclusion. But now he was here, with the killer, and was able to accuse him to his face.

The face of the killer didn't seem put out in the slightest.

'Of course they were.' de Boise clearly didn't think who the bits belonged to was of any importance. 'I got the mad old druid to give them to the next messenger with a nasty little curse as well.'

'So you were trying to provoke the king to come to Wales seeking your killers.'

'And he's usually so easy to provoke,' de Boise complained. 'He'd have set off without a moment's thought, or preparation, and I'd have been waiting for him.'

'Just you?' Hermitage thought that was very unwise, knowing William the way he did.

'I had to get some men together. I found the druids and the gold but couldn't risk trying to fight off William completely alone. Unfortunately, the best I could do was Bermo and his men.' de Boise pointed out the rather sorry bunch who were mooching around towards the back. 'Not that I was going to risk a frontal assault with that lot. I'm not stupid. I've got an excellent plan. A nice ambush and an arrow in the back. Then I'd have the gold and could buy a whole army.'

'But the king didn't come.' Hermitage nodded and shook his head at the same time.

'No he didn't,' de Boise snapped. 'So he obviously needs some more provocation.'

'I don't think killing us will bother him in the slightest,' Hermitage pointed out.

'In fact, if you let him know how you're planning to do it, he might come to watch,' Wat added with resignation.

'Ah, but it all adds up, doesn't it?'

'Adds up to what?'

'Adds up to more dead people. The king might be able to ignore one dead knight, but when his investigator and the weaver go as well, he's bound to think there's something going on.'

'Something going on,' Hermitage tutted at taking death so lightly. 'How do you know about the King's Investigator anyway?' he asked.

'Oh, he's always boasting about how he has his own investigator.'

'Is he?' Hermitage felt a swell of pride.

'Said he would send his personal investigator to sort out Martel and the gold if it went on too long.'

Hermitage was about to say that that was nice. Then he remembered that it wasn't.

'Of course he hasn't got a clue what it means or what it's for,' de Boise went on. 'But then he boasts about how he's got his own privy man as well.'

Hermitage's despair when he found out about the true depths of people's deceit came back as a familiar friend. The whole business had been a ruse from one end to the other.

'So when the king didn't come looking for your killer, you thought you'd wait for the investigator and then you could send bits of me back as a further provocation.'

'Good, isn't it?'

'Isn't it a bit,' Hermitage searched for the word, 'mad?'

'Shut up,' de Boise snapped back. Hermitage had clearly touched a sore spot. Touched it with something hot and pointy judging from de Boise's reaction.

'I am not mad,' the Norman insisted. It sounded like he was trying to convince himself as much as anyone.

Hermitage thought it best to change the subject. 'And I suppose you sent the druid Gardle in advance to bring us here?'

De Boise laughed heartily at this. 'Oh, yes, that was easy, not that I knew you were already on the way. The old druid, the one who's more plant than person?'

'Lypolix?'

'That's the one. Complete idiot. After I'd killed the messenger I came down from the cave through the wretched mist they always have here, the old loon started dancing about saying I was a God come down from the sky.'

They all turned to look at Lypolix, who didn't seem in the least put out by the attention.

'And what are you going to do if someone thinks you're god?' de Boise asked.

'Put them on the correct path,' Hermitage explained.

'No. You're going to milk it for all it's worth. That's what you're going to do.'

Hermitage just sighed and tutted, which of course had absolutely no effect on a slightly disturbed Norman warrior. 'I even came up with the idea of the sacrifices all on my own,' de Boise was very proud.

'How nice,' Wat said. He noticed that the Arch-Druid and Lypolix were now engaged in deep conversation.

'Yes. I reckon if William isn't provoked by his own precious investigator being sacrificed by a bunch of druids, then the man's already dead. Bound to bring him galloping across the country at full speed.'

Hermitage shook his head slowly. 'I really think you've overestimated William's concern about me. His concern about anyone really.'

'Not his concern about gold though. Put it all together, Martel, gold, investigator, deaths piling up.'

'I think even that would come second on list of things to do when killing people was in there as well.'

'Well never mind.' de Boise was clearly getting a bit impatient with them not seeing that his idea of sacrifices was a good one. 'We'll get on with it anyway. Then, if your bits don't bring William running, I can send Martel in pieces as well. I'll just have to settle in here with all the gold and start my own Kingdom. Might be a bit of a bigger battle when he does turn up, but I'll be well prepared by then.'

They were all pushed along the path by de Boise's new found army. None of whom seemed to have any concerns about the plan.

'And you Banley?' Wat asked. 'Are you going to participate in sacrificing a monk and sending his bits to William?'

Banley looked at Wat and gave the obvious answer. 'Have you seen how much gold there is?'

'How much gold does there need to be?' Hermitage asked solemnly. 'How much gold do you need to look the other way while your brothers are put to their deaths?'

Banley thought carefully about this. 'Some,' he said.

'Some?'

'Yep. There has to be some gold. And there is.'

'Is that all it takes?'

'Yes,' Banley was very sure of this.

268

'Why don't you let us go?' More piped up in de Boise's face now. 'I mean, if you only want to kill them two, there's no need to put the rest of us to all this trouble.'

'Let you go?' de Boise looked astonished. 'Actually,' he pondered carefully, 'that is a thought.'

More nodded happily.

'I've only sent dead bits to William so far. If I sent a live person who could explain everything it might work better.'

'Explain everything?' Wat asked with incredulity, 'More? Explain everything? He can't explain his own beard.'

'Hm,' de Boise thought some more. 'Perhaps I do need to send someone a bit more intelligent.'

'Good luck with that then,' Wat scoffed.

De Boise was clearly irritated by this, 'Listen weaver,' he pointed a large gloved finger at Wat. 'You're going to be a hole in the ground with a rock on top in a minute, so I'd shut up if I were you.'

'Right,' Wat nodded slowly. 'If I behave you'll lower it gently, will you?'

They were approaching the gaggle of huts now and the ridiculous idea of being sacrificed under a large rock took on a sudden reality in Hermitage's mind. This really was ridiculous. People did not get sacrificed under rocks these days. Not that he had any recollection of days when it was commonplace.

'What in the Gods' names is going on here then?' Hywel came forward from the huts to face the parade of the tied-up. 'Who are you?' he asked de Boise, who seemed to be in charge.

'Your new king,' de Boise announced.

There was coughing from the back as Bermo and his

men seemed to find this a bit of a surprise.

'Or I will be, once William is out of the way. Who are you?'

'I am Hywel, head man of this village. I don't know anything about a new king.'

'Well you do now. We've brought this monk and his friend to be sacrificed under the stone.'

Hywel looked around the crowd that was now gathered in his village. There were more people than he'd be able to see off on his own. And the men of the village were still up in the hills mucking about with Wulf's stone.

'What's Wulf doing tied up?' Hywel asked cautiously, noting the large sword and other weapons hanging from de Boise's person.

'We're going to do him as well.'

'A druid?' Hywel was shocked. 'You can't sacrifice a druid.'

'We can, you know. Even your Arch-Druid seems to think it's a good idea.'

Hywel couldn't see the Arch-Druid at the moment but would certainly be checking this.

'Well you'll have to wait,' Hywel folded his arms. 'There isn't a stone here, or a hole to put it in.'

De Boise looked about the place, annoyance on his face. 'You, druid,' he looked hard at Wulf. 'Where's this stone?'

Wulf said nothing.

'You, ugly old druid, where's the stone?' this time he asked Lypolix

'Upon the mountain,' Lypolix cackled and pointed up to the hills.

'What's it doing up there? I want it down here on top

of the monk.'

'It will be, it will be,' Lypolix did some sort of gyration, which he obviously thought explained everything.

De Boise was looking to the hills, hand on hips and irritation on his face, when Wem and Caradoc appeared from behind the farthermost hut. They were pulling a rough cart, on top of which was a collection of flat stones. Every few yards they stopped, took two of the stones from the cart and laid them on the ground. They didn't just drop them anywhere, they placed them carefully, looking back up the hill to make sure they had got them in line with one another and with the quite impressive trail of flat rocks that was now laid across the valley floor.

Everyone watched this small procession without saying a word. It was such a bizarre sight that there was no obvious explanation for what on earth the men were doing. They were completely oblivious to their audience and carried on, happily dropping rocks on the ground and moving on.

Eventually, they arrived at Hywel's hut and looked at their cart with some frustration. There were no rocks left now, and the two men puzzled over the gap between the trail and the hut.

'Now what's going on?' Hywel broke the silence, striding over to the men and examining their rock road.

'Oh, hello Hywel.' Wem dragged his attention from his construction. He smiled happily at the village head, but then his face dropped when he saw the huge group of people were gathered by the hut. 'What the Gods?' he asked.

'That's what I'd like to know. I've got a village full of strangers who eat all the food and do no work. Some foreigner who claims to be the king and you putting rocks down all over the place. Has the whole valley gone mad?'

'It's for the stone,' Wem explained his rocks. 'We've discovered that the rollers work much better on a flat surface. So we've made one. Clever eh?'

'I hope you haven't damaged any crops,' Hywel scowled.

'Not really,' Wem looked away. 'It is a sacred task after all. Deliver the master stone.'

'The one you're going to drop on the monk?' de Boise demanded.

'That's it,' Wem confirmed, happily.

'And where exactly do you think this stone is going to go?' Hywel said, condescending from his position of authority.

'Wulf told us,' Wem was still smiling. 'It's all sorted out.' He looked to Wulf who, despite his being tied up, found somewhere else to look.'

'So now you need to dig a big hole,' Hywel pointed out, noting that there wasn't yet a big hole in the village. 'Causing more trouble.'

'Yes.' Wem looked back at the end of the rocky road. He turned back to Hywel. 'Do you want to move your hut, or shall we throw it in the bottom of the hole with the monk?'

Caput XXIX: Digging for Bones.

There was much protestation from Hywel at the final location of the master stone but he was outnumbered. He was outnumbered by druids who said it had to go there, by men of the village who had built a road to deliver it to just the right spot, and by quite a large number of men with weapons.

de Boise, keen to get on with things, instructed what he now called "his men" to start digging. This they did, heedless of the fact that the place for the hole was the place Hywel lived.

Hywel had tried a basic, "you cannot touch my hut", but when some of de Boise's men started to do exactly that, he stepped forward and tried to stand in their way. Holding his arms out to bar their progress, he watched as they walked round his outstretched arms and started to dismantle the back wall.

Dismantling involved kicking the rude walls of the hut until they started to crumble. The roof was in danger of coming down before Hywel dashed inside to retrieve his possessions. As these were very few, it didn't take long, and it wasn't a few moments before Hywel was standing by his small pile of possessions looking at the much larger pile that used to be his home.

'This is outrageous,' he wailed. 'You simply cannot do this to the hut of the village headman,'

de Boise looked at Hywel and at the heap that was his hut. 'We just did,' he pointed out. 'And now that I'm king, I think I want a new village headman anyway.'

Hywel looked horrified.

'Someone who doesn't let their own home get kicked to pieces,' de Boise scoffed at Hywel's inadequacy.

Hermitage noted that de Boise had gone from planning to be king to declaring himself as such. He looked around and thought that being monarch of this place was not exactly the pinnacle of regal achievement. He also noticed unsettled grumbling in the group of local men with the sticks, led by the one de Boise called Bermo. Even if they took against their new ruler, Hermitage could see there wasn't much anyone could do. de Boise was well-armoured and had the weapons to go with it. The only one who might face him was John. And John had disappeared altogether.

Typical. Just when you're going to be sacrificed, the one person who might be able to do something about it is nowhere to be seen.

'Now dig,' de Boise instructed.

It wasn't clear who he was instructing, and so everyone stood around waiting for someone to arrive and start the digging.

'All of you,' de Boise yelled, drawing his sword and waving it menacingly. 'Dig.'

Still everyone stood, each individual expecting the one next to them to be the one de Boise was talking to. It was only when he smacked Banley on the backside with the flat of his sword, and moved towards the other observers that they got the idea that "all of you" actually meant all of them.

The ones not tied up approached the site of Hywel's demolished hut and started to drag bits of it out of the way.

'What do we dig with?' one of the robbers asked, when the ground was clear.

'I'll dig with your head if you don't get started,' de Boise explained, helpfully.

Wem held up his hands to call a halt and ran off to the village store, coming back with a few picks and rough tools, most of which were used for the crops or for woodwork. The main digging implements still being up the mountain with the stone. He didn't like to point out that they wouldn't have to dig very deep round here before they came to solid rock.

Tools distributed, the team got to work and had soon made a reasonable impression on the ground.

'How big is this rock?' de Boise demanded. 'I hope it's big.'

'It is pretty big,' Wem confirmed as he dug into the ground.

'Bigger than a monk?'

'Oh yes, much bigger than a monk.'

'Excellent.'

Hermitage didn't think it was excellent at all.

'Surely they aren't really going to do this?' he asked Wat. He still couldn't believe they'd got this far.

'Don't see how de Boise can send our bits to King William if we're buried,' Wat noted, encouragingly.

'He'll probably only realise that once the stones are in place,' Cwen mocked the Norman's stupidity. 'Then he'll make us all dig the stones up again, just so we can get at you.'

'Sorry to put you to any bother,' Wat said, dryly.

de Boise still had questions. 'Are we going to get them all under one stone, or will we need more for the weaver and the druids?'

'What druids?' Wem asked.

'We're doing a couple of druids at the same time,' said

de Boise. 'Killing monks and druids and weavers with one stone would be good.' He seemed quite pleased with the efficiency.

Wem looked rather worried at this, 'I don't think you'll get them all under the one rock. It is big, but not that big. Er, why are we doing druids?'

'Because I say so,' de Boise explained. 'Not that the king will be interested in bits of druids, but every little helps.'

Wem looked around the faces for some guidance on this, but everyone looked away.

The digging proceeded with little enthusiasm before, as expected Wem made his announcement. 'We've hit rock.'

de Boise stepped over to look at the hole. 'Well, that's not very deep is it?'

The hole was only about four feet deep, which was actually quite good for these parts.

'Does it need to be?' Wem asked.

De Boise thought about it. 'I suppose not,' he concluded. 'If the monk is lying on a rock when the rock falls on him, it'll be much more effective.'

The monk in question thought that the time to speak up was really getting quite close now.

'Where's this stone?' de Boise demanded, seeing no sign of it.

'I can signal the men to get it on the road,' Wem offered, with little enthusiasm.

'That would be good.' de Boise made it clear that the next stone would be for Wem if he didn't get on with it.

Wem climbed out of the hole, turned towards the mountain and gave a piercing whistle through two of his fingers.

After a moment there was an answering whistle.

'It's on its way,' Wem confirmed.

'How long 'till it gets here?'

'No idea. We've never done this before.'

De Boise looked up at the mountain, looked at Wem and then leant forward and simply punched the man in the face.

'Ow, bloody hell,' Wem complained from the ground where he now sat. 'What was that for?'

'Many things,' de Boise said. 'Consider it a punishment for impudence. It's also setting a very good example of what I'll do to anyone else who causes trouble. Mostly it's because I've just about had enough of this place, and it made me feel better.'

The rumbling of Bermo's men died down a little in the face of this naked aggression.

'Bring the monk and the weaver,' de Boise commanded.

One of Bermo's men, who happened to be closest, hauled Hermitage and Wat to their feet and pushed them in the direction of de Boise and the new hole in the ground.

Cwen tried to get to her feet to do something about this, but was pushed back by another of Bermo's men. Quite what she hoped to achieve wasn't clear. Perhaps she wanted to get in the hole with Wat.

'Er, Wat?' Hermitage asked.

'Yes?'

'Now would be a good time to think of something.'

'For once, Hermitage, I agree with you.'

Hermitage thought that was very nice, but actually the thinking of something was more what he had in mind.

They were pushed and shoved over to the edge of the

hole and made to stand by de Boise.

'This really is ridiculous,' Hermitage protested. 'There's a much easier way to challenge the king than sending bits of people he knows all over the country.'

De Boise turned to him and looked expectant.

'You simply challenge him,' Hermitage explained. 'You just send a messenger, a whole live, breathing one, with word that you challenge the king. You have the gold and if he wants it, he'll have to come and get it.'

'Idiot,' de Boise responded.

Hermitage couldn't see why he was being an idiot.

'If I did that he would come with full force, wouldn't he? This way, he'll think it's just a bit of local trouble and come alone, or with a handful of men. Then I can get rid of him. I wouldn't be able to kill him if the whole army turned up, would I? Honestly, you really should try to think things through you know.'

'If we took word,' Wat offered.

de Boise looked again, although this time he was clear that Wat was just making things up to escape his fate.

'We could go back to the King and tell him that we tried to get the gold but that the druids are fierce and won't let it go. We say that they killed Martel and you and that we didn't have the men to deal with them. All he needs to do is come with a small force and it will be his.'

'I don't know where you two have been, but you don't seem to have the first idea,' de Boise was dismissive. 'I'm not going to let you go because then I wouldn't be able to kill you, would I?'

'But you don't need to kill us,' Wat explained.

'But I want to,' de Boise countered.

There seemed to be no arguing with that.

'Now.' de Boise rubbed his hands in eager anticipation.,

'Shall we pop you in the hole now?' He gave it a moment's thought. 'No, you might try and get out. We'll wait until the stone gets here, then do it all in one go.'

He paced up and down. The pace was that of an impatient man who cannot wait for his giant stone to roll down from the hills so that he can crush a monk and a weaver to death.

'Well?' he eventually demanded of Wem,

'No, not really,' replied Wem, who was in no mood to cooperate.

de Boise was about to unleash his mailed fist again, when a noise caught his attention.

They all heard it, a sort of low, grinding, rumbling noise, accompanied by some splintering sounds and the distant shouts of men. It was no natural sound at all. It was most akin to a fight between a large number of masons and an equally large group of carpenters, both of whom were running away from giant with a significant flatulence problem.

'Aha,' Wem said with some satisfaction. 'It's coming.'

All eyes turned up the valley towards the hillside, and waited for something to appear. They all knew that it would be a large rock on rollers, trundling down the path of flat stones. As no one had ever seen anything like that before, they were keen to get first sight.

'It's definitely coming,' Wem confirmed. 'Coming pretty well by the sound of it.'

'Excellent,' de Boise said. 'When it gets here we'll pop these two in the hole and then tip it on top of them.' He smiled to himself at the prospect. 'Oh,' he said with a sudden realisation.

'Problem?' Hermitage asked, hoping there was quite a big one.

'How am I going to get your bits if you're buried under a rock?'

'Well,' Wat began, 'we didn't like to say anything but it is a bit of a problem. That's why sending us with word to the king is a much better idea.'

'Got it.' de Boise ignored Hermitage and Wat completely. 'If the monk can leave an arm out, and you leave a leg, I can get them without having to move the stone again.'

'A leg?' Wat asked.

'Or anything else you like. As long as it's vaguely recognisable.'

'There!' Wem called and pointed. 'It's coming.'

They all followed his finger and saw the men of the village emerge from the brush. They were emerging very quickly indeed and didn't look at all happy.

'It's coming.' Wem nodded authoritatively.

'It's coming,' the men of the village screamed as they ran to keep up with their charge.

Wem looked puzzled and took a step forward. His eyes widened as the sight of the stone coming down the valley became clear.

The rocks and the rollers were working very well indeed, so well that the rock was travelling at a very good walking pace, but with such weight that it was clear stopping it was going to be the problem.

'We released the holding brace,' Caradoc yelled as he ran to keep up. 'And the bloody thing set off.'

It was clear that the stone was large. Quite large enough to finish off a monk and a weaver. And quite large enough to finish off the entire village, with its inexorable speed.

It was also clear why the men of the village were

running around to try and keep the thing under control. One slip or missed roller and the sacrifices would be scattered all over the valley floor.

At regular intervals several of them would run to the back of the stone to retrieve a roller that had been discarded like some giant toothpick. They heaved this round to the front of the stone and laid it down on the road, usually just before the stone arrived, looking forward to crushing their hands - and arms and anything else that got in the way.

'That's very impressive.' Hermitage was quite taken with the very clever use of materials which enabled such a huge stone to be moved and at such a rate.

'It'll be even more impressive if we're standing in its way when it gets here,' Wat pointed out.

'Hm.' Hermitage was considering something else. 'You know what?'

'There's a bloody huge rock about to crash into us?'

'No.' Hermitage was thoughtful. He had his head on one side and was considering the approaching piece of mountain. 'I don't think the hole is big enough.'

'Oh dear,' Wat said, not giving this any importance at all.

'The rock is very large and I don't think it will fit in the hole. It might go in the top but it certainly won't sink to the bottom.'

'So?' Wat almost shouted as the audience began to scatter in all directions.

'It means there will be a gap at the bottom. If we are in the hole, I think we could be quite safe.'

'Apart from having a monstrous rock on top of us, which we won't be able to move?'

'We could dig our way out,' Hermitage was quite

happy at the prospect.

'I'd rather not.' With hands tied behind his back he tried to nudge Hermitage with his shoulder so they could get out of the way of the approaching rock.

'We're quite safe here,' Hermitage said. 'The path is guiding the passage of the rock very effectively, and the floor of the valley is flat and so the stone is slowing.'

Wat looked and saw that there did seem to be a bit less unstoppable force to the rock as it drew closer.

'And if it does get here, we simply step out of the way.' Hermitage nodded to himself. 'In fact I don't know why the men with the stone are making such a fuss.'

'Perhaps they wanted to warn the villagers that their death was hurtling down the hill.'

'Ah.' Hermitage was grateful for Wat's explanation.

The slowing of the stone was quite noticeable now. The great behemoth had dropped to a walking pace as it approached the site of Hywel's hut.

'That really is very clever indeed,' Hermitage nodded in satisfaction. 'It would be most diverting to consider the practicalities behind the scheme; angles and weights and such. I don't mean to put these villagers down, but I'm not sure they'd have the wherewithal to calculate this to such a degree of accuracy.'

'I'm pleased you think they've done so well,' Wat said in that tone he had.

They were all gathered now at the edge of the hole as the massive stone slowed more and travelled sedately on to its terminus.

de Boise looked very happy indeed, probably with the size of the rock compared to a monk.

Wem looked very content that his plan had worked to such a high degree of accuracy. The rest of the crowd looked on, very impressed that something very impressive was happening.

As the stone reached the end of its paved path, it had just enough momentum to take it over the edge of the hole. The entire journey couldn't have happened better and there were smiles all round. Apart from Hermitage and Wat, of course.

The stone, the great, master stone, hewn from the side of the hill and brought to this place to fulfil the destiny Wulf had seen in his vision, edged its way over the hole a few inches more.

It was a few inches which was just enough to increase the weight hanging over the hole so that it was slightly more than the weight on the earth. The whole thing began to slowly tip up.

'It's going to tip,' Wem said in wonder, 'it's going to tip straight into the hole.'

'Quick,' de Boise barked, gesturing towards Hermitage and Wat. 'Throw them in.'

Caput XXX: There Goes the Stone.

ywel was first to move. He had a look that said he had had enough of all this and was going to take action to bring it to an end.

Almost simultaneously, the Arch-Druid stepped forward from where he had been mingling in the crowd, the look in his eye was firm and resolute.

Lord Bermo came up for the ceremonial moment, his look was a bit confused but it seemed to have some sort of purpose.

Finally, from behind a hut, crouching low so that he would not be spotted, came John.

All of this was unseen by Hermitage and Wat as they waited for their fateful moment. Despite Hermitage's confidence that the stone would not, in fact, crush them to death, the actual experience of falling into the hole, just before the rock did the same, was quite uncomfortable.

The stone was now at its very tipping point and de Boise gave the fateful order. 'Now,' he screamed.

He screamed again as Hywel, the Arch-Druid, Bermo and John, simultaneously pushed him into the hole in advance of the falling rock.

With a finality as heavy as only a very substantial part of a welsh mountain can deliver, the master stone swung its awful weight up and over and came to a halt with a muffled thud as its sides ground into the mud.

'Oh,' Hermitage said as he looked around and realised he was not under the rock at all.

'There.' The Arch-Druid dusted his hands at a job well done.

'Come here, call himself King?' Bermo said in disgust. 'What do you think of the squirrel now?' he shouted at the rock - which made everyone frown.

'New headman indeed,' Hywel said with a smirk.

'One less,' John said, rather ambiguously.

Wat and Hermitage just looked at one another. And then at the rock.

'What have you done?' Hermitage asked, appalled at what had come to pass.

'Put the Norman under the rock instead of you?' the Arch-Druid replied, not seeing why Hermitage needed to ask.

Hermitage's selfish thought was that this was a good thing. But pushing people under rocks had to be bad, generally speaking, so shouldn't be encouraged. He tutted in a rather non-committal manner.

The robbers were now the only ones left with any loyalty to the man under the rock, loyalty which they abandoned as fast as a rock sliding down a welsh mountain. Under Banley's direction they scurried among the captives, releasing them from their bindings, and acting as if this had been their plan all along.

Bermo's men helped out and there was a lot of mutual scowling and growling between the two bands.

Ellen and Cwen, joined Wat and Hermitage at the rock. Ellen was talking loudly and had the ear of Leon. She had it between her fingers and it had turned very red.

She paused in the tirade against her son. 'Cor,' she said, looking into the hole. 'What a way to go.'

'Yes,' Wat agreed. 'And rather him than us.'

The various faces stared at the rock with different thoughts. They were all inscrutable but ranged from Hermitage's sorrow at a life lost, to Leon's wish that his mother was under the rock as well.

'Help.' They all turned as they heard a distant cry. Perhaps one of the robbers had decided to carry on being a robber, or Lypolix was carrying on with the sacrifices regardless.

Among all the people milling around, pilgrims, robbers, Bermo's men, stragglers, villagers, no one seemed to be in distress. Even More was distracted. He was using a stone and a small beetle to demonstrate to one of the village children what happened when a rock fell on you.

'Help.' The cry came again and no one could locate it.

'Someone get this thing off me.' Now the voice of de Boise was recognisable.

'Good gracious.' Hermitage looked at the rock, partly in alarm that the man was alive under there and partly in satisfaction that he had been right, the hole was too small.

'Ha, ha,' Ellen laughed and gave the rock a friendly kick. 'Get yourself out of that then.'

Hermitage looked cautiously at everyone else and knew that his next suggestion was not going to be well received. Nonetheless, he could not keep it in. How would he live with himself?

'We must get him out,' he said.

No one moved.

'He's trapped,' Hermitage pointed out.

'As you would have been,' Cwen said. 'And I don't think de Boise would have dirtied his hands digging you out.'

'What he would do is one thing. What we would do is another. And what we would do is what must be done.'

'Eh?' Ellen looked confused.

'There is a man trapped under a rock. It is our Christian duty to get him out.'

'Says so in the good book does it?' Ellen asked.

'Yes.' Hermitage was confident.

'Says a lot about digging bad men out from under rocks?'

'Not exactly,' Hermitage confessed he didn't have any accurate references for exactly this situation, but the principle was clear.

'He may be a bad man, but he is in need.'

'What if he's evil?' Ellen asked.

'I beg your pardon?' Hermitage wasn't really prepared for a theological discussion. Which was unusual.

'Yeah, what if he's evil and we've buried him under a rock? God would be pleased with that.'

'He's not evil,' Hermitage said. 'As such. Just, erm, bad. Anyway, we could always disarm him before we let him out, then he'd be harmless.'

'He's more harmless under the rock.'

'There's no point Hermitage,' Wat spoke up. 'We couldn't move this thing even if we wanted to.'

Hermitage frowned at this. 'These men got it down from the mountains. I'm sure we could move it a bit from here.'

'You said we could dig our way out anyway,' Wat pointed out.

'Ah, yes. But that rather depended on being thrown into the hole with a reasonable selection of tools.' He looked for the man in charge of stone moving and beckoned him over.

'de Boise is trapped under here,' he explained. 'If we could lift it a bit, he could hand his weapons out and then we could rescue him.'

Wem stroked his chin. He then walked round the rock, giving it desultory kicks every now and again. He emerged from the other side shaking his head and sucking the air in through tight lips. 'Tricky,' he said.

'You got the rock into the hole,' Hermitage pointed out.

'Ah, yes,' Wem acknowledged. 'Getting rocks into holes is one thing, getting them out again is something else altogether.'

'I'm sure you could come up with something.' Hermitage pleaded.

'Tell you what, I'll give it some thought, have a chat with Caradoc and the others and see what can be done. Get back to you in about a week?'

'A week?' Hermitage was horrified. 'He'll be dead by then.'

'Oh, yes.' Wem showed little concern.

Hermitage watched in disappointment as the man wandered away.

Wulf now came up and laid his hands on the stone. 'This is just how I imagined it,' he whispered in awe.

'There's a Norman buried underneath,' Hermitage pointed out.

'Yes,' Wulf acknowledged with slightly distant gaze. 'This is the master stone you know,' he explained.

'We'd heard,' Wat said.

'Now a great stone circle will be built around it.'

The Arch-Druid joined his stone seer and they admired the standing stone, ignoring the muffled pleas that were coming from underneath it.

'I had a vision you know,' Wulf explained to Hermitage.

Hermitage nodded politely, hoping that this wasn't going to get awkward.

'There will be a ring of magnificent standing stones.'

He gazed into the sky as he described his dream. 'Not like Lypolix's little things. These will all be as big as this master. They will stand sentinel, creating gates to the Gods. Some will even have great cross-pieces hauled upon their heads, under which we will make our obeisance.'

The Arch-Druid and Wulf were standing solemnly, with heads bowed.

Hermitage frowning at a recollection this brought to mind. 'In a circle, you say?' he asked Wulf.

'That's right,' Wulf nodded.

Hermitage hesitated, 'One circle of great big stones like this, with, as you say roofs on some of them, and then perhaps a smaller circle outside.'

Wulf frowned at this heathen who was describing his circle.

The Arch-Druid glowered, 'How do you know of the Grand Complication?' he demanded.

'Is that what it's called?' Hermitage liked the sound of the name. He didn't like the fact that these druids didn't seem very happy any more.

'Speak,' the Arch-Druid commanded.

'Ah, well, it's nothing really,' Hermitage smiled. He could tell they weren't going to let this go. He tried to sound as nonchalant and disinterested as possible. 'It's just that it erm, sort of sounds a bit like the one they've got down south?'

The two druids were utterly silent. Which did not seem good.

The Arch-Druid spoke very slowly, 'What "one they've got down south?"'

Hermitage was now all enthusiasm, surely they would know about the circle. 'Oh, yes,' he gushed. 'Great big thing. In the fields near Salisbury. Just like you said, big stones, roof on some of them, a big one like this in the middle.' Hermitage now looked at the rock with newly informed eyes. 'In fact it's exactly like this one. Isn't that remarkable?'

'And you've seen this? With your own eyes?' the Arch-Druid sounded a bit disappointed now.

'Absolutely,' Hermitage confirmed happily. 'I was sent from my monastery to study the druids and er, others, and spent some time with a charming fellow who told me all about it.'

'A charming fellow?'

'Yes,' said Hermitage. 'In fact he was a druid as well. Perhaps you know him?'

'Hardly likely,' the Arch-Druid huffe. 'There are a lot of us, we don't all know one another.'

Hermitage wished these people would make their minds up. First they're happy, then they're grumpy. There was no pleasing them.

'Chap called Theletrix?'

The Arch-Druid and Wulf immediately knelt at Hermitage's feet.

'Oh, I say,' Hermitage didn't know what to do.

'You,' the Arch-Druid almost stumbled over his words. 'You met the great mage? And spoke to him?'

'Who?'

'Theletrix, the great mage of the druids?'

'Oh, is he? Yes, I suppose so. He didn't mention any mages.'

'Lord Theletrix is the great mage of all the druids.' Now the wretched Arch-Druid was impatient.

'Is he? Ah, jolly good.'

'And you say he knows of the circle to the south?'

290

'Absolutely. He said it was built thousands of years ago, which is obviously ridiculous.'

'Thousands of years ago?' Wulf almost sobbed. 'They built the Grand Complication thousands of years ago?' He found a glare from somewhere and threw it at the Arch-Druid.

'So he said.' Hermitage gave a light laugh at such a patently stupid idea. 'But he didn't say it was a Grand Complication or anything.'

'What, erm, what did he say it was?' The Arch-Druid sounded like he didn't really want to know.

'What did he call it?' Hermitage wracked his memory, 'It was a very strange expression. Oh yes, a timepiece.'

'A timepiece?' The Arch-Druid had a crack in his voice.

'Yes, that's it. He said they would be able to tell what time it was whenever they wanted. Day or night. They'd also know what day and month it was and everything. Sounded very clever to do it all with rocks. But an awful lot of trouble when all you need to do is write it down anyway.'

'Write it down?' It was Wulf who was now sounding very despondent. His glare at the Arch-Druid deepened.

'We will have nothing to do with writing,' the old druid announced.

'Really?' Hermitage couldn't believe anyone wouldn't be fascinated by reading and writing.

'We carve our sacred runes upon the rocks and that is all that is needful,' the Arch-Druid was announcing this solemnly. 'We have heard of this writing on animal skins and the like, but it is against the will of the Gods.'

Hermitage gave one of his best tuts. 'Much easier to keep track of the time if you write it down. No need to move rocks about at all.'

'You,' Wulf hesitated. 'You write down the time?'

'That's right,' Hermitage explained. 'Every monastery has a monk who keeps count.'

'Keeps count?'

'Of course. How else would we know when the devotions are due? The monk gets up every morning and writes down what day it is. That's pretty easy, it's basically the last one plus one. Then he checks when the sun rises, when it's high and when it sets and lets everyone know. He sets his candles to measure the passing hours and then rings the bell.'

'And he doesn't have a stone circle at all?' Wulf had some hope in his voice.

'Of course not,' Hermitage laughed lightly at the very idea. 'We sometimes use a sundial.'

'Sundial?'

'Yes, a plate of metal with a spike in the middle. The shadow of the sun cast by the spike tells the hour.'

Wulf was looking at Hermitage in wonder. 'That's how the stone circle works,' he paused. 'Of course you need to see the sun, which doesn't happen much round here. And this metal plate is of magnificent size, like a stone circle?'

'Oh, no,' Hermitage said. 'quite small really. You can carry it around.'

'Carry it around?' Wulf sounded so disappointed he was on the point of tears.

'I've heard rumours that some monks are working on a magnificent device of wood and metal which actually tells the time all on its own. Even in the dark.' Hermitage couldn't wait to get the details of this as soon as it was available. 'But we still use the monk to write it all down anyway. And then once a year a monk comes from the church and checks that our monk is on the right day.'

'And what do you call this monk of yours?' Wulf was really in his boots now.

'Anything you like really,' Hermitage couldn't see it mattered. 'The last place I was at we had a name for him because he looked out for the passing days and hours. We called him the watch.'

'The watch,' Wulf threw his hands in the air. 'We were going to build a bloody great circle and all we needed was a watch!'

'Writing,' the Arch-Druid grumbled as if it was a disgusting habit. 'And lord Theletrix's circle did not open a gateway to the Gods?' he asked.

'No,' Hermitage was firm on that nonsense.

'I can tell the time perfectly well with the circle we've got,' Wulf seemed to making some explicit criticism of the Arch-Druid. 'Why would we need a Grand Complication at all?'

The Arch-Druid was thinking, 'Perhaps we should travel to see this great circle the Lord Theletrix has. You could see if it makes a difference,' he suggested to Wulf.

'Be a lot quicker than building our own,' Wulf said, rather sulkily.

Hermitage really didn't have much of a clue what was going on any more. Everything was confusing; the people most of all.

The Arch-Druid and Wulf seemed buried in their thoughts. de Boise was by definition buried under the rock, and his complaints were gradually becoming fainter. The crowd in the village were sorting themselves back into their groups, presumably to decide what to do next, which made Hermitage wonder what he should do next.

'What do we do now?' he asked Wat plaintively, as he realised the complexity of their situation. 'We've found the gold and we've found Martel.'

'What's that?' Martel had heard his name being mentioned.

'I was just saying that we've sort of completed our mission to find you and the gold.'

'And what do you do next?'

'That's just what I was asking,' Hermitage turned to Wat for the answer.

'Well,' the weaver mused. 'The king thinks Martel is dead.'

'Probably for the best, really,' Martel was despondent. 'I thought he might be pleased if I said there was gold. Should have known better.'

'And Le Pedvin was being his usual deceiving self, not saying what he really wanted.'

'Le Pedvin?' the quake in Martel's voice was clear for all to hear. 'I'm not going anywhere near him.'

'The cave it is then,' Wat said, which didn't seem to cheer Martel at all.

'I don't think the druids will want to part with the gold,' Hermitage observed. 'And we are not just taking it,' he added before Wat or Cwen could make the suggestion.

'It's easy enough then,' Wat said. 'With de Boise under the rock, we go back and tell William the truth.'

That sounded good to Hermitage.

'Well, some of the truth. We say Wales was full of gold and the druids had it, but de Boise wasn't dead at all. He had deceived William and came to steal the gold for himself. He's bound to believe that. After all, he thinks everyone is as bad as he is. We just say de Boise ran off with it. To Ireland probably. That should stop William bothering the welsh for years.'

'And you'll make sure he thinks I'm dead,' Martel urged.

'If you want.'

'I'm not sure he'll believe any of this,' Hermitage fretted.

'What choice does he have?'

'He could kill us,' Hermitage pointed out.

'Ah,' Wat said knowingly. 'Not now that we know how proud he is of his personal investigator.'

This did not cheer Hermitage. 'What are we going to with this lot?' He nodded his head to the village which was still pretty much swarming with stragglers, pilgrims, robbers, Bermo and his men as well as the druids, John and More and all the villagers. It looked like a pretty busy town. 'We can't turn up with a troop of twenty odd people following on.'

After all their trials with King William and Le Pedvin, getting to Wales, being nearly killed by a largely mad Norman and some strange druids, Hermitage felt that the most difficult task was still ahead; getting people to stop following them.

They left the master stone and headed into the crowd, the foundations of the monolith quietly moaning behind them.

Caput XXXI: End of Sorts.

ermitage sought out Ellen, who he thought seemed to be the most intelligent of the group - if one of the most scary. As they approached they could see that she was in heated conversation with Leon, which was turning out to be one of the main features of her family.

'I told you,' Leon was insistent. 'Lord Bermo has offered me a job. I'm going to be a guard. I want to be a guard and there's nothing can do about it.' He stamped his foot.

'A guard!' Ellen wailed at the air. 'You want to be a guard? You'll be killed.'

'But if I'm a guard we'll get regular food and stuff. We might even be able to get a little hovel of our own.'

'We've got a perfectly good hovel at home.'

'I hate it,' Leon burst out. 'And I hate you. You're ruining my life.' He stomped off.

Ellen turned to see the others arriving. She tried to look calm and in control.

'Well.' Wat rubbed his hands together. 'It's been nice to have you straggling us, but we're off now.'

Ellen had a thoughtful look. 'Straggling you has been quite interesting, actually. And we got fed. I think we might carry on.'

Hermitage thought that was a very bad idea indeed. He liked being on his own and it had taken him a long time to get used to just having Wat and Cwen around. If he was going to be straggled for the rest of his life, he might just go mad.

'Good idea,' Wat agreed. Hermitage regarded him with some horror. 'I'm sure King William and the whole Norman army will be really pleased to meet a bunch of Saxon stragglers.' Wat wore a curious smile. 'After all, he does so love Saxons in large numbers.'

Ellen's look remained thoughtful. 'Or then again, we might stay here.' Hermitage sighed his relief. 'After all, the village looks like it could do with some fresh blood.' Hermitage hoped that the druids wouldn't take that too literally.

Ellen adopted a new expression as she looked around the place, one that said Hywel clearly wasn't up to his job, and what the village really needed was a woman in charge. 'My son's been offered an important job in lord Bermo's army you know.'

'Really,' Wat sounded very impressed. 'All turned out well in the end then.

Cwen stepped forward, looked Ellen up and down and then the two women exchanged heartfelt hugs with many pats on the shoulder. 'You look after yourself girl,' Ellen said.

'And you, old woman,' Cwen replied.

The two sniffed and wiped their eyes.

'Don't you take any nonsense from these two,' Ellen instructed. An instruction Hermitage considered to be completely unnecessary.

'And you keep this village in order,' Cwen responded.

Hermitage looked on in complete bewilderment. Surely these two hated one another. What on earth was going on? He looked to Wat for an explanation.

The weaver's expression said that there probably was an explanation, just not one they would understand.

They left Ellen issuing orders to people who didn't

know who she was. 'That's stragglers dealt with,' Wat said. 'Just robbers, pilgrims, John and More to go.'

They found Banley next. He and the rest of his band were sitting around outside the large village hut, comparing sticks with Bermo's men.

'I imagine you'll be staying here,' Wat said to the leader. Hermitage didn't know why he'd conclude that. After all, the robbers had followed them half way across the country.

'Oh, yes,' Banley confirmed. 'I think we have a duty to make sure that the poor, defenceless druids don't get any of that gold taken off them.'

'By some band of ruffians,' Wat prompted.

'Exactly.' Banley nodded and his men grumbled their agreement. 'And it was such a lot of gold.' Banley went rather misty eyed, and Hermitage had some doubts about the man's sincerity.

'I don't know whether to wish the luck to you or the druids,' Wat said as they left.

'Wat,' Hermitage hissed in the weaver's ear. 'I have a horrible feeling they plan to rob the druids.'

'I have a certainty they plan to rob the druids.'

'Then shouldn't we do something?'

'Such as?'

'Oh, I don't know. Tell someone?'

'There are so many reasons not to do anything,' Wat explained. 'One; I don't think that lot are capable of robbing cow dung. Two, the druids haven't done us any favours, so why would we care?'

Hermitage thought that was a most uncharitable thought.

'And three, I think John has found himself a new job as well.' He nodded over to the edge of the woods where the druids were in conversation.

The Arch-Druid was addressing Wulf and Gardle, Lypolix was presumably scampering in the woods somewhere. There was a large woollen blanket at their feet, tied up into a bundle. It was pretty clear that the bundle contained the gold, which had been recovered from the sacrificial field.

By their side stood John. The man was upright and proud, rigid and very fearsome. His largest sword was held in front of him, point down, and he was surveying the village as if inviting someone to try and take the gold so that he could chop them to bits.

'He did seem to be in thrall to the druids,' Hermitage commented.

'He's probably as glad to be out of Norman clutches as the rest of us,' Wat commented. 'Being a sell-sword to Le Pedvin must be a precarious occupation.'

Hermitage felt a tug at his habit and turned to find Elard, Lanson and Pord standing in a neat row.

'We were just going to look for you,' Wat said. 'We're leaving now.' He looked Lanson in the eye. 'And you're not coming with us.'

Hermitage winced at the rudeness.

'That's right,' Elard confirmed happily. 'Sorry about that, but you'll just have to manage without us.'

'I think we'll cope.'

'What are you going to do then?' Hermitage asked. 'This is a heathen country, the nearest shrine must be miles away.' He then thought this through. 'Except, of course you don't go to the real shrines anyway.'

'We're not doing shrines anymore.' Elard smiled.

'Well, I'm pleased to hear it.' Hermitage was happy that they might be heading towards the right path.

'No.' Elard shook his head, 'We're going to be druids.'

Wat gave a short, sharp laugh. Hermitage didn't understand.

'What do you mean, you're going to be druids?'

'Have you seen them?' Elard was as puzzled as Hermitage. 'They get robes and food and even gold.'

'But, but,' Hermitage tried to get his thoughts in order. 'It's not just a case of deciding to be something. Druids believe in Gods and spirits and trees and mushrooms and things.'

'We can do that.'

'No, you can't.' Hermitage was appalled. 'You can't just say you believe in something. You have to actually, you know, believe it.'

'I do,' Elard said.

'Me too,' Pord and Lanson added.

'Well, I don't believe you.' Hermitage folded his arms.

'Yes,' Elard noted this. 'But you don't matter. The big druid with the beard has said he'll take us.'

'The Arch-Druid,' Hermitage said.

'If you like.'

'The one whose every word you have to obey.'

'That's right,' Elard agreed, but he sounded a bit less sure.

'The one who just tried to sacrifice his own druids.'

'Erm.' Elard now looked to Lanson and Pord.

Wat patted Elard firmly on the shoulder. 'I think you're making the right decision. And if we're ever in this part of the country again we'll pop by and see if you're still here.'

Elard gave a weak smile.

'Or if there's three new stones sticking up with some moaning coming from underneath them.' He pulled

Hermitage and Cwen away, leaving the erstwhile pilgrims to consider their options.

'This is going really well,' Wat said. 'Nearly shot of the lot of them. I think we just sneak out now. No one else needs to see us go.'

'I've got a feeling More will find out and follow us anyway,' Cwen said. 'After all, he's no earthly use to this place.'

They headed off back towards the master stone and the path that led back over the hills, away from the village.

Hermitage could hardly believe it was all over. Of course there was still the king and Le Pedvin to deal with, but as they were so many miles away he felt confident that Wat's story would be accepted. He was also confident that at each mile post on the way to Derby he would leave a little bit of that confidence behind.

They were close to the stone now and it seemed they would get away without More spotting them. Hermitage did feel bad not saying goodbye to More. But then saying hello had not been exactly fulfilling.

'Bye then,' More's squeaky voice, wafted across the grass. The ancient boatman didn't sound in the least concerned that they were going without him.

Hermitage looked at the master stone and saw More and Martel, sitting comfortably with their backs against the rock, feet outstretched.

'Ah, yes, goodbye,' Hermitage stumbled over his words. 'You're, erm, staying here then?'

'Oh, no,' More shook head and beard. 'Me and mister Martel got a plan.'

'Really?' Even Hermitage's curiosity, rampant as it was, showed no signs of interest in any plan these two had come up with.

'We're going to run a ferry,' More announced proudly.

Hermitage scanned the village quickly, in case there was some large body of water he'd missed.

'Not here,' More scoffed at Hermitage's idiocy. 'The village headman says there's a big river over the other side of the hills.'

'Where?' Hermitage asked.

'No,' More said. 'Why.'

Hermitage was lost. 'Why what?'

'No, not why what, Just Why. The river's called the Why. Why you'd call a river the River Why I don't know. Pretty stupid if you ask me.'

More should know, thought Hermitage in an uncharitable moment.

'And the best thing about it is that the ferryman just died.'

'That's the best thing?'

'Oh, he didn't drown or anything.' More reassured Hermitage. 'I'm going to run the boat, 'cos I can do that, and mister Martel is going to do all the money and stuff.'

Martel smiled at the plan. Hermitage thought it would at least be better than living in a cave. Although running a ferry with More was not a task he'd take on.

'And have you got a boat?' he asked

'There's usually one around if you look hard enough.' More grinned at the complexity of his plan.

As they lapsed into silence, Hermitage, Wat and Cwen quietly contemplating that the people of the River Why didn't know what was coming their way, a quiet moan could be heard emerging from the ground.

Hermitage suddenly recalled that de Boise was still down there. In all the goodbyes and partings, he'd completely forgotten that they'd just buried a Norman noble under a rock. Surely they couldn't walk away and just leave him there? He imagined the man would be motivated to dig himself out once he got hungry enough.

Wat squatted down at the base of the stone, 'Well,' he shouted at the rock. 'We're off now, so good luck with everything. The stone and the like.'

'Get me out of here,' de Boise found some of his old strength.

'Oh no, we're not going to do that. And if I were you I'd stay there. Once we've told King William what you've been up to he'll chop your head off as soon as say hello.'

'I'll find you and kill you,' de Boise shouted.

'No, you won't. If you did that William would know you weren't in Ireland. And I don't think there's an army in the world could stop him dealing with the man who stole all his gold.'

Hermitage tutted in disappointment at this dishonest dealing.

All de Boise could do was let out a muffled shout of frustration.

As they were about to leave, the muffled shout became a scream.

'Good Lord,' Hermitage turned back. 'What's happened?' He thought that the stone might have slipped in the hole and really done for de Boise. What an awful thought.

Even More and Martel leaped up and took a step away from the stone.

'Get me out, get me out,' the Norman noble was positively hysterical.

'What is it now?' Wat asked wearily.

'There's something in here with me.' De Boise sounded

as scared as a normal person.

'What could be in there?' Hermitage asked. 'It's probably a mole or a rat or something.'

They all pressed their ears against the stone to see what they could hear.

The blood of three people turned as cold as the stone itself as they recognised the noise.

From the base of the stone, from the tomb in which de Boise was sealed came a familiar and disturbing cackle.

'It's only me,' Lypolix's voice could be heard, 'I've bought some berries.'

Finis

The woes of Brother Hermitage continue as he goes to Shrewsbury to tackle some nuns:

Read on…

Hermitage, Wat and Some Nuns

Howard of Warwick

Hermitage, Wat and Some Nuns.

An Introduction

And it came to pass that Brother Hermitage did visit Shrewsbury; a place that would gain renown for the workings of the medieval monk detective - just not this medieval monk detective.

Caput I

The year was surely one to be written in all the history books of the land. It would be remembered for centuries, such were its momentous events. Men and women in a thousand years would recite it as a pivotal moment in English history.

1068.

The year Gilder died.

In and around the town of Shrewsbury, where he had held sway as its leading merchant and land owner (and house, hovel, peasant and slave owner as well), not a dry eye could be found. In the streets and the markets, in the taverns and the houses, in the churches and even among the monks of Bromfield and the nuns of Wenlock tears were shed and chests were beaten.

There was wailing and there was howling. The name of Gilder was in nearly every conversation and someone had even created a little rhyme in his memory. It was all the people of the town could do to stop themselves going to the body itself to hoist it aloft and carry it in procession. There never would be such a day as the day Gilder died and the little children were being told to remember it.

The town was not ready for such a shock. Gilder had held the place together for more years than many could remember. It was only under his rule that people had finally stopped sacking the place every few weeks.

For centuries past it had been the Danes. When the Danes went back to wherever it was Danes came from, the Welsh popped over. And if neither of them were available even the English would have a go - just to make sure there was nothing left for the Danes to sack.

It was all very well being grandly swapped between the Kingdoms of Wessex and Mercia when someone married someone else, but either realm would be more use if a king actually turned up now and again to stop invaders taking everything of value away in their sacks.

Gilder had put a stop to that. He had erected some walls around the place to act as a deterrent but all they really did was stop those who used to simply walk in and help themselves to whatever was lying around. Any more committed invader would bring a couple of ladders and it was business as usual.

No, Gilder had other methods as well, and they seemed very effective. Nobody was quite sure what they were, which was worrying considering the man was no longer available to deal with attackers, but they had worked. He usually just went and had a word with groups who started bothering the gates of the town and they would go away. It was marvellous.

Sometimes the discussions lasted long into the night and involved the consumption of large quantities of food and ale - the town's food and ale. The result was always the same though. The would-be pillagers would leave pillage-less. Often they were grumbling and clearly unhappy but as the saying goes, "better three pillagers in the woods than one in your parlour".

It was only now occurring to the town moot, that gathering of the great and good of Shrewsbury, that they had not a clue what it was Gilder said to these people that made them behave so reasonably. Perhaps his son, young Balor, knew the secrets of the merchant but just now it was not decent to go enquiring about such things. There would be plenty of opportunity - always assuming no one came to plunder Shrewsbury in the meantime.

But Gilder was old, there was no doubting that. He would have to go sometime, everyone acknowledged, but now? There had been no time to prepare. No long, lingering days leading ultimately to demise. The suddenness of the event was doubtless causing as much of the turbulence as the fact of the death itself.

If the town was in a state of turmoil, it was also nervous. As the hours stretched into days, minds turned from the shock of the departure to its implications. Ordinary folk started to discuss how they would manage now that Gilder was no more. Who would be their leader and protector? They would have to be extra cautious in dealing with anyone who wanted to come into the town. Extra cautious usually involved giving the town guards extra arrows.

This particular sunny and bright summer morning would not be a good time for strangers to arrive at the gates seeking entrance.

So it was that the three strangers who arrived at the gates this morning seeking entrance were somewhat put out by their welcome.

'How can three of us plunder a whole town?' the smart looking one called up to the guard in his wooden tower. 'One of us is a monk and one's a woman.'

'I could plunder them if I wanted,' the young woman whispered, as if insulted by having her plundering abilities doubted.

The guard peered down, noting that the small figure who was supposed to be a woman was giving him a look that could stop a charging bull. She might appear young and slight, but the dark hair was pulled back a bit too tight and the fists were clenched a bit too fiercely for comfort.

'A monk?' the guard enquired, choosing his subject carefully.

'Yes,' the well-dressed one replied wearily, brushing a fall from a mop of curly black hair out of his eyes. 'This bright young fellow here? The one wearing the monk's habit and with the haircut of a monk who looks just like a monk? He's a monk.' He straightened his immaculate jerkin and sighed heavily.

'Brother Hermitage.' The monk introduced himself to the guard with an enthusiastic nod. He also had an enthusiastic gleam in his youthful eyes and an enthusiastic smile on his lips. The enthusiasm seemed to hover around him like a miasma, just waiting for the opportunity to enthuse about something. Or anything, really.

'Funny name for a monk,' the guard observed, suspiciously.

'A lot of people say that,' Brother Hermitage replied brightly. 'And this is Wat the weaver,' he went on, indicating Wat at his side. 'And this is Cwen, she's a weaver as well.'

Cwen glared.

'A very good weaver,' Hermitage added. 'I can assure you we mean no harm.'

'Well, what do you want?'

'We'd like to come in please,' said Cwen, making it quite clear she thought the guard some sort of idiot for not realising what people who turn up at gates generally want.

'Why?'

'Because we are travellers on our way to Derby, and Shrewsbury is in the way,' said Wat, a tone of impatience creeping in.

Hermitage was about to suggest that the guard could come out to talk to them if he didn't want to let them in when he heard footsteps approach from behind. Perhaps, if there was a queue of people trying to enter the town this morning the guard might be more cooperative.

'Excuse me,' a female voice joined the conversation. It was the sort of "excuse me" that was more command than request. This person was going to be excused whether you liked it or not.

Hermitage turned and saw the new arrival. He turned back to the gate. Then he turned more quickly back to the woman. Yes, there was no doubt. He had been right the first time. It was a nun. He supposed there was no reason why a nun should not be on the road and seeking entrance to the town but it was the last person he'd been expecting. His mind asked him who the first person might have been but he managed to silence it. Perhaps it was a woman dressed as a nun, who wasn't one really? He considered it even more unlikely that a woman pretending to be a nun would be on the road. Or anywhere else, come to that.

'Sister,' he nodded acknowledgement.

The nun gave him a look that said how offended she was that the empty air had the temerity to speak. It was hard to tell whether her stern expression was the result of a wimple so tight it was making her eyebrows look like earmuffs, or whether she was naturally stern. She had the build to do stern very well indeed. She was tall and broad and looked as strong as an ox - and Hermitage had always been nervous of oxen.

She didn't have to repeat the "excuse me", she just naturally made them all step back to allow her through. As she did so she gave Hermitage a specific glance. It was more of a blatant stare of inquisition and all he could think of was to smile. This was clearly the wrong thing to do as the nun looked very puzzled.

When she approached the gate she looked at the guard and had him scurrying from his post.

In only a few moments, after the noises of various bits of gate paraphernalia being rearranged, a gap appeared as one wooden door was drawn back sufficiently for a single person to pass. It seemed even the wood of the gate wanted to get out of the way of this arrival. Mayhap, as a young sapling it had had a bad experience with a nun.

Hermitage, Wat and Cwen stepped forward to follow, only to find the gate shut in their faces.

'Well, really,' Hermitage complained.

'Open this gate,' Cwen shouted, kicking it to emphasise her request.

Wat was more contemplative. 'I'm sure I've seen her somewhere before,' he mused.

Hermitage thought it extremely unlikely Wat would have met a nun before. He had met very few himself, and was happy to keep it that way. 'On the road somewhere?' he suggested.

'Hm,' Wat frowned, 'could be.'

'They do all tend to look alike,' Hermitage commented, 'dressing the same like that. It's amazing anyone can tell which nun you're talking to.'

Wat cast a very peculiar glance at Hermitage, his eyes clearly pointing out Hermitage's habit. The one which was the same as most other monks.

'This is Benedictine,' Hermitage pointed out. 'It's

completely different.'

'Now,' said the guard, popping back up at the top of the wall, 'where were we?'

'You were about to let us in,' Wat explained.

'No,' said the guard, thoughtfully, 'that wasn't it.'

'Like you did for the nun,' Cwen pointed out.

'Ah, well, got to let her in,' the guard explained.

'Does she live here then?' Hermitage asked.

'Sort of,' said the guard, which Hermitage thought was a bit odd. 'That's sister Mildburgh and she gets really cross if you don't do what she says.'

Definitely a nun then, Hermitage thought.

Cwen spoke up, 'I think you'll find we'll get really cross if we don't get let in.'

'Oh, yes,' said the guard, ignoring Cwen completely. He faced Hermitage. 'Did you say he was a weaver?' He gestured at Wat.

'Oh dear,' Hermitage mumbled, 'I know where this is going.' He addressed the guard, 'Yes, that's right. Weaver.'

'Wat the weaver?'

'That's the one,' Hermitage said quickly, 'and I am a brother originally from…'

'The Wat the weaver?' The guard was not being put off.

'Yes,' said Hermitage with resignation.

The guard turned his attention to Wat and stared, long and hard. Eventually he decided what to say. 'You dirty devil,' he leered.

Wat shrugged.

'But those days are behind him now,' Hermitage explained. 'He has forsworn making any more tapestries of dubious content.'

Wat didn't look happy at being reminded of this.

'The one I saw wasn't dubious at all,' the guard commented with a grin. 'It was downright rude.'

'I'm sure,' said Hermitage, hoping to get the conversation back to the question of their entry into the town. 'But the works of Wat are more wholesome now.'

'And nowhere near as profitable,' it was Wat's turn to mumble.

'Oh,' said the guard, 'that's a shame. Still. Great admirer of your work sir,' he called. 'Honoured to meet you.'

Hermitage tutted, 'Perhaps you'll let us in then?'

'I liked that one in the bath house,' the guard mused, his mind somewhere else altogether.

Hermitage sighed at the lack of progress.

'Perhaps we should tell him you're the King's Investigator?' Wat suggested. 'And that you demand entrance.'

Hermitage was alarmed at the prospect. 'I'd really rather you didn't,' he said in a low voice. 'You know I never wanted to be King's investigator. It was only that William made me.'

'William the King,' Wat pointed out, unhelpfully.

'These people might not be impressed by that. We don't know how far the Norman influence has extended.'

'Norman yoke, you mean,' Cwen corrected.

'Be that as it may, I think we should keep it to ourselves.' Hermitage was anxious not to be known as the King's Investigator. It was bad enough that he had to look into the widest range of horrible events at the behest of the King and his henchman, Le Pedvin. He'd much rather be investigating some particularly troublesome text or other.

But he was away from the King now. Miles away. The people of Shrewsbury would have no need whatsoever of a monk who went round investigating things. The very idea was ridiculous.

'Alright,' the guard had emerged from his reverie, a reverie about which Hermitage wanted to know nothing at all, judging from the look on the man's face. 'You'd better come in then. Can't keep the great Wat the weaver loitering outside.'

The news was very welcome, even if it was only for Wat.

The guard disappeared from sight and there was the sound of heavy steps descending a wooden staircase. This was followed by muffled instructions to someone else within the walls and the sound of timbers being moved aside.

Chains followed, clanking their way across the ground. Then there was a deep thud, probably some heavy counterweight being dropped to the ground. This was immediately followed by the shout of someone who had just had a heavy counterweight dropped on their foot.

The noise of an altercation drifted over the gates, reaching three sets of bemused ears. The manipulator of the counterweight was being taken to task in a most unseemly manner. His suitability for the role was seriously questioned along with his parentage. The three new arrivals exchanged looks. Only Hermitage blushed at the language.

The sound of a head being knocked against the inside of the gates of Shrewsbury caused eyebrows to rise. The subsequent impression of an unconscious body being dragged away was perfectly clear.

The footsteps on the stairs returned, this time getting

closer.

A new face appeared at the top of the guard's tower.

'Yes,' the face asked, 'what do you want?'

Wat contained a small scream. 'We want you to open the gates so the three of us can come in and plunder the town.'

'What?' said the new guard. 'One bloke, a monk and a girl?'

'That's right,' said Wat. 'We're very fierce.'

'You're certainly very something or other,' the guard snorted.

'So, can we come in?' Hermitage asked, trying to sound meek and harmless - which in any event was his natural demeanour.

'Please yourselves,' the guard replied. 'It's opening time anyway.'

'Argh.' Wat let his scream out and walked round in a very small circle.

The guard waved to someone below and the final sounds of the town's night defences being moved aside drifted over the great wooden gates of Shrewsbury which swung majestically open. Well, they started to open before getting stuck, at which point two men appeared and put great effort into kicking the great wooden gates of Shrewsbury to get them moving.

'We're going to have to do something about those hinges,' one of the men commented, taking no notice of the visitors waiting to come in.

'Goose fat,' the other replied.

'Goose fat!' the first one coughed. 'That's your answer to everything.'

Ignoring the fact that the gates weren't fully open, Hermitage, Wat and Cwen sidled their way past the struggling doormen and entered the town.

Hermitage felt immediate relief at having walls around him instead of being in open country. He spent most of his time being nervous about something or other, but the three of them walking alone from Wales to Derby really gave him something to work with.

Another wretched mission as King's Investigator had sent him across the border and now he had to get back to Wat's workshop in Derby to meet the Normans and confirm he had completed his work. [8] If he didn't, they had promised they would kill everyone and burn the place to the ground. Of course they might do that anyway, it seemed to be their preferred way of letting people know they'd arrived.

But they were ahead of time. There should be no problem getting to Derby so a sojourn in Shrewsbury was both affordable and a great relief.

Hermitage looked at the simple, rough houses gathered around the gate. People were already on the move at this early hour and it felt good to be among friendly faces once more, with a large and solid wall of wood between him and the outside world.

They would find lodgings, they would eat and drink and shrug the trials of the journey from their shoulders. Perhaps there might even be time for him to locate the nearest monastic house, find out about it and then perhaps consider paying a visit. Even Hermitage, in his innocence had learned to look before he leapt. He wasn't going anywhere near a strange monastery without being well prepared; he knew what monks were like.

---

[8]
    All explained in the volume entitled Hermitage, Wat and Some Druids, which is about Hermitage, Wat and Some Druids.

His last house, the monastery in De'ath's Dingle, had been the most appalling place, full of the most appalling people - all of them monks. He was still grateful not to be there anymore and would now hesitate before crossing the threshold of any monastery without some advance information. He was sure there would be people in the town who could help him.

The three of them wandered away from the gate and towards the centre of the town. The streets sloped gently upwards and the houses became progressively finer. Merchant houses proclaimed their importance from great height, their upper stories extending over the street as if casting everyone into their shadow.

More humble dwellings, the wattle and daub clear for all to see, nestled at the shoulders of their greater cousins.

The street itself was as rough and dirty as any street would be, but at least it was dry, the summer heat having baked it hard.

As the day shrugged off the infested blanket of night, doors were opened, businesses began their trade and the holler of the tradesmen started to fill the air.

The people who passed on the street gave the new arrivals the attention any stranger would deserve: frank staring and a look of disbelief that there was someone they didn't recognise. The examination was normal enough but something was not quite right. The stares did not linger long enough. The appraisals were not rude enough and the children did not point and laugh.

Even Hermitage, seldom able to understand why people did any of the things they did, or pick up on the most blatant expressions of emotion, implicit or explicit, now noticed that the people were not behaving quite right. For him to pick up details of human behaviour was pretty unusual.

He turned to Wat and Cwen who had clearly noticed this long before and were looking carefully at the faces of those passing them, or just going about their business.

'What is it?' Hermitage asked, quietly. He always turned to Wat for explanations of what was going on in the world around him. He had explanations of biblical texts or the issues surrounding the post-Exodus prophets to hand should the weaver ever want them. But the weaver never did.

'They're all odd,' Cwen observed.

'A whole town can't be odd,' Hermitage replied.

'I can think of a few,' said Cwen.

'What's the matter with them?' Hermitage rephrased his question.

'Let's ask,' said Wat, piling straight in in his normal, confident manner. He reached out and grabbed a passing boy who was otherwise intent on some errand.

The child looked surprised and shocked to be arrested so abruptly. He glared demandingly at Wat. This was alarming as there were tears streaming down the cheeks of the child, who must be at least ten and so should know better.

'What's going on?' Wat asked. 'What's wrong with everyone?'

The boy sniffed a bucket of something soft and sticky up his nose and choked out the words, 'Gilder is dead.'

'Gilder?' Wat repeated, a worried look on his face. 'Gilder of Shrewsbury? The great merchant?'

'That's him,' said the boy, wiping the tears from his eyes. He took a swallow and then grinned broadly at them all. 'Isn't it wonderful?' The tears of laughter sprang back to his face and he used Wat's moment of surprise to jump away and skip off down the street.

On his way, he bumped into an old maid who was coming up the path with a small load of kindling in her arms. She immediately dropped this and grabbed the child in a hopping dance. They pirouetted along the path, laughing and crying at the same time.

Now they had some clue, they saw that virtually everyone had the same look of gloriously happy relief.

There were tears everywhere but they were falling down broadly smiling faces. People were clapping one another on the back, shaking hands in happy congratulation at their luck and generally striding about the place filled with joy that Gilder the great merchant of Shrewsbury was finally dead.

The rest of the tale can be found in the book of the same name - funnily enough.

Printed in Great Britain
by Amazon

35036211R00187